Praise for the Novels of Jennifer Scott

The Accidental Book Club

"Will have you laughing and crying at the same time."
—Fresh Fiction

"The still-evolving relationships between the various women are touching. . . . Scott has drawn an affecting tale of family, love, and forgiveness."
—BookNAround

"An entertaining read, and book clubs will enjoy the characters and the story."
—Drey's Library

"Establishes Jennifer Scott as a powerful voice in women's fiction."
—Silver's Reviews

"Another nice read from Jennifer Scott. The characters were engaging and lively, and the issues that Jean was going through with grieving for her husband were heartbreaking and real."
—Luxury Reading

The Sister Season

"Emotionally honest and psychologically astute, *The Sister Season* is ultimately an uplifting story about the pull of the past, the need for forgiveness, and the redemptive power of familial love."
—Liza Gyllenhaal, author of *Bleeding Heart*

continued . . .

"*The Sister Season* is a powerful, honest look at the harm that ripples out from every unkindness, and the strength inherent in the sisterly bond."

—Heidi Jon Schmidt, author of *The Harbormaster's Daughter*

"A fantastic story about the (often dysfunctional) ties of family."

—Examiner.com

"Scott did a great job with these characters . . . illustrating the way sister dynamics can be so complicated." —Book Addiction

"Carefully crafted, with pivotal moments carefully placed in a solid plot that moves." —The Best Reviews

Praise for the YA Novels of Jennifer Scott Writing as Jennifer Brown

"A compulsive read."

—Gail Giles, author of *Right Behind You* and *What Happened to Cass McBride?*

"Authentic and relevant . . . one to top the charts."—*Kirkus Reviews*

"The book's power—and its value—comes from the honest portrayal of characters." —*Publishers Weekly* (starred review)

"A nuanced novel. . . . Brown creates multifaceted characters as well as realistic, insightful descriptions." —*Booklist*

"*Thousand Words* is a powerful, timely, and compulsively readable story. . . . This is an excellent choice for book discussions and a must purchase for all libraries." —*VOYA* (starred review)

SECOND CHANCE FRIENDS

Jennifer Scott

NAL
ACCENT

NAL Accent
Published by the Penguin Group
Penguin Group (USA) LLC, 375 Hudson Street,
New York, New York 10014

USA | Canada | UK | Ireland | Australia | New Zealand | India | South Africa | China
penguin.com
A Penguin Random House Company

First published by NAL Accent, an imprint of New American Library,
a division of Penguin Group (USA) LLC

First Printing, May 2015

LIBRARY OF CONGRESS CATALOGING-IN-PUBLICATION DATA:

Scott, Jennifer, 1972–
    Second chance friends / Jennifer Scott.
        pages cm
    ISBN 978-0-451-47323-3 (softcover)
    1. Female friendship—Fiction. 2. Life change events—Fiction. 3. Domestic
fiction. 4. Chick lit. I. Title.
    PS3619.C66555S43 2015
    813'.6—dc23   2014047035

Printed in the United States of America
10 9 8 7 6 5 4 3 2 1

Set in Bell MT
Designed by Spring Hoteling

For Scott, always

ACKNOWLEDGMENTS

I've always been fascinated by the way the universe brings people into our lives. And when it comes to writing books, I am both fascinated and grateful for the people who've been brought into mine.

Thank you to Cori Deyoe for always trusting my vision and turning an open ear to my voice, and for never telling me not to pursue an idea. Thank you to everyone at 3 Seas Literary Agency for your unending support and for making me feel like a welcome family member. Huge thanks to Sandy Harding for loving the story and helping me make it the best it could possibly be. I'm overjoyed to add you to my "friend" list. Thank you to everyone at NAL for all you do to help bring my books to life—from reading to editing to sales to cover design, you are all awesome!

Acknowledgments

Thank you to the kid crew—Paige, Weston, and Rand—for your continued patience and love. And, Scott, you are my best friend for a lifetime. I love you all.

Finally, I want to thank you, my readers, for reading and sharing my books, and for e-mailing me with kudos, encouragement, questions, and story ideas. You are the best!

PROLOGUE

The breakfast rush at the Tea Rose Diner typically began at around 6:20 a.m., when the early risers came in for bagels and cream cheese to go, or English muffins and jam to go. And rivers of coffee, strong, to go. Then came the elderly, up before dawn and looking for a little social time, and the blue-collar guys—a legion of workers in flannel and steel-toed boots, toting scuffed plastic gas station mugs as big as their heads, hoping for refills after their hash browns and sausage links, requests that Annie, the owner of the Tea Rose, always obliged. It took most of a whole pot to fill up those monsters, but what Annie lost in coffee, she more than made up for in customer loyalty. Being the only traditional diner in sleepy suburban Caldwell, Missouri, had its advantages.

Sometimes the early risers were the white-collar guys, shirts starched and cologne heavy, spoons balanced over their pinkie rings as they dipped into bowls of oatmeal with raisins and read their newspapers or their laptops or their smartphones, always so busy, busy.

Often, due to the Tea Rose's location, which just happened to sit at an intersection less than half a mile away from Caldwell High, the early risers were teenagers, stopping in for cinnamon rolls on their way to school, their parents waiting in the parking lot, checking their watches impatiently behind the wheels of their still-running cars.

Rush almost always ended at 8:47 a.m., precisely thirteen minutes before the first school bell rang, and then the diner would be ghost-town dead until dinnertime. Such was the rhythm of the suburbs.

But on September 2, the rush ended early. Probably because it was the Friday of Labor Day weekend. Probably because the kids had other things to do, such as wake up late and tie themselves into bikini tops that would get peeled off during pontoon parties later in the day as their wearers gave the official sayonara to summer. Probably because the Friday before the first day off of the school year just didn't include early rising and cinnamon rolls.

September 2 was a slow morning. Only three customers were at the Tea Rose at 8:38 a.m.

A woman in a back booth, small, wearing an EMT uniform, just finishing up a plate so huge the cook wondered aloud where she was putting all that food.

A woman at a table by the door, mid-forties, listening

intently to a long-winded caller on her cell phone, her free hand wrapped around a cup of coffee, which she had mentioned while ordering that she desperately needed, but had not yet touched.

And a young woman seated at the counter, effortless and beautiful, wrapped in a wrinkled long-sleeved button-down, even though it was already north of eighty degrees outside, with the promise to get hotter. She looked nervous, as if she was awaiting someone she didn't want to meet. Or maybe as if she wanted to be anywhere but at the Tea Rose, yet had nowhere else to go. She fitfully shoveled bites of Boston cream pie into her mouth.

It was so slow, Annie had plenty of time to do a walk-in inventory and write up her produce order a full day early. Slow enough that the one waitress could duck out for a smoke break, sitting next to the cook on empty crates just outside the back door.

Forget slow—it was downright dead at the Tea Rose at 8:38 a.m. on September 2. Dead as it had been in a long time.

It was beautiful outside. September beautiful. Was there really anything more perfect than September in the glorious Midwest? Tina Shore didn't think so. Especially when the September day in question also happened to be a Friday and the start of a long weekend. She should have been anxious about all these darned days off the school district gave their students—she and her husband were hardly Rockefellers. No work meant no pay, and after a whole summer with no pay, they were starting to feel the squeeze. Lester sure seemed to be concerned. *No paycheck for three months and already a day off,* he'd railed when she'd reminded him that Labor Day was coming up. *We'll starve to death with all these holidays!*

But the holidays were so worth it to Tina. She had come back to work in August rested, sun-kissed, and skinny, just like she'd been when she and Lester had first met. She was convinced that moving to Missouri and taking the job driving the elementary school bus had been her best decision ever. If only Lester could relax about the money, like she did. Although she was willing to bet that as soon as he got his hands wrapped around a beer bottle on Monday afternoon, he'd become a fan of Labor Day real quick. She hoped to talk him into taking a quick camping trip up to Smithville. Nothing better than cold beer around a warm campfire in September, the noise and hustle of Kansas City shut out by twenty miles of sleepy small towns and trees. Nothing better at all.

Just one more day. Half a day, really. She'd already picked up everyone. She just needed to get them to the elementary school, and then she would be one afternoon route away from working on that campfire.

The kid at the last stop had forgotten something and darted back inside his house just as she'd pulled up. He'd taken his time, even though she honked and yelled out the window that she was going to have to leave him if he didn't come quickly. She hated leaving behind a child, though. She always felt guilty when she had to do it. It was her job to get them to school just as much as it was theirs; at least that was the way she saw it. So, threats aside, she'd waited for him as the minutes ticked by. And now she was the late one. Late, but making up time on this beautiful September day.

Traffic was busy for Caldwell, and the kids were acting crazy. They felt anticipation, too. Only in school two weeks, and already they were salivating for a day off. Practically bouncing off the bus walls. Yelling, some of them singing, switching seats. It was as if they'd never ridden a bus before, as if they'd forgotten all the rules. She tried to ignore it, to give them a break. She tried to zone out on the beautiful weather, imagine herself sitting in a lawn chair with a fishing pole and a diet margarita with a colored straw, but the kids just got louder and louder.

Some kids had opened windows. The wind screaming in only added to the noise. And then, out of the corner of her eye, she saw something in her side mirror—a book flying through one of the windows and onto the street. She heard a *"Give it back!"* and then saw a fistful of pencils bounce on the pavement after the book. And then came laughter.

"Hey!" Tina shouted, her foot instinctively letting up on the gas. She flicked a glance at the clock on her dashboard—shit, they were really behind now—and pressed back into it. "Cut it out!" The kids at least had the decency to look caught. They stilled, big-eyed. Some of the girls used their hands to cover their giggles. "You can't be throwing things out the window! Y'all know that!" she said, gazing at them in the mirror, trying to catch the eyes of the kids she guessed were the most likely culprits. "It's

Friday! You don't want to end up at the bus barn on a Friday."

Several of the kids scoffed. The bus barn hadn't been a threat since Tina herself was a kid. Seemed nobody was afraid of authority anymore. And maybe they didn't even call it that here in Missouri. Maybe they called it the *garage* or something else a little more official sounding. For all she knew, that was the case. She hadn't been here long enough to learn much of anyth—

Tina turned her eyes back to the windshield and gasped, panic slamming into her. She'd misjudged where she was on the road, had thought she was much farther back than this. The stoplight ahead was red. There was a line of cars waiting. And she was going way too fast to stop in time.

The little girl in the seat right behind her shrieked— she heard that much as she stomped on the brake, pressing down as hard as she could, the bus jerking right and veering into the turn-only lane. But then she heard nothing but the hollow moan of tires trying to grip pavement and the shuddering of the bus around her.

And then she heard nothing at all.

Every stoplight seemed interminably long to Michael and Maddie Routh. They were nervous, jittery, but it was an excited kind of nervous. They couldn't talk to each other. When they tried, all that came out were giggles, so they pumped up the radio volume and sat with their feet and thumbs keeping time to the beat. They were adorably matchy—faded jeans and Converse low-tops, his gray, hers pink—an accident they found themselves guilty of often. The stoplight seemed to go on forever.

They'd been trying ever since they got married. It had been so easy for all their friends. Most of them were already complaining about being up all night with newborns or choosing paint colors for their nurseries. Michael and Maddie had to sit through endless dinner parties that featured long name-choosing conversations, all the time Maddie pretending that seeing a friend rubbing a swollen belly didn't make her so jealous she could spit. They'd brought flowers to hospitals and tiny pink and blue rattles decorated with celebratory ribbons. They'd held wiggling little ones in their inexperienced hands, trying not to let every crinkle of diaper stab them in their hearts. It had been so depressing, and they'd begun to talk about possibilities: fertility specialists, procedures, even adoption if it came down to it.

But it hadn't come down to it. Maddie had the proof right there in her hand, her nails a pale pink that matched her shoes, and now it was just a matter of getting the test confirmed. How ironic, she'd thought, that this was *Labor* Day weekend. A good omen. If they ever got there, that was. They had a nine o'clock appointment, and this stoplight was really taking so long.

"Why are there so many stoplights in the world?" Maddie said, slouching down in her seat. "We're going to be late. You think we'll be late?"

Michael grinned. "You're already late. That's the good

news," he said, and there came the giggles again. He reached for her hand and squeezed it.

"That's not what I—" But she never got to finish the sentence.

They never saw or heard the bus coming until it plowed into Michael's door.

Suddenly everything seemed to explode around them. Glass flew, and there was noise, so much noise, and Maddie felt a sensation of moving, of jostling and tumbling and flying, and there was no time even to scream. It felt like being grabbed and shaken, eyes unable to focus on anything, mind unable to grab sense of what was happening. And then there was the horrific sound of hissing and creaking and thunking as their car settled into place. And then the awful silence. Only they weren't in front of the stoplight anymore.

They were upside down. She could feel the seat belt digging into her shoulder, her hair sticking to one side of her face. She felt a tickle on her cheek and hastily swept at it. Her hand came away covered with blood, but she didn't know where it had come from. There was no pain, only shock and confusion and deep, deep fear.

"Michael," she croaked, surprised to hear that her voice worked. She fumbled, trying to orient herself, and reached for him with the hand that still held the positive test stick.

She knew. Right away, she knew it was bad. Blood, there was so much blood, and his eyes were open, but he wasn't moving. His mouth worked, but he wasn't saying anything.

"Michael!" she croaked again, only louder this time,

and she shifted, grasping for the seat-belt buckle, but she couldn't move. The door had caved toward her and the buckle was wedged into a tiny space that her hand couldn't make sense of.

She looked around wildly. A school bus lay on its side about ten feet away, the back windows shattered, its front end rutted into the ground near the windows of a diner. As she watched, three people barreled through the diner door, racing toward the bus.

"No," Maddie said, though she knew her voice wasn't loud enough. "Over here. Help us over here."

She watched as one of the people—a tall, slender woman—climbed the bus and stuck her head and arms through a window. A few seconds later, she came out with a child who was crying, holding one arm up against her tiny side, but otherwise unharmed.

"Come over here," Maddie said, louder this time. She felt throbbing begin to set in. Her head, her shoulder, one trapped leg. "We need help."

The woman passed the child to two other women, who took her and sat her gingerly on the ground. She dipped back into the window and came out with another. That child was fine, too. Blood ran into Maddie's eyes.

"Help!" she cried, tears mingling with the blood. She felt panic rise as the woman extracted yet another child through the window, and one of the others managed to pull open the back emergency door to let more children stream out. "Oh, God, oh, God," she said, breathing heavily. "Help us, please! Michael." She turned toward him again. Reached for him, but her arm was so tired now, so heavy. "Michael, please talk to me."

He continued to stare at her, his face pale as she'd ever seen it. He blinked, but it was lazy and far away, and that was all it took to unleash the panic full force.

"Help!" she screamed. "Help us, please! Over here! Look over here!" She thrashed with every ounce of energy that she had, bumping around in the cramped and crumpled space. "Help us! Help!" And then as quickly as it had come, the energy drained from her and her screams turned to sobs. "Please help," she said. "He's dying."

She saw the woman who'd opened the bus door turn her head, and then say something to the other two, motioning toward Maddie's car. The one standing on the overturned bus slid off. Together, they rushed to the car, a younger woman coming to Maddie's side, and an older woman going to Michael's.

"Sir?" she heard the older woman repeating. "Sir? Can you hear me?"

The younger woman was a flurry of activity, reaching in and trying to get to the seat-belt buckle, asking Maddie questions, saying things to her, but it was as if the world had ended. Maddie could feel herself talking, screaming, crying, but on the inside she was only watching as the older woman held Michael's head in her hands, catching his blood as he drifted away from them.

ONE

Karen gazed through the plate-glass window, her eyes wandering over the divots in the ground where the bus had crashed a month ago. She rubbed the side of her cell phone absently, her fingers bumping over the volume buttons, her fingernail scratching up against the SILENCE switch. Oh, how she'd love to "accidentally" flip that switch. If she never heard the phone ring, she wouldn't have to talk to anyone, right? She wouldn't have to answer the next time Kendall called. But she knew even if she did silence it, the peace would be short-lived. Kendall would only show up at her house or, worse, at her job, expecting her to pull strings she didn't have to make things easier for a son whose hide she wasn't sure she wanted to save anymore.

The girl had been calling all morning, congested with tears, begging. Blaming. Always blaming. As if Karen didn't do enough blaming for herself. You'd think, as a mother, Kendall would know that. Yet Karen had awakened to Kendall's tears and blame at the most ungodly hour, had been ripped out of a dream with it.

"Mom?" the voice on the other end had said.

Karen's heart had sunk. For one, she wasn't Kendall's mom. She was Travis's mom, and Kendall just happened to be the girl he was living with at the moment. Just as with Jessilyn and Margarite and that trashy girl whom Karen only ever knew as "Tag," Kendall's calling Karen "Mom" wasn't going to make her any more permanent in his life. Travis wasn't the permanent-girl type of guy, as much as Karen wished he would be. For another, anytime Kendall was calling her "Mom" on the phone at—she had leaned over and checked—4:42 in the morning, it was not going to be good news.

"What's going on?" Karen had asked, wiping her eyes with her free hand, then slipping on her glasses. The world had sprung into focus and, just like that, her day had started.

And now, an hour and a half later, she sat at the Tea Rose avoiding her not-daughter's phone calls, because she knew what the calls were about. Travis was in jail. Again. Drunk and fighting. Again.

Only this time he did a real job on the guy. This time the guy might not pull through.

Dear God, would that make her son a murderer? Was

that how it worked? Someone went from hothead to killer in the flip of a switch?

You'd think she would know. She'd worked at Sidwell, Cain, Smith & Smith for twenty years. Surely they'd defended drunk guys who had accidentally beat other guys to death in that amount of time. Kendall clearly thought Karen should know what to do. *You've got to help him. You've got to get him out of jail. There's the baby to think of, you know.*

Oh, yes, *that* much Karen knew. Her one grandchild. Her grandson, to be exact. Sweet little Marcus, born approximately eight minutes after Travis dumped Tag, seemed to be one of the few good things to come from her son in years. But that also made Kendall more permanent than the others, a fact that Karen wasn't ready to live with just yet. Kendall certainly wasn't any worse than those girls, but she wasn't any better than them, either. She hadn't shown it full-on just yet, but Karen suspected the girl had a shifty side to her. And a vengeful one.

Yes, they had the baby to think of, and Karen had her own baby to think of. It didn't matter if your child was two or twenty-two, she decided—you still hated to see him suffer, even if he brought it on himself. And if this man that Travis had beaten up was to die, Travis would be suffering for many years, she feared. She didn't even want to think of what that road would look like for her. A son in prison for life? How would she ever admit that to anyone?

On cue, her phone rang, and even though she'd been expecting it, she still jumped when it vibrated in her palm, causing her to slosh a dime-sized dollop of coffee onto the table. Predictably, Kendall's name flashed across the screen. For a moment, Karen considered upending the phone into her mug, letting French vanilla crème drown out Kendall.

But in the end, she couldn't do it. Abandoning Kendall would mean abandoning her son. What kind of mother could do that? *The kind whose son is in jail every other weekend could do that,* her mind nagged her. *The kind who should have toughened up on him long, long ago.*

She held the phone to her ear. "Hello?"

"Mom? It's me." Karen could hear the baby crying in the background. She focused on it. Tried to conjure the scent of the top of Marcus's head, the clench of his fist around her forefinger. Concentrating on Marcus helped calm her, helped remind her why she hadn't already washed her hands of the whole Kendall situation. "You find out anything?"

"I haven't even gone in yet."

"But it's a special circumstance."

I wish, Karen almost said. *I wish this was something that rarely happened.* "Nobody will be there at this hour," she said instead. Though that was a lie. As far as she could tell, Mr. Sidwell practically lived there. She'd found him sleeping on his office couch more than once.

"Well, will you call me after you've talked to them? Be sure to tell them Travis was in fear for his life. And he's got witnesses, too. I can bring the witnesses right to you. Be sure to tell them that."

Karen pushed her finger into the drop of coffee, let it sit

there for a moment, and then swiped the stain away, wiping her thumb dry on her sensible—translation: law-firm stodgy—brown skirt. "Honey, I've told you. I'm a recruiter. Human resources. I don't really work with the attorneys. I rarely talk to them. I don't feel right asking for favors."

"You work in the same office with them every day," Kendall said.

"But it's not like we're on a first-name basis or anything. I don't even work in the same hallway with the others."

"Just ask," Kendall said with finality. Karen heard the baby's cry get closer to the phone, as if Kendall was picking him up, and then settle into sniffles and grow silent. "If Travis goes to prison, Marcus and I won't be able to afford to live here. We'll have to move, and who knows where we'll end up?" Ah, there it was. The shifty, vengeful thing she'd suspected was lurking underneath.

Karen closed her eyes and pressed her thumb against one, and then the other, not even caring if she was smudging her eye shadow. She was already getting a headache and could feel the backs of her knees begin to sweat inside her panty hose. It was going to be a very long day. A long, stressful one at that. She let out a breath she hadn't even been aware of holding. She understood the threat clearly. Pull some strings at work to get Travis off the hook, or never see sweet Marcus again. "I'll ask," she said.

But when she hung up, she wondered whom. Whom at Sidwell Cain would she feel comfortable asking for help in getting her son off on a potential manslaughter case? God, the humiliation. She could just throttle Travis for putting her in this position.

"Please don't die, whoever you are," she said, her eyes turning toward the window again. She could see a shadowy reflection of herself, the outline of her hair. She spent way too much time curling it every morning, but it was short and unremarkably grayish brown, and hairstyle was the only style she really had going on anymore. Even though she was trim, middle age was starting to take its wrinkly, saggy toll, and the dress code at Sidwell Cain could be described as "litigation drab." She felt like she needed to make a daily effort of some sort, and if that effort was a curling iron and half a can of hair spray, so be it. Absently, she fluffed at a flat spot of her hair, her gaze shifting to the lawn on the other side of the window instead.

"Still doing okay over here? You haven't even touched your coffee. I was going to top it off." Sheila, the Tea Rose's only waitress worth her salt, leaned a hip against the booth. She rested the coffee carafe on the table and followed Karen's gaze out the front window.

"Hard to believe it was a month ago already," Sheila said. "The grass is even starting to grow back."

Karen nodded. This was where she'd been sitting when the crash had happened. She'd seen the whole thing as it unfolded one month ago—the bus screaming toward the intersection. She'd known it was going too fast. She could tell, even from her table, that it wasn't going to be able to stop in time. She'd watched as it wobbled and jerked on its shocks. She'd watched as it hit the other car. She'd watched as both skidded into the grass, spraying chunks of sod onto the window right next to her. She'd watched without flinching. She'd been too rooted by horror to flinch. But she'd been flinching every day since.

"He died right there," she whispered, and though she was sure Sheila had heard her, she wasn't saying it for Sheila. She said it to herself every day as she revisited her booth, unable to scrub away the memory of what had happened. Unable to forget Michael and Maddie Routh, the sweet couple in the red car, on their way to an early-morning doctor appointment. Unable to forget holding Michael's head in her palms as he died, catching his blood, catching his life.

"It seems so surreal," Sheila said. But Sheila hadn't been there that day. She'd been on vacation. The other waitress—what was her name? Indie? Andie? Karen couldn't recall—had been there. She'd been out back smoking a cigarette, but had run inside upon hearing the noise and called 911 while Karen and the other two customers had rushed outside to help.

"Yeah," Karen said. "'Surreal' is a good word for it." She gathered her purse and pulled out a few dollars. "I should get to work. Can't lollygag around all day."

"A day off would be nice, though," Sheila said.

"What are you talking about? You just got back from vacation," Karen teased. "Some of us never went."

In fact, Karen could barely even remember what a vacation felt like, it had been so long since she'd taken one. Raising Travis by herself, she had no extra money for travel. And then by the time he was raised and out of the house, she'd been too lonely to take one. The idea of sightseeing without someone to point out the landmarks to seemed so terribly sad.

Sheila rooted through her apron pockets until she found Karen's check. "It's a double-edged sword, though, you know? You get away, and by the end of your trip you start thinking about how good it'll feel to get home again. And then you get home and all you can think about is how amazing it was while you were away. This diner seems extra dingy ever since I got back. I want to smell sunscreen again."

"I'll be sure to wear some next time I come in," Karen said. She scooted out of the booth, then paused to offer Sheila a smile and a quick pat on the arm. "See you tomorrow. Try not to skip off to any tropical paradises while I'm gone."

"You didn't even touch your coffee today," Sheila said. "You sure everything's okay?"

Karen thought about Travis, tried to picture him in jail, his shaved, tattooed head gleaming under fluorescent jail lights. Miserable, in danger, but alive, breathing. She thought about the man whom Travis had beaten, hooked to tubes in a hospital bed. His family already grieving their loss.

No, things were not okay.

Her eyes roamed to the divots in the grass again.

Things were not okay, but she wasn't Maddie Routh, now, was she? And she wasn't that poor bus driver, God rest her soul.

"Guess I was just in it for the company today," Karen said. She waved and headed to her car.

TWO

Recently, Melinda had been particularly struck by how truly easy it was to live a lie. How frighteningly simple it was to love someone, be totally and undeniably committed to him, build a life with him, and still be hiding a major life fact. Hard emotionally, perhaps. But in execution, a breeze.

She thought about this every morning at this time, studying herself in the scuffed bathroom mirror, washing her face, tying her hair into a limp ponytail (the only trick her hair seemed to know how to do), brushing her teeth, and unceremoniously popping that tiny white pill into her mouth.

Chewable. They made them chewable now. Which meant she had to think about it every day, not just wash it down along with her feelings of guilt. Tiny white pill; tiny white lie.

Baby, baby, baby, her jaw muscles seemed to creak at her while she chewed. Or more like, *Nobaby, nobaby, nobaby.* Door locked, pill packet crammed back into the bottom of the tampon box, where Paul would never look. Easy and done. She licked her teeth clean and gave one last study of herself in the mirror, faking a smile. She didn't look like a liar. She could forget the deceit had ever happened. Until tomorrow, when she had to do it again.

Paul was still sleeping. Curled around his pillow like a child, with his bare back, soft and warm as a biscuit, poking out from the top of the sheets. His cowlick knocked free by sleep once again. Melinda studied him while she wrestled earrings into her earlobes. He was perfect, really. The most perfect man. She was so incredibly lucky to have him, and she knew it. Most of the time, she waited breathlessly for him to figure it out and leave her. If he ever did, it would destroy her, yet she would somehow still understand.

He'd been her first. God, how embarrassing it was. Almost as bad as admitting it to the guys at work. *A twenty-four-year-old virgin,* they'd crowed. *If you need any volunteers,* they'd offered. *If you want some pointers. Ha! Get it? Pointer? I'll happily volunteer my pointer!* The comments were humiliating, but she didn't take them personally. It was part of working with mostly men. They meant it no more seriously than when they razzed one another. In a way, it was an honor that they treated her like one of them.

She'd saved herself for Paul. She hadn't known that was

for whom she'd been saving herself until after they'd done it. And then she'd realized that, yes, this was the one. This was the man who was meant to take her virginity. This was the man who wouldn't abuse it, even if things didn't ultimately work out between them.

When Paul had lowered himself over her that first time, she'd lain there like a corpse, afraid to so much as touch his cheek. She'd cried, too, not because it hurt, but because it had finally happened and her chest felt so full of feeling for him she couldn't contain it. But of course he'd been afraid he'd hurt her. He'd pulled her into him and petted her hair, his bare feet finding hers.

"I'm so sorry," he'd murmured over and over again. "I never want to hurt you."

And she'd let him think that it was physical pain that had caused her tears, because she was too afraid of how fast and how fully she'd fallen for him. She'd half cried over the anticipation of the pain she'd feel when he came to his senses and left her for someone better. She didn't want him to know that even if he walked away, she'd still have felt it worth it to give herself to him.

A lot had happened since that first night. Dates where he swept her off her feet. Arguments after which she was shocked and thrilled to find he still wanted her. That Christmas when they accidentally gave each other the same gift— DVD copies of *Fiddler on the Roof*, to commemorate their first date at an outdoor theater—and then Valentine's Day of the very next year when they accidentally did it again, this time with gold cross pendants. The engagement, the wedding, the I-love-yous and the promises that Melinda could feel Paul really, really meant. House hunting—they found their perfect house on the first day—and furniture shopping, which should have taken agonizing months, but instead took only a few hours for the two of them to fall in love with exactly the same couch, the same bedroom set, the same dining room table, without having to really even talk about it. Slow dances in the living room, and fast dances at parties. Over time, she had come to accept that this perfect man did want plain-faced, simple her and her only—they were soul mates—though occasionally that same fear, that same unwarranted pain, crept through again. Most notably, every morning when her deception started anew.

She shut her jewelry box, and Paul stirred, turning over sleepily and opening one eye.

"Hey," he said, breathing in deeply, as if he'd just come up from underwater rather than from a dream. He reached over and turned the alarm clock so he could see it He rubbed his face. "It's early. I thought you were off today. Come here." He swept a muscled arm open as invitation.

"Babysitting, remember?" she said, going to him, standing at the side of the bed. "My sister has jury duty."

He curled his arm around her lower back and pulled her so that her thighs were butted up against the mattress and she was about to topple over on him. "Ah, babysitting is good practice," he said. He reached up into her shirt and laid his warm palm flat against her stomach. "Who knows? Nine months from now we may be needing your sister to babysit our little guy."

Melinda wriggled out of his grasp, tugging on the hem of her shirt. "Well, you know, it hasn't happened yet," she said. She turned away, afraid he'd see guilt on her face, and pretended to look for shoes tucked under the bed.

"We can always try again right now, if you think last night didn't take. Hedge our bets." Paul pulled himself to sitting, the sheet falling around his waist. He was still nude from the night before, and part of Melinda wanted nothing more than to slip under the sheets with him, to feel him against her.

But it hadn't been that way lately. It'd been purposeful, and in some ways relentless. She'd felt afraid every time he touched her these days, irrationally so. She knew that it wasn't going to happen. It wasn't going to work. The tiny white pill she took every morning made sure of that. But it was the fact that he so wanted it to happen, that he was so sure it was going to happen, that made it seem scarier, as if the pill would somehow be rendered ineffective just by the force of his desire.

"I'm late," she said. "Sorry. Rain check?"

He let out a pouty sigh. "I was afraid you'd say that." He pulled himself all the way out of bed and kissed her on the temple as he headed for the bathroom. "Have fun with the kids. I love you!"

Her heart tugged. "I love you, too," she said. She paused, then went to the bathroom door and rested her forehead against it. "I really do."

He opened the door. He'd put on a pair of boxers and stood in the light, scratching his chest. "Good," he said. "I really do, too. Now, go, or I won't let you go."

• • •

Her cell phone rang the minute she pulled out of the driveway.

"Where are you?" Holly demanded on the other end. Ever since they were little, Melinda's older sister seemed to have only one volume setting: loud and bossy. They were opposites in just about every way. Where Holly's hair was long, thick, and glossy black, Melinda's was shoulder length, thin, and blah. Where Holly was tall and curvy, Melinda was short and flat-chested. Where Holly was a palette of color on porcelain skin, Melinda was plain and makeup free on honey skin. But they were sisters—close, despite their differences. Or maybe close because of them.

"I'm on my way. Sorry, I'm a little behind," Melinda said.

"Oh, great. Well, I'll just tell the judge that you were a little behind. I'm sure he'll feel sorry for me right before he tosses me in jail for contempt of court."

"You're not going to be late. You live half a mile from the courthouse. And I seriously doubt they lock people up for being tardy to jury duty. Besides, if he tosses you in jail, I'll bail you out if it takes me a hundred years to do it."

"Gee, thanks," Holly deadpanned.

"That's what sisters are for," Melinda said, grinning.

"Okay, well, since I'm obviously going to be leaving the second you get here, let me tell you some things now."

"Shoot."

"Mitchell has engineering camp today at the university. You have to have him there by nine."

"Engineering camp? Is that a thing? He's eight. What about school?"

"Shush, I'm not finished. I've packed him a lunch—just grab it out of the fridge before you go. Reenie was up teething all night, so good luck with that. She can have more Tylenol at noon, but I wouldn't expect her to eat anything at all today. And Gregory is . . . well, he's just Gregory."

"Got it."

"You sure? Maybe I should write some of this down. I'll write it down."

"No, come on. This isn't that complicated. Gregory goes to basketball camp, Reenie has a lunch in the fridge, and . . . what's the name of your third kid again? The one with the hair?"

"Darn it, Linds, it's not a good day to mess with me! I've had three hours of sleep, there's spit-up on every item of clothing I own, and with my luck I'll spend the night in the clink because my inconsiderate sister doesn't think being late to jury duty is any big deal."

Melinda chuckled. "Relax, Hols, I'm just teasing you. I've got this. But listen, I'm on the road, so I need to go."

"Okay, okay, Safety Officer Sam, I'll let you go. But hurry up."

Melinda hardly ever talked on the phone while driving. And never texted. She'd seen the result of those decisions too many times. Someone thinks he's making an innocent phone call to say he's on his way home and wraps his car around a tree and dies. Blip. Just like that. Nothing that she, or any of the other paramedics, could do about it. The worst was when they got to a scene and the victim's hand was still wrapped around the phone.

Scratch that. The worst was actually when they got to a scene and the victim's hand was still wrapped around the phone, and the phone was still working.

Of course, there were so many things that could go wrong in a car. Things people really couldn't control. She'd probably seen them all. Bad brakes, someone falls asleep, a squirrel runs out into the road. Once a rollover accident she'd been called to had actually begun as a fistfight in the driver's seat. And there was the time a guy had a seizure and ended up sitting in his car in a stranger's living room.

But cars weren't the only way to go. Not even the most surprising, Melinda supposed. People died all the time from accidents they could never have prevented in a million years. Hell, for that matter, she could choke on one of her clandestine birth control pills and die in the bathroom with sexy, naked, sleeping Paul clueless on the other side of the locked door. Wouldn't that be a surprise for him? So many layers of surprises, he wouldn't know what to do with them all.

"God, morbid enough, Melinda?" she said aloud, and flipped on the radio. She was going to be spending the day with two rowdy boys and a teething toddler—she needed to lighten up a little or it was going to be a very long day.

The song ended and a local newscaster came on. "Today, on the one-month anniversary of the deadly school bus crash in Caldwell, parents of the injured children have announced that they intend to file suit against the school district. . . ." Melinda's attention perked. It had been a month already? How was that even possible? She hadn't been back

to that diner since the crash. It had seemed like only yesterday, though.

She listened to the rest of the newscast, and then turned
the radio off.

"One-month anniversary," she muttered. "Like it's a
celebration."

As if on autopilot, she found her car turning onto For-
est, and then Shady Tree, and finally onto Highway 32,
heading toward the intersection where the crash had happened.

Melinda knew she was on borrowed time, and that
Holly was ready to kill her as it was. But Caldwell was a
small community. You could get from one end to the other
in just a few minutes, especially this early in the morning.
You could drive from your house to the Tea Rose Diner, for
example, in plenty of time to still arrive at your sister's
house before jury duty convened.

She couldn't explain it, but she felt pulled. Like she
needed to see it, to be back at that scene on this one-month
milestone. Like she needed to kneel next to those god-
awful divots that everyone could see from the highway. The
city really should have filled those in.

She'd still been clutching the stick, for Christ's sake.
That girl, that Maddie Routh, had still been holding the
white stick so tightly her nails were digging into her palms.
Her husband's whole body had been crushed, the car flattened, every window busted out, every door sunk in, but
she didn't drop the stick. It had been covered with blood—
whose? hers? Michael's? who knew?—and her hand was

slicked with blood, too, but she would not let it go. The pink plus sign was crowded out by the crimson, but she would not release it. Even after they freed her from the vehicle, she held on to that test stick. As if it would save her from something.

Melinda didn't think she would ever forget that pink plus sign.

She didn't think she would ever eat hash browns and sausage and banana pancakes again.

She didn't think she would ever be able to pull into that parking lot another time.

But she was wrong. She was pulling in. She was getting out of her car. She was walking toward the divots. The grass was starting to regrow in them. Soon nature would do what the city had not done. Time would fill in the ruts, and there would be nothing left. No reminder of what had happened that day.

Except for the memories in her heart.

Paul hadn't understood. Of course he hadn't. *Thank God Melinda was there to help,* he'd told people, proudly. *She's used to seeing these things. She knows how to handle it.* He'd assumed life would go on as it had. They'd keep trying to have a baby, keep trying to start their family.

But he'd been wrong.

Yes, she was used to seeing these things.

And that was precisely why she couldn't carry on as normal.

That stick. That bloody stick with the pink plus sign.

She nearly bumped into a woman in a dowdy brown

skirt coming out of the diner and then did a double take. How weird. Melinda hadn't thought of the woman since the day of the accident and would never have been able to describe her if anyone asked—it had been such chaos she couldn't focus on anything other than the impossible task of trying to keep Maddie Routh calm—but she knew the woman the minute she caught her profile in her periphery. She was tall, but thin, wore clunky-heeled shoes, a pair of cheap stud earrings poking out from under her short grayish brown hair.

"Hello?" she asked, stutter-stepping toward the woman.

The woman paused, and Melinda could see recognition set in her eyes. "Oh," she said. She half waved with a hand that was gripping a cell phone. "I was in my own world there, I guess. How are you?"

Melinda nodded, and then instantly wished she'd never spoken to the woman at all, as she didn't know how on earth to follow up the hello. It seemed like there should be more, but the more was so weighty and enormous, how could one say it to a stranger?

The woman gestured toward the divots. "It's been a month, today," she said.

Melinda nodded. "That's why I stopped. They were talking about it on the radio." She squinted into the sun, which was the warm beautiful orange of morning. "Probably stupid to come back here. Nothing to see."

The woman shrugged. "I come every day." She pointed with her cell phone at the nearest window. "Sit right there, right where I was sitting when it happened."

Second Chance Friends

Melinda turned and gazed at the window. To watch the sun rise over those marks in the grass every day. It seemed so . . . "Pointless," Melinda muttered. The woman didn't hear her, but she burned with apology anyway. She offered a grin. "I don't suppose you've heard anything about what happened to her," she said. "The girl in the wreck? Maddie Routh?"

The woman shook her head. "I wonder about her all the time. I hope she's okay."

Melinda nodded and turned to stare at the divots again. If she didn't know better, she'd swear the new grass was a different color. Richer, somehow. A deeper hue. "Yeah," she said, unable to tear her eyes away.

"And I hope the baby's okay," the woman added softly.

"Yeah," Melinda said, and, without realizing it, gripped both arms around her stomach tight.

THREE

Hiding was exhausting. It sounded so easy. After all, hiding was full of don'ts. *Don't go to work. Don't call in. Don't answer your phone when they call you. Don't go home to Sunday dinner. Don't go to rehearsal. And, whatever you do, don't go out with the cast on a Friday night.* What was simpler than inactivity?

But the truth of the matter, as far as Joanna Chambers could see, was that *don't* wasn't as full of inaction as it seemed. There was willfulness behind shrugging off the most important parts and pieces of your life. It stuck in the pit of your stomach and leapt in your heart. The phone never rang to indifference.

Not that she'd answered her phone in a month. Not that

she'd checked her missed calls, and especially not her voice mail. The last time she'd done that was a mistake.

Voice mail #1 had made her toes go icy: "Joanna, hello, it's Max. Not sure what's going on with you, but we're really missing you here at LaEats. Stephen told us you're sick with the flu? It's been a long time. Hope you're okay. Listen, I don't want to fire you. But Leese will probably really start going apeshit if you don't at least call. Stephen's been taking your shifts. Call soon."

Voice mail #2 had made her swim with guilt: "Joanna, it's Stephen. What the heck is going on? It's like you dropped off the face of the earth. Is this about that night with the wine? It's okay. It really is. I don't even remember most of it anyway. I was stupid to say something. I was drunk. It's fine. . . . I wish you'd answer your phone. I can't keep covering you forever. Leese is on the warpath. Plus I'm afraid you're trapped in a hole or something. If you don't answer by the end of today, I'm going to come to your apartment. I love you. In a nonweird way, okay? Please answer."

Voice mail #3 had crushed her: "Yes, I'm calling for Joanna. This is Eliot, your stage manager? Stan said to tell you you're off the cast. And to, uh, never audition for him again. Uh, sorry. Good-bye."

Voice mail #4 had broken her heart: "Hey, sweetie, it's me. Your father and I are wondering if you might have time to come to dinner this Sunday. We know you're busy with the show, but it's been so many weeks now, we've forgotten what you look like. Just kidding, a mother could never forget such a precious face. Come home. We miss you."

Voice mail #5, she couldn't even listen to: "Um, hi. It's Sutton. You probably know that. . . ."

Hiding was such a bad idea. She should have known that. She'd tried it before. It didn't work out then, so why would she have any reason to expect it to work out now? She'd hidden so well the last time that she'd disappeared from college for what, so far, looked like would be forever. Was she prepared to disappear from acting forever? From working? No, according to her bank account, she could disappear from working for only about two more months, and then she'd be screwed.

Not that LaEats was going to keep her job open for two more months. Not that Stephen was going to cover her shift for that long.

God. Stephen.

He might not have remembered most of what happened that night with the wine, but she did. She remembered every single second of it. She remembered him showing up for their standing Friday night movie date, a box of Franzia under his arm. His turn to buy; her turn to cook.

"Whatever you're making, it better go with . . ." He'd paused, checking the box as he followed her to the kitchen. "Red."

She'd bent, pulled a cookie sheet out of the oven with flourish. "Pizza pockets. I believe red is, in fact, the proper pairing."

He set the box on the counter. "What the hell? Frozen pizza pockets? I made beef bourguignon for you."

"It was delicious."

"It took me all day!"

"Whatever. You just made it because you like saying it." She'd scraped the pockets onto a plate.

"Saying what?"

"Beef bourguignon. Sounds like *boof.*"

"It's French," he protested.

"It's naughty, and that's why you love it." She stuffed a bite of pizza pocket into her mouth. "Get the glasses. I'm thirsty. And I've got vintage Sandra Bullock cued up."

They'd sat on her couch, munching on pizza pockets and popcorn and Skittles, and drinking way too much wine. They watched *While You Were Sleeping,* talking over the movie, trying to decide which of their LaEats regulars would be most likely to be the subject of secret marriage fantasies.

"Got one," Stephen said, taking a huge gulp of wine. "The girl with the pointy boobs. The one who always starts with the Irish Nachos?"

"Oh!" Joanna, more than a little drunk, had snapped her fingers a few times, trying to drum up the girl's name. "Ugh. I can't remember. The one Bryce calls Patty O'Furniture."

"Yes, that one! She might be secret-fantasy-worthy. She's got a nice face above those cone boobs."

Joanna curled one lip. "Not my type," she said. She'd

been saying that about all the girls he brought up, a part of her hoping it could provide a good segue. Maybe wishing he would ask: *What do you mean, not your type? Do you have a type of girl?* She always did this when they drank too much together. She always felt the truth sitting right there in the back of her throat, begging to come out, and looked for ways for it to conveniently slip. She wanted so badly to tell her best friend. If only one other person in the world could know, maybe the weight on her chest wouldn't be so heavy. Maybe she wouldn't walk around feeling so ashamed all the time, and so silly for feeling so ashamed. And so angry that there should be shame involved at all.

Stephen leaned forward to refill her wineglass. "There's another girl," he said. "She's definitely fantasy material."

"What girl? Don't say Mani-Pedi Woman. It's bad enough how Bryce goes on about her. She's not all that he thinks she is."

"Nope, not Mani-Pedi Woman." Stephen sucked a drop of spilled wine off his thumb and sat back, a blot of wine licking over the top edge of the glass and bleeding into his shirt. He didn't notice. "She is cute, though. Bryce is totally going to get her number next time she comes in."

"Plain. And she has a ring tan."

He got wide-eyed. "How did you notice that?"

She shrugged, feeling her face burn. The truth was, Bryce wasn't wrong. Mani-Pedi Woman was cute. But she was also a cheater. And gay. The ring tan was on her right hand. Of course Joanna noticed.

"So who's the girl, then?" she asked, sipping her wine, not noticing that the credits were now rolling on the TV.

"She's not exactly a regular customer," Stephen said.

"Barfly? You know I don't pay attention to those. They're so pathetic with their mow-hee-toes and their lame get-laid lines. Hey, baby," she mimicked in a drunken voice, "I don't suppose you could help me with this zipper? It's stuck." She made an exaggerated pouty face.

Stephen laughed and bumped her shoulder. "No. None of the barflies." He shook his head a little too fast, causing him to lean hard into her. "She works there."

Joanna's eyes grew wide. "Oh my! You've been holding out on a work crush? Who is it? Is it the new bartender? It has to be the bartender. She's got all those tattoos. I never took you for a tat man." She jostled his shoulder with hers. "Tell me. Do not leave me hanging here."

Stephen leaned his head against her shoulder, and then turned and rubbed his nose shyly against her shirt. "You," he said.

Joanna had laughed out loud, sure it had been a joke. Stephen calling her secret-fantasy-worthy was like calling a sibling secret-fantasy-worthy. "Yes, I am such a dream. A nice face above these pointy boobs."

Stephen turned his head to gaze at her, his eyes faraway and swimmy, their faces just inches apart. "No, I'm being serious," he slurred. "You're the crush."

"You're drunk, Stephen Wilkinson," she said, bumping his shoulder again. "This is going to be hilarious tomorrow."

"Yeah," he said. "I am and it will. But that doesn't change the fact."

"What fact?" She rolled her eyes too elaborately, talked too loudly, shrugged too high, she knew. But her heart was pounding and she felt a restless fleeing sensation in her legs. She wanted Stephen to turn this into a joke. Please, a joke. As much as she would have liked to have reason to tell him the truth about her, this wasn't the way.

"This fact," Stephen said instead, and leaned over and kissed her.

It was nice, as kisses went. Soft and warm, and she would've been lying if she said she'd felt nothing at all. Of course she did. She loved Stephen. Being kissed by someone you loved felt good, no matter who you were and what kind of lies you told yourself and the world.

But there was a difference between feeling good and feeling right. This kiss could never be right. She'd pulled away, trying to be gentle about it.

"You're drunk," she repeated, much more softly this time, licking her lips. She could taste Stephen's wine on them.

Stephen gazed at her sleepily, grinning sadly. "And I'm not your type," he said.

"It's not that. . . ." She leaned forward and set her wine-glass on the coffee table. Suddenly, none of it had felt right. Not the food or the wine or the romantic movies. Suddenly it all felt like she was leading him on. Of course he would become confused. It was all her fault. "I mean, it is that, too. It's just not . . . I need to tell you something."

Nervous—she was so nervous. She'd never said the words aloud. She'd never told anyone the truth. And a part of her had convinced herself that she wouldn't have to, that it was painfully obvious, the stuff of stereotypes. A part of her wished it would never need to be spoken. There was ease in others guessing.

Apparently, she'd been wrong. A guy had fallen for her, regardless of how painfully obvious she thought the truth was.

But Stephen—good old Stephen; God bless Stephen— simply smiled and set his wineglass down. "You don't need to say anything. It's no hard feelings." And he reached up and tweaked the end of her nose lightly, the way he'd always done when he felt playful. He'd stood and swayed. "Woo. Looks like you're going to have a houseguest tonight. Damn that wine. Pretty sure you slipped bourbon in it so you could have your way with me."

He headed toward the spare bedroom, the one that had only ever been occupied by him.

"Night," he called over his shoulder.

"Night," she'd said, and then had downed the last of her wine, poured another glass, and downed that one, too, trying to wash away the lump in her throat.

The next morning, she'd made sure she was gone before he awoke, as her only goal was to disappear. She'd declared herself officially in hiding and had gone to the last place she could think he would look for her—that greasy diner off the highway. They served Boston cream pie there, a weakness of hers.

And then the accident had happened, and she had gone into a weird mourning over some guy she didn't even know.

And now, after a month of hiding, she was exhausted. Mentally, emotionally, physically. She couldn't sleep; she wasn't eating well; she was jittery. And it didn't help that the news was showing that grainy cell phone footage from a month ago. Its graininess was her only saving grace— you couldn't tell who was who in that video. Apparently, even her best friend and her parents didn't recognize her. She didn't have to endure any "hero" conversations or have everyone thinking she was traumatized and "needed to talk."

But of course she'd recognized herself in that video. She'd watched herself all morning, running out of the diner, her shirt untucked, looking as hungover and miserable as she'd felt that morning. She saw herself run toward the school bus, which had landed on its side. She saw her arms stretch up to climb, saw them reach through the open windows, the broken windows.

Every time she saw the footage, she remembered new things—the cries of the kids inside, the relief she'd felt that all the kids seemed to be able to cry, the adrenaline strength that coursed through her as she handed bruised and bloodied kids to two women who seemed to have materialized out of nowhere and were standing next to the bus.

The feeling of dread when one of those women called them both to a crumpled car, so wadded up she hadn't even noticed it before the woman had pointed it out.

The nausea and helplessness of seeing the man behind the wheel of that car.

What had been their names? Route? Roush? A young couple. A cute couple. They'd been heading to an early doctor appointment, she remembered. They'd had big news to confirm.

Joanna aimed the remote at the TV and pressed the power button, snuffing the grainy video into silence.

But it didn't help. She still felt agitated, like she—finally—needed some human interaction. And maybe some more Boston cream pie. Or maybe just proof that it really had happened, that she really had been there. That it wasn't some other lost-looking girl in the video footage.

She grabbed her keys and headed down to the parking garage.

She saw the two women as soon as she pulled up to the diner—an older woman in office attire and a younger one in chinos and a T-shirt. They were standing on the sidewalk, their arms crossed and their elbows nearly touching, staring at the bumps where the bus had carved up the earth on its approach. They seemed to be talking, and while it seemed unlikely that she would run across them here, today—her first time out since the crash—it somehow also made sense that she had done exactly that.

She parked her car and watched, her legs suddenly filled with ice water over the thought of human interaction. She could do this, right? You didn't just become unable to live among people, did you? These women were not Stephen, not Sutton, not Stan, not her disappointed parents. She didn't have to hide from them.

The younger one saw her first. She put her hand on the shoulder of the older woman and said something, and the older woman turned as well. Their faces didn't change. Now she had been spotted—she had to say something.

"Hello," she said, coming toward them on the walkway. "I didn't expect . . ." She didn't know how to finish the sentence.

"Yeah, looks like we all had the same idea today," the younger one said.

Joanna crossed her arms, curling her fingers through the belt loops of her shorts. "I didn't really plan to come. It just suddenly seemed like the right thing to do."

"Same here," the younger one said. "I should be at my sister's house right now. She's going to be furious when I get there. But I couldn't help it. I felt pulled."

The older woman shifted her weight. Her phone rang and she looked at her hand quizzically, as if she wasn't really sure what she was holding. She pressed a button on the side and it went silent. "It's been haunting me a little," she said. "Somehow being here makes me feel a tiny bit better. I was just saying I still wonder about Maddie all the time."

"Maddie?"

"Routh," the younger woman added. "The woman in the car. We were just talking about the pregnancy, wondering how it's going."

"Oh," she said. *Routh*. Maddie Routh. That had been it.

Maddie and Michael. She remembered now. How could she have ever forgotten? Awkwardly, she extended her hand. "Joanna, by the way."

The younger woman smiled and took her hand. Joanna felt a jolt of something unexpected. Connectedness, maybe? Had she been hiding for that long? "Melinda."

They shook, and then she turned her hand to the older woman. At first dazed, she seemed to shrug herself out of it, and then took Joanna's hand. Again, she felt the electricity of human contact.

"Karen," she said. "Freeman." Her phone rang again and she shut it off immediately, without looking, a frustrated crease appearing on her forehead. "I should go."

"Me, too," Melinda said. "My sister is going to be livid. It was nice meeting you, Joanna." She shrugged. "Again, I guess."

"First time didn't really count," Joanna said, and then wondered if she'd sounded too flip. She hated how she second-guessed everything that came out of her mouth. "I mean . . . I'm sure I wasn't good company. . . . It was just a rough scene. Nice talking to you both."

The women turned, leaving Joanna alone on the sidewalk. "So you'll be here tomorrow, huh?" she heard Melinda ask Karen as they walked.

"Every day," Karen answered. "I don't know why. It just makes me feel better."

Joanna stood in the early sun, goose bumps popping up on her shins despite the humidity that was already in the air. She watched as the two women found their cars and said their last good-byes, got inside, and each drove away. She felt very alone, while at the same time she felt surrounded by ghosts. The ghosts of the bus driver and Michael Routh. The ghosts of her past, of her present. The ghosts of her secrets.

A few diner patrons walked in and out, maneuvering around her, but she couldn't uproot herself from the pathway. She had a sudden desire to belong again. Not to anyone in particular, but to society as a whole. She wanted to go to the farmers' market on Wednesday mornings and to the movie theater on Friday nights. She wanted to eat at the chain chicken place across the highway and buy screws at Home Depot. She wanted to jog in the park with the retirees and the stay-at-home moms. She wanted to fit in. Of course she had ghosts. She was so hidden she was practically dead. Living people had no haunts following them, did they?

It seemed so absurd to her that grass had grown while she'd been gone from reality. So blatantly defiant. You could hide from life all you wanted; it would still keep going without you. It wouldn't even notice you were gone. To her, that fact felt sadder than death itself.

She started moving, her feet scuffing in flip-flops along the walk, the goose bumps fading, her armpits becoming damp with sweat.

She wasn't even surprised to find that her flip-flops took her away from the door and into the grass instead.

She ignored her craving for Boston cream pie and instead found herself walking to the edge of the bumps. She lowered herself to the ground, sitting cross-legged inside a divot.

Coming here every day had made Karen feel better, she'd said.

Joanna closed her eyes and slowly brushed her hands over the new grass, feeling it tickling her palms.

Yes, she could definitely see how it would.

FOUR

As far as Karen could tell, all law firms were high on the snoot scale. But Sidwell, Cain, Smith & Smith, where she'd worked for nearly twenty years, seemed to blow right through the roof of snoot and on into full-on snotty. The floors were polished marble and the chandeliers were copious. Seemed every room you walked into had crystals dripping from the ceiling right above your head. The main receptionist, Evvy, spoke in a whisper and had one of those smiles that turned down at the edges as if she pitied you rather than enjoyed you. The attorneys barked orders at their secretaries—especially the ones they were not so secretly sleeping with—and nowhere was there a single visible photo of a child or a favorite pet. God forbid the errant clipped cartoon. It seemed to Karen as if they were all argyle-clad drones with their sensible shoes and their pencils tucked behind their ears and their dreadful bow ties.

It had been hard for Karen, at first, to accept the culture of Sidwell Cain. She hated that nobody laughed out loud in the employee lounge, and she hated the blind attorney, Mr. Cain, who wore a chip on his shoulder so large it was almost impossible to fit in the same hallway with him. And she hated the commute downtown. Caldwell was a suburb only ten miles or so away from the heart of Kansas City, but some days it felt like a million.

Had it not been for Antoinette, Karen might not have lasted twenty days at Sidwell Cain, much less twenty years.

Antoinette was the other inhabitant of what they'd lovingly dubbed the Hiring Cave, separated from the rest of the firm in a secluded hallway on the bottom floor, sandwiched between the copy room and the employee lounge. There was not a single chandelier to be found in their part of the building; no client would happen upon them on purpose, or even by accident. At first, Karen had felt insulted that Sidwell Cain had thought so little of their HR department. She felt hidden away like a dirty little secret. But once Antoinette schooled her in the fine art of Getting Away with Stuff the Others Can't, she began to feel at home in the Hiring Cave. Better—she began to feel comfortable. They regularly shouted conversations between their offices. Sometimes they played music—something that would never have been allowed upstairs. And each of them kept fluffy house slippers tucked beneath their desks for when they were doing paperwork. And on the first Monday of every month, Antoinette and Karen shut their doors for "payroll meetings," which were actually daylong festivals of lattes, Cheetos, and celebrity gossip, during which they gathered around an old mini tube TV that Antoinette had smuggled in several years ago to catch up on daytime talk shows.

In some ways, the only way Karen could handle the snootiness of Sidwell, Cain, Smith & Smith was by retreating to her separate world downstairs.

"So, what are you going to do?" Antoinette asked as they hurried over to Wong's Café for lunch a few days after Kendall had awakened Karen with Travis's bad news. "Ignore, ignore, ignore?"

"I can't," Karen said, half out of breath, even though she'd changed into her sneakers for the walk over. Antoinette was child-sized—one of those fireballs of energy in a little package of muscle and enviable waist-length wiry black hair—but she could move on those matchstick legs. Even in heels. "If I ignore her, who knows what she'll do? Take the baby and hide, probably."

"You know it's only a matter of time before she disappears with that baby anyway, right?" Antoinette said. She plunged through the door of Wong's, which was shoulder-to-shoulder packed, as usual.

"I don't like to think about that." Karen stepped inside behind her friend. But of course she knew it was true. Travis wouldn't keep Kendall around any longer than he'd kept any of the others, and as much as she'd like to believe she'd raised her son better than to let his baby be smuggled off to God-knew-where, she had serious doubts that would be the case. In some ways, she'd been steeling herself for the day Marcus went away since the day he was born, hugging him extra hard, absorbing his scent extra long. "But, yes, I know."

"Sorry, I don't want to be depressing, but it is what it is. You going to talk to Mr. Sidwell about getting Travis out?" She turned to the counter. "Pork lo mein," she shouted over the din of the crowd. "And don't put any of those disgusting baby corns in it." She turned and made a face at Karen. "Those things are unnatural. You want to split an order of spring rolls?"

Karen shook her head. "I'm not all that hungry. Just some soup, Mr. Wong," she called out. "A small." She turned back to Antoinette, who was loading soy sauces and napkins into her purse. "I don't think so. What am I supposed to do? Hi, Mr. Sidwell, I know you don't know me—I'm one of the drones you hide in the basement—but I'm wondering if you could get my son off on a possible murder charge? At a discount?"

At the words "murder charge," Karen touched her fingertips to her temples. She hadn't heard from Kendall in several days, so she had no idea whether the mystery man on the other side of the bar fight was still alive. Surely if he'd died, Kendall would have blown up her phone with calls and texts. Unless the girl had already moved on, and not bothered to tell Karen about it. She wouldn't put it past her.

"So you're going to let him cool out in the clink this time?" Antoinette asked, reaching over the counter to snag her order. "I think that's the right thing to do. He's never going to learn if you keep bailing him out, you know."

"I know," Karen said miserably. Mr. Wong placed her soup on the counter and she grabbed it, then passed her credit card to the impossibly young-looking girl who always ran the register. Her arm was jostled by a man distracted with his cell phone, but she felt too numb to care. "Let's change the subject."

"Excuse us," Antoinette snarled, shoving past the man, never too numb to give it back to what she considered the overly rude, me-first business crowd.

Karen followed Antoinette toward the door. Mr. Wong's was so crowded now, the line held the door open, and they had to shimmy sideways through it. Once on the sidewalk, Antoinette stopped short, Karen nearly smashing her soup cup against Antoinette's back.

"Okay, new subject," Antoinette whispered, tugging on Karen's sleeve with two fingers and gazing pointedly at the middle of the line. "Guess who's back?"

Karen followed her friend's gaze, and when she saw the subject of the stare, she sighed. "Come on," she mumbled, aiming her face to the sidewalk and walking quickly ahead.

But Antoinette lagged behind. "Oh, hey," she said, sounding mortifyingly fake to Karen's ears. "Long line today, huh?"

Karen stopped, resigned, and glanced up. There he was, looking right into her eyes, just as she knew he would be. She swept as much of a smile as she could across her face. "Hi," she said.

"Hi, there," he answered in that voice of his that somehow managed to be soft-spoken and confident all at the same time. Like his ideas were so good, he didn't need to be loud about them.

His name was Marty Squire. Mid-fifties, built like a thirty-year-old, with meticulously combed salt-and-pepper hair and light blue eyes that went so deep, Karen couldn't hold his gaze for more than moments at a time before feeling like she needed a life vest. He worked at an accounting firm on the fourth floor of their building, but he dressed like a lawyer, in navy suits with power ties and shoes so shiny they were like he was walking in little black pools.

Karen knew all of this through Antoinette, who Karen had always suspected had missed a lucrative calling in private investigation. Antoinette always knew everything about everyone and never apologized for snooping. And if you asked her something that she didn't know the answer to, you could guarantee that within the day she'd have it sniffed out.

"Eating at the desk today?" Marty asked, motioning to the foam soup bowl Karen held.

She looked down, blushed. She hated it when she blushed around him. It was like she was a teenager again—*oh, no, a boy talked to me!*—but the last thing she wanted was for Marty to mistake her for interested. "Oh. Yeah." She lifted up the bowl as evidence.

"It's crowded as balls in there," Antoinette said, and Karen blushed again, on her friend's behalf. If only she had half the ease in conversation that Antoinette did . . . and if only Antoinette could be a tiny bit more reserved. "If you're planning to eat in there, you better strap on some hockey gear. You're going to have to fight for a table."

The line inched forward, thankfully causing Marty to have to take a few steps, leading him away from them. "Nope. At the desk for me today, too," he said. "I've got a hot date with a calculator and a very messed-up audit."

"Good times," Antoinette said. "I cannot be trusted with anything that might take a calculator to figure. Thank God I have Karen here—"

"Well, have fun with that," Karen said. She grabbed Antoinette's arm and started pulling her down the side-walk back toward Sidwell, Cain, Smith & Smith.

"Okay, maybe we'll get a chance to eat together tomor-row," she heard Marty say, but she didn't slow her stride.

"If I can talk the workhorse here into it," Antoinette called over her shoulder. "If it weren't for me, she'd never leave her desk."

"Not true," Karen said under her breath, but she didn't slow down, and didn't let go, until they had rounded the corner.

Antoinette giggled. "You are so adorable when you're in lust."

"I'm not in lust."

"Oh, really? Is that why you're sprinting down the side-walk with soup in your hand? Did you take a sudden inter-est in marathon running?"

Karen hadn't really thought she'd been jogging, but now that Antoinette mentioned it, she was panting a little.

And Antoinette was having to skip a few steps to keep up with her. "I've got work to do," she said.

"Uh-huh. Well, he, my friend, is in lust, whether you are or not."

"Oh, please. Does your mind go nowhere else?"

"From your lips to Sal's ears," Antoinette said. "He thinks he's the most neglected husband in all of history. If my mind went there, he'd probably go to mass and light a candle." She slowed, and Karen was forced to slow alongside her. "Come on, Karen. What's so bad about Marty? I think he's kind of cute."

"I haven't noticed." They'd reached the Sidwell Cain building, and immediately her gut had turned sour again. What would she tell Kendall when (if?) the girl ever called back, wondering what the attorneys would do for Travis?

"I call bull on that one," Antoinette said, her heels clacking on the shiny marble vestibule floor. "He's adorable. You'd have to be dead not to notice. And you'd have to be dead not to notice that he's into you."

"I am dead." She punched the down button on the elevator. "In the romance department, that is."

The truth was, she hadn't ever been alive. After she'd found out she was pregnant with Travis, the boy she'd been messing with—Doug—had run for the hills, never to be seen or heard from again. Not that she wanted his loser, pot-smoking carcass hanging around her baby, anyway. It hadn't been love between Doug and her, and it hadn't been love—or even anything close to it—for her and anyone since. She loved Travis, and he was enough. And after he'd moved out, she was just too tired for it. And out of practice. And scared to take lessons.

The elevator doors opened and Karen and Antoinette stepped in. They were alone, Karen noticed with a pang of regret.

"Well, that's just sad," Antoinette continued. "You have a lot to offer. You're cute, you're self-sufficient, you're funny, you have a great ass. . . ."

"And I have a son in jail," Karen reminded her. "Don't forget to add that to my selling points."

"That's not your fault."

"Isn't it?"

The elevator settled to the basement level with a thump. "Marty just wants to have lunch. What's wrong with lunch?"

Fortunately, the doors opened, and Karen sprang through them, taking her soup to her office, where she closed the door and sat before her computer, pulling up another search for "fight manslaughter legal options." After a few minutes of searching, she opened the soup, but it looked cold and congealed, as unappetizing as bile. She re-covered it and threw it away.

She leaned back in her chair, closing her eyes and sighing. She tried not to think about what it meant that Kendall wasn't calling. She tried not to think about how Travis was doing in jail—if he was getting tormented or stonehearted or if he was suffering withdrawal from drugs. She tried not to think about Doug, which she rarely ever did, and how he'd gotten off so easily when he'd walked out on her life. What if he was a rich surgeon now? Or happily married with an entire brood of doctors to call his own? What if one of Doug's other kids was a warden in the jail where Travis was currently sitting?

"God, don't think, Karen," she whispered to herself. "Just don't think at all."

But she couldn't help it. Her mind turned to Marty, standing there watching her back as she hightailed it away from Mr. Wong's, practically dragging Antoinette by her hair. Did he feel hurt by her rudeness? She didn't want him, but she didn't want him to be offended, either.

Antoinette didn't get it. It wasn't *just lunch*. It would never be *just lunch*. It was so many other things. It was sharing. Sharing a meal, sharing information, sharing a heart, sharing a life. And Karen had never been too keen on sharing. Not with anyone. Not with her aloof brother or her cold mother or her absent father or Doug the Runner. She was settled. She was set. She'd managed to escape even a single date for all these years, and she didn't intend to change that now.

She didn't have time, or the mind, to share.

FIVE

Paul had slipped a pamphlet under her cereal bowl before he'd left for work. He'd attached a sticky note to it: *See you at two!* With three *x*'s lined up next to the exclamation point—three kisses. If she'd been out of the shower before he'd left, he would have planted those kisses right in the middle of her forehead. He would have pulled her in close, whispered into her hair something positive and encouraging—something about them getting answers today. She knew it as well as she knew him. Instead, she'd lingered, waiting until she heard the roar of the garage door opening and closing, and then leaned into the scalding water stream once more before getting out.

She'd dressed like the traitor she was—furtively, behind a locked bathroom door—before digging into the tampon box and pulling out the pills. She'd held one in the palm of her hand, considering. Last night they'd made love. And then again this morning. He'd switched to boxer shorts, on his mother's advice. He'd urged Melinda to take cough medicine—also on his mother's advice. For a woman who'd never even graduated high school, she sure seemed the expert on fertility. Melinda wished she would stay out of their business, out of their bedroom, but then again, she'd come with advice only when Paul had gone looking for it. He'd gone to so much trouble, such worry, all the while ignorant to what was really going on.

It was this realization of just how much a baby would mean to Paul that made Melinda pause and stare at the little white culprit in her palm that morning. The guilt was eating her alive.

But then she thought about the SIDS babies they'd gotten calls on over the years. Only a few of them, but a few dead babies were more than enough. She could still see the looks of astonished, helpless grief on the mothers' faces every single time. No, *grief* wasn't a strong enough word for it. *Implosion* was more like it. An implosion of the heart, the back draft sucking the soul into such recesses of existence as to never appear again.

She'd tossed the pill into her mouth and chewed, grimacing. Paul wouldn't understand, and maybe it was wrong, but it was done, and she wouldn't have to wrestle the wrongness again for another twenty-four hours.

With trembling fingers, she pulled the pamphlet Paul had left out from under her bowl. On the cover was a beige brick building, in front of which stood a serenely smiling man and woman—the man standing behind the woman and both of them lovingly cradling her pregnant belly.

"'Women's Care Reproductive and Fertility Center,'" she read aloud. She gave a sardonic chuckle. "For when your birth control pills are doing a stellar job."

She dropped the pamphlet facedown on the counter. How could they look so damned happy about it? How could they not be terrified? Maddie Routh had probably once had that happiness, but the terror in her eyes the day of the wreck was nothing that Melinda ever wanted to experience. It was a terror not only of losing her husband, but of losing something more. Something all-encompassing. Did she smile when she wrapped her own hands around her belly? She must be going on three months along now. *If, that is, the baby survived the crash.*

Suddenly, not knowing the fate of Maddie Routh's pregnancy was an indignity Melinda could no longer bear.

Her mind turned to the older lady she'd run into last week at the diner. Karen. She'd said she'd come to the Tea Rose every day, sat in the same booth she'd been in the day of the accident, said it made her feel better. Maybe she'd sleuthed out information about Maddie.

Melinda put her clean cereal bowl back into the cabinet and slid the pamphlet into her purse, first folding those smiling faces in on themselves—what she couldn't see couldn't hurt her, right?—and then grabbed her car keys.

Karen was just where Melinda expected her to be, sitting in the same booth, a cell phone cupped in one hand, a cup of coffee steaming in front of her. But she wasn't alone. At first Melinda walked to the counter and started to pull out a stool, feeling intrusive, but then she got a good look at who was sitting across from Karen—the pretty blond girl who'd pulled the children out of the bus that day. Joanna, she'd said her name was.

Guess Melinda wasn't the only one with this idea.

Guess the diner was a draw to all of them.

She pushed the stool back in, offering a sheepish grin to the waitress who'd just shown up with a menu, and walked over to the booth.

Joanna saw Melinda first, and the recognition seemed to dawn on her as slowly as it had on Melinda. Karen followed Joanna's gaze.

"Oh, hi," Karen said.

"Melinda," she reminded her.

"Yes, of course," Karen said. "I remember."

Melinda gestured to the booth seat Joanna was sitting on. "Can I join you?"

Joanna scooted over, and Melinda sat, just as Karen said, "Sure!"

"I was just telling Joanna here that I'm waiting for a call from my son's girlfriend, so I apologize in advance if I should jump up." She flicked her eyes worriedly to the phone, which she still gripped tightly, as if she could squeeze a ringtone out of it.

"No problem," Melinda said. "I'm actually on my way to an appointment." She checked her watch, even though she knew it was hours before she was expected at the center.

A waitress appeared with a plate that she set down in front of Joanna. "Can I get you anything?" she asked Melinda. "Coffee?"

"Just some orange juice," Melinda said, feeling a wave of anxiety push in on her stomach as she remembered Paul's note under her cereal bowl. She doubted she'd even be able to handle the orange juice. Wouldn't Paul be filled with hopeful delirium if she were to show up to the fertility clinic vomiting? The waitress left, and Melinda watched as Joanna stared down into her plate.

Bacon, eggs, biscuits and gravy, two sausage links. Melinda swallowed a few times, her hands never leaving the bench, where they pressed into the vinyl on either side of her.

"That looks delicious," Karen said. She sipped her coffee, one eye sliding over to the screen of her cell phone.

Joanna unrolled her silverware and smoothed the paper napkin over her lap. She leaned forward to dig in and noticed Melinda staring at her.

"Everything okay?" she asked.

Melinda swallowed again, tried not to inhale the scent. "Yeah," she said, forcing a smile. "Fine."

Karen narrowed her eyes. "You sure?"

Melinda nodded, tearing her eyes away from the plate. She tried not to think about the greasy egg coating her tongue, the back of her throat. Tried not to hear the children's cries when she looked at the school bus yellow of the yolk.

Joanna and Karen looked alarmed, Joanna's fork poised over her plate.

Melinda tried to laugh, but it came out sounding more like a cough. "It's just that's what I was eating that day. The day of the crash. Big breakfast."

"Oh," Joanna said. "I can . . ." She gestured to the booth behind them, indicating that she would move to it.

"No, no, I'm just being stupid," Melinda said. "Kind of a bad morning. I'll be fine. Please. Eat."

"You're sure?" Joanna asked, and Melinda nodded, waving her off. *Get a grip, Melinda—you look like a freak,* she thought.

Joanna took a few bites and Karen sipped her coffee, and soon the orange juice arrived, and Melinda thought it a good thing after all. The juice was cold against her throat, which she hadn't realized was burning, and the sugar actually helped calm her stomach.

Finally, Karen let out a lengthy sigh. "Well, I guess I'm not going to hear from her this morning after all," she said, letting her phone clatter to the table. She rubbed her forehead with her palm. Melinda noticed that the older woman didn't wear a wedding ring. "This is so ridiculous, you know?" she asked, peeking through her fingers with one eye, and groaned, let her hands drop back to the table. "Coming here every day, I mean," she finished. "I come here, I sit at this table and stare at the grass. The whole time I'm telling myself it makes me feel better to be here, but the truth is, it doesn't. I feel . . ." She trailed off, rested her chin in her palm for a moment as she stared out the window, shaking her head. Joanna dropped her fork and reached across the table, putting her hand on Karen's arm.

"Like you can't forget her," Melinda said quietly. "Right?" she said louder, forcing the other two to turn back to her. "Maddie Routh. You can't forget about her. At least that's how I feel. I came here today because I can't stop wondering about the baby."

"Me, too," Joanna said. "I think about her all the time. I wonder if I could've saved her husband if I hadn't been helping those kids."

"You had to help the kids," Karen said. "Who wouldn't help the kids first? It's natural. We all did."

"I know," Joanna said. "But I was the first one out there. And he died."

They all gazed out the window again. Melinda would never forget how Maddie Routh had sobbed as her husband lost consciousness.

He's gone, isn't he? Talk to him. Michael! Michael, say something! Tell him. Tell him to stay with me. Tell him the baby needs him. Oh, God, she'd cried.

It'll be okay, Melinda kept saying over and over again, because it was all she could say. She'd been trained to deal with these types of situations. She handled them every day. She knew how to save lives, and she knew when a life was too far gone to the other side to be saved. She'd seen the look in Michael Routh's eyes so many times before, and it was never good news. *Calm down. We're going to get you out. Be calm,* she'd repeated.

"I prayed with him," Karen said, interrupting Melinda's thoughts. "It was the weirdest thing. I haven't been to church since I was ten years old. I never pray. But somehow

I knew it was the only thing I could do for him. So I prayed the Lord's Prayer, because it was the only prayer I could remember. Ever since, I've prayed it every night before bed."

"I heard you," Joanna said. "I thought that was what you were doing."

"It still doesn't help," Karen said, and she picked up her coffee and took a long sip.

"Do you know anything about the baby?" Melinda asked. "Have you heard anything? Do they know anything here?"

Karen and Joanna shook their heads, and Joanna went back to eating, only the bites were very small and tentative now.

"I should go to work," Karen said. "I can't be late. I've got some favors I might need to call in." She wadded up the napkin on her lap and placed it on the table.

"Where do you work?" Joanna asked.

"A law office," Karen said. "But I'm not a lawyer, so you don't have to start hating me." She smiled wanly. "You?"

Joanna chewed, swallowed, seemed to consider what she might say. "I am unemployed at the moment. I kind of abandoned my job. My life, really. This is the only place I've been in a month. My parents are starting to worry I've died. I should call them."

"Yes, you should," Karen said. "Take it from me, it drives you a little crazy when you don't hear from your adult kids." She picked up her cell phone and waggled it in the air before dropping it into her purse. "Although I guess if my son's worst problem was unemployment, I would throw a party."

"Well, that's probably not my worst problem," Joanna said blandly. "But that's a story for another day, I suppose."

Melinda drained her orange juice, almost shocked to see it empty, and shook her head emphatically. "I've got to know," she said. "I can't just keep wondering forever what happened to him."

"Who?" Joanna asked.

"The baby. Maddie Routh's baby. I have to know if he survived. I want to at least be able to say he survived. Isn't it eating you up?"

"I wouldn't say 'eating me up,'" Joanna said. She pushed a lock of hair behind one ear. "I mean, I've thought about them, but it's not, you know, keeping me up at night."

"It's kept me up," Karen said. "Not every night, but I've been up thinking about them." She looked at Melinda. "You said 'him.' Do you know that it's a boy?"

"No, that's just what I was picturing," Melinda said. She scooted the empty juice glass on the table between her fingers, knowing, but unable to admit to herself, that this was only partly about the Routh baby. It was mostly about her own. "But I can't just keep picturing for the rest of my life. I can't imagine myself at eighty years old, wondering whether the Routh baby is getting ready to retire, or died young, or—I don't know—anything at all." She pushed the glass away, exasperated, and leaned forward. "I can't explain it, but I feel like when that crash happened, something happened to me. Or to us, maybe. The baby and me. Or, hell, I don't know, maybe all of us." She swirled her finger around to indicate herself, Joanna, and Karen. "A month and a half ago, I'd never met you before, but here I am sitting with you now, acting like a crazy person. I'm not sure how to put it in words, exactly. It's just like—"

"It connected us," Joanna said for her.

Melinda nodded. "In a sense, yeah."

Karen's phone beeped and she jumped. She reached into her purse, checked the caller ID, seemed torn, but then pressed a button to silence it and dropped it back into her purse.

"I thought you were waiting for that," Joanna said.

Karen waved her off. "She'll call back," she said, though her face seemed to say otherwise, and it occurred to Melinda that she didn't know these two ladies at all. Not really. So why did she feel like she could crash in on them at the diner whenever she felt like it, plop down in a booth with them, and start talking crazy stuff about the Routh baby? Was it that Joanna was right—that they were somehow connected by the crash? Because, try as Melinda might to make this meeting appropriately uncomfortable or awkward . . . it just wasn't.

"I'm sorry," she said. "I didn't mean to take you away from your phone call. I'm sure you have your own stuff to worry about, without me bringing up the crash over and over again."

Karen shook her head. "But it's not as if I wouldn't think about it if you didn't bring it up. I'm the one who's here every day, remember? And, yes, I have my own stuff. A lot of stuff. But this is important. I think I understand what you're saying about that baby. I feel it, too."

Joanna pushed her barely touched plate away from her. "I do, too," she said. "But what are we going to do about it? It's not like we can find Maddie Routh and just demand to know how the pregnancy is going."

Melinda leaned back against the booth, chewing her upper lip. Karen hoisted her chin up with her palm and looked out the window again. Joanna picked up her fork and idly swirled it through the gravy on her plate. Time ticked by, and even the waitress seemed to hover, but not interrupt.

"Well, why can't we?" Melinda finally asked. "Really. Why can't we look her up? It can't be that hard to find her. We know her first and last name."

"What if she's had her number made private after the crash?" Joanna asked.

"Then we'll have to look harder. We'll ask around."

"And then we just show up?" Karen asked, though it didn't sound like she was arguing.

Melinda shrugged. "Why not?"

"It's not like we want to hurt her," Joanna said.

"No," Melinda agreed. "We want to help her. Don't we? Or am I just being selfish?"

"Of course we do," Karen said. "I'm sure she could use some help, with Michael being gone."

"And if she's offended or whatever, we'll just go away. We'll see that she's all right, and then we'll leave her alone."

"Yes, definitely," Karen said, pointing at Joanna. "I think it's really important that we give her the right to privacy. She's still mourning."

"Of course," Melinda said.

Karen's phone rang again. She grabbed it and checked the ID. "I should probably take it this time," she said. "We'll talk more about this tomorrow?"

Melinda and Joanna both nodded. "Sounds like a plan," Joanna said.

Karen scooted out of the booth, answering her phone as she went, and after a few awkward minutes Joanna and Melinda both agreed it was best that they move on with their day. Melinda tried not to think about what that meant for her—her anxiety over meeting Paul at the fertility clinic had abated, but she was sure it would be back. She went to the cash register and paid for her juice, then plunged outside, calling a good-bye to Joanna over her shoulder.

She gave the divots only a glance as she walked by on her way to her car. The divots seemed unimportant now.

Now that they had a plan to see Maddie herself.

SIX

Joanna could hear the strains of "Luck Be a Lady" before she even got close to the amphitheater. She hummed along as she walked the paved park trail, yanking the visor of her baseball cap farther down over her eyes and pushing the oversized sunglasses up on her nose, adjusting the hem of her runner's shorts, in which she always felt so exposed and uncomfortable. She much preferred maxidresses and flip-flops to this getup.

She probably looked ridiculous. She didn't fit in with the other park-goers at all. She wasn't health-conscious, nor was she a young mother looking for some fresh air and a way to exhaust a busy toddler. She'd never been great at blending in with her surroundings—which she always considered a by-product of feeling constantly hidden within her own life—but right now she looked like the stalker she was as she plodded along the trail toward the piano chords.

She knew the production by heart. She'd been one of the Hot Box girls in her high school production, a part with which she'd never felt comfortable—giggly and shimmying and wrapping feather boas around herself. She'd secretly pined to play Adelaide, and so when the community theater announced its plans to run *Guys and Dolls* for its fall season finale, she'd jumped at the chance to audition. She'd turned her East Coast accent up to its highest decibels, had put extra swagger in her hips, had mooned over Nathan Detroit like no one else.

Instead, they'd cast her in the part of straitlaced, straight-faced, stern, and sexless Sarah Brown. She'd been disappointed, but more than that, she'd felt exposed, as if everyone knew she could never pull off a sex kitten role, swooning for a man. She might as well have been wearing a neon sign that flashed the words *CLOSET LESBIAN* across her chest. And then, of course, she felt ashamed of herself for finding the prospect so distasteful.

She'd considered turning down the part, actually. Even though she knew all of Sarah Brown's songs and could follow the fold as straight-faced as a nun. But then she saw who was cast in Adelaide's part, and the result was so mesmerizing, she couldn't have argued with it if she tried.

Sutton Harris. Long, swoopy hair the color of decadent dark chocolate, skin so smooth and white it invited touch, and an easy smile. Sutton looked amazing in sweatpants tied loose and rolled up at the cuffs, and she looked amazing in jeans with jewels on the back pockets, and she looked amazing in her Hot Box dresses, and she even managed to make feather boas not look ridiculous.

Joanna knew instantly that she was in trouble. She'd felt this once before, for a girl named Alyria in college.

Alyria Payne—a name meant for the stage, and that was exactly where Joanna had met her. And where she'd fallen in love with her, as well. On the set of *Little Shop of Horrors*, in which neither of them had much more than a bit part.

Not that Joanna was terribly surprised that she'd fallen in love with Alyria. She'd had stirrings of feelings for girls as far back as middle school. Hell, maybe even further, if she wanted to be really honest with herself. But she'd always dated boys. It wasn't difficult. She was blond and athletic and cute, and when she put on makeup, she was actually sort of pretty without even really trying. The harder part was making boys believe that she had some deep moral grounds for being so hands-off. In truth, she just didn't understand what was so exciting about kissing boys. They seemed so big and clumsy and rough, while girls' lips looked soft and inviting and flavored with sweet glosses.

Just to be sure, she'd finally let it happen with a boy, her junior year in high school. Dusty Caine, whom she'd dated for more months than even seemed possible, and who seemed to take it more and more personally each day that she wouldn't put out for him. She'd finally let him take her one afternoon on his living room floor while his parents were at work. He'd fumbled around on her, sucking and pinching and grabbing and twisting like a monkey trying to open a jar of pickles, and then there'd been pain between her legs, but before she could even register it, he was collapsing on top of her, gasping for sweet Jesus. And then it was over.

She knew then for sure. Or at least she thought she did. She never understood why it was all so confusing.

Still, it wasn't a surprise when she found herself sitting on the makeup table, back pressed against the mirror, kissing Alyria and feeling all the things she never felt with Dusty. She was in lust. Worse, she was completely and totally in love. With a girl.

And it scared the crap out of her.

She'd quit the production. And then, when Alyria had taken to waiting for her in the parking lot before class, she'd quit school entirely. It had nearly broken her parents' hearts, and had frightened her, but being afraid of what would happen to her future, careerwise, was nowhere near as scary as what could happen to her lovewise. Dear God, her mother was dying to plan her a wedding, was positively dripping with grandchild fever.

Joanna had never gone back to school, not even after Alyria had moved on. Instead, she'd gotten a job waiting tables at LaEats and had artfully hung out in Waiting Mode. She didn't know what she was waiting for, and she had a gut-yanking feeling that maybe what she was waiting for was to become un-gay, even though she knew it was ridiculous and pointless. Even if she could convince herself that she was no longer in love with Alyria (and she could), there would always be another Alyria. There would always be another girl.

Still. She'd felt herself aging. Stagnating. She missed the theater. She missed the fake accents and the heavy makeup and the silent catastrophes that took place backstage during performances. She missed late-night fried egg dinners after closing night. She'd missed acting.

Two seasons ago, she tried out for the community theater, which had been auditioning for an outdoor summer performance of *The Music Man*. She got the part of Mrs. Paroo. She had kept her head down and fallen in love with nobody. She was as sexless as she'd pretended to be in high school. She'd tried out for the next production, and the next one, and by the time *Guys and Dolls* came around, she wasn't even vigilant about her colleagues on the stage anymore.

And then, boom. There was Sutton. Sutton as beautiful, sweet Adelaide.

Joanna picked up her pace as she reached the end of the trail that was closest to the amphitheater, until she was actually at a jog. She wasn't doing this to fit in; rather, she was hearing the opening notes of "A Bushel and a Peck" and couldn't contain herself. She was like a dog hearing the telltale garage door rumble of her owner coming home.

She veered off the trail and through the grass, up the short hill that obscured the theater from the path and vice versa. She felt her quads burn as she powered up the hill, her breath coming in hard and uneven now. But the moment she popped over the top of the hill and saw the stage, she stopped, bending forward with her hands on her knees, trying to steady her breathing.

She was too far away to make out details, but she was close enough to see the cascading hair. They were practicing in costume now, and Sutton's dress was tight and leggy. Joanna felt even more breathless at just the sight of her. It had been more than a month, but the feelings clearly hadn't changed.

Slowly, she walked toward the amphitheater, glancing around to make sure nobody noticed her. There was a smattering of onlookers perched in the seats—what Joanna would have derided as freeloaders once upon a time, but whom she now was grateful for, as she would stand out less.

She sank into a seat near the back, watching intently as Sutton shook her hips and crossed her arms over her chest, flirty, owning the Adelaide role. Once, she could have sworn that Sutton had seen her there—that her eyes had lingered just a little too long in her direction, and that her smile had gotten just a little too relaxed—and she slid down farther in her plastic seat. But then Stan had stormed onto the stage, stopping the music abruptly, and had taken Sutton into quiet, wildly gesturing consult, and Joanna's fears subsided. She watched as they started the number over, stopping and restarting it again two more times, and had to sit on her hands to keep from applauding when Sutton was finally finished and allowed to leave the stage.

She probably should have left then. But she couldn't tear herself away, partly because she was afraid the moment she'd leave, Sutton would come back onstage, and she'd miss a chance to study her one more time.

She'd been so engrossed in watching the girl who'd replaced her screw up all her lines and look totally wooden onstage, she didn't even notice that someone was approaching her from the aisle.

"Joanna?" she heard whispered, and her head whipped to the side.

Sutton was coming toward her, in full makeup, her costume swishing against the seats. Joanna's heart plummeted somewhere beneath her feet, and she felt all her blood leave her head. She felt dizzy and had to remind herself to take a breath.

She plastered a smile on her face. "Sutton. Hey," she whispered back. "You were amazing. As usual."

Sutton looked confused. "What are you doing here? Eliot said you quit."

Joanna shrugged. "Kind of got fired is more like it," she said. She gestured to her shorts. "I was out for a jog and thought I'd see how progress was going. It looks great. You look great."

Sutton blushed, brushed at the front of her costume. "It's a little retro-femme for my taste," she said.

"You pull it off," Joanna said, but then trailed away as the tension felt heavy in the air. This was how it always was between her and women she fell for. Was it this way for other girls with men? She could talk so easily to Stephen, but then again she didn't see Stephen as anything more than a friend. She could feel blood begin to rush to her own cheeks, certain she'd said too much, had laid her cards too boldly on the table. What if she'd misread Sutton all this time? Or worse, what if she'd read her correctly? She wasn't any more ready now than she'd been with Alyria.

"Thank you," Sutton said.

The music stopped abruptly, and Joanna could hear Stan giving animated instructions, punctuating his point by pounding his foot in a specific spot on the stage over and over again. Joanna's replacement stood with her hands tucked into her stomach, nodding vigorously, looking overwhelmed. She almost felt sorry for her—Stan could overwhelm even the most seasoned community theater actor.

"I should probably get back to my run," Joanna said, edging out of the aisle.

"Oh. Okay. Yeah," Sutton said. "I suppose I should get . . ." She gave an awkward backhand wave toward the stage.

"See you."

"Okay."

Joanna had stepped out of the aisle and started back toward the jogging path, her heart already heavy in her chest. This was a mistake. Coming here was such a colossal screwup. How could she have expected it to go well? How could she have expected it not to break her heart to see Sutton again?

"Hey, Joanna?"

She turned. Sutton hadn't moved from her spot.

"You sure everything's okay?" Sutton asked. She took a few steps toward Joanna.

"Yeah, everything's great."

"You sure? It's just that I asked around and nobody's heard anything from you in like over a month. You're not, like, sick or anything, are you?"

Joanna felt a sad grin tug at one corner of her mouth. As happy as she was that Sutton had cared enough to ask around, she was suddenly embarrassed that people were talking. She didn't know what exactly she'd expected—that she could really just disappear for a month and nobody would notice?—but she found that she didn't like Sutton to think of her as weak, flawed. She wanted to be everything to Sutton, even if she knew she would never allow herself to be anything to Sutton.

Of course, had nobody noticed that she'd disappeared, how would she have felt about that? To be so disposable.

"I took a . . . sabbatical," Joanna said lightly. "I've been away." Not technically a lie. She'd been away from everyone else. It was a sabbatical of sorts. It had been meant to be a time of rest.

"Oh, I bet that was nice," Sutton said. "I would love to do something like that. Did you go somewhere fabulous? A beach, I hope?"

"Nah. It was—"

Fortunately, the music ended onstage, and Stan began bellowing for the whole cast to assemble onstage, bailing Joanna out.

"Oh, shoot," Sutton said, biting her lip and turning toward the stage. Joanna's heart leapt—Sutton's lip-biting habit was part of what had attracted her so much. "Stan is on the warpath today."

"Sounds like it," Joanna said. "You probably shouldn't get caught talking to me. I'm not his favorite person right now."

Sutton rolled her eyes. "Who cares what he thinks, anyway? He'll get over it. Word is he's doing *Grease* next summer. You have Pink Lady written all over you. Maybe even Frenchy."

Joanna felt herself blush. "More like Riz. But I doubt he'll forgive me between now and then."

"Well, I hope you at least try. You're really good. And . . . I really miss you," Sutton said. Stan barked her name, standing on the stage and shading his eyes to look into the house.

"Nobody's paying you to gab, Adelaide!"

"Nobody's paying me at all, Stan!" she yelled back, and then turned back to Joanna and giggled. "It's fun to give it back to him sometimes."

Sutton turned and edged her way down the row of seats, back to the middle aisle. "Come back, okay?" she hollered over her shoulder to Joanna before jogging back to the stage.

Joanna stood in the grass, her heart beating so hard she could feel her pulse in her toes. She watched as Sutton's hair fluttered behind her, as she took her place back on the stage, as she seemed to turn her eyes directly to Joanna, even from there. Joanna's legs felt too weak to climb even the shallow hill back to the walking trail. She wanted to sit back down, to watch Sutton dance and listen to her sing and think about all the things that they could be together, all the subtle hints that Sutton had dropped. She was into Joanna—Joanna could feel it. She could hear it, Sutton's desire, thrumming beneath her sentences, could feel it beating against her face every time Sutton turned her eyes to study her.

She knew it, yet at the same time, she was afraid to allow herself to know it. She wanted Sutton, but what was more, she wanted the ease Sutton showed in her expression. She wanted to be proud of who she was. She wanted to own it.

But she could never be proud. She could never be at ease.

Slowly, she trudged through the grass, the sounds of the cast's curtain call giving way to the delighted screeches of children playing tag, swooshing down slides, being pushed in their swings by their devoted mothers. She stopped at the tip of the trail and watched as one mom hoisted her chubby daughter to catch hold of monkey bars, standing below, a palm's reach away from her daughter's body as the girl inched along. She gazed at the smile on the woman's face. It was so easy. It was so filled with love.

Joanna plodded along the trail, head down, watching the concrete as it slipped past her shoes, at first in a walk, and then in a jog that felt like escape more than anything.

Maybe that was all she wanted. Maybe it was just the love she was craving. That was what had been missing for her, and for so long, and maybe she was just unclear. It wasn't that she was in love with Alyria and Sutton—it was that they were easy and comfortable to tag that love onto. Love was a complicated thing, after all—you couldn't just go around attaching yourself to everyone. You had to be comfortable with the person you loved. She'd been confused, was all. She'd been mixed-up. She could have that love, that sticky-faced-toddler-kiss love that she'd seen in the mother's eyes at the playground. She could have that— she just had to get her act together.

Immediately, she missed Stephen with a depth that felt endless, and was practically washed away by the guilt of having hidden from him all this time. She missed his jokes, his devotion, even his kiss. It had been so soft, so full of goodness. He would never hurt her, she knew that. She'd wanted to confide in him, had wanted to tell him her biggest secret. What bespoke love more than that? She loved Stephen, and he loved her back. He had admitted it, but even if he hadn't, he'd shown it. For years.

She'd just been too blind, too caught up in this gay thing, to see it.

Her jog turned to a run as she rounded the last curve. She could see her car at the end of the straightaway, and she pushed, kicking back her legs as hard as they would go, shoving out thoughts of Sutton and Alyria and letting memories of Stephen in. So many memories she almost felt light-headed.

She reached her car, gasping, pacing, feeling tingles rush up her legs and into her lungs. She walked a quick few laps around her car, hands on hips, until her breathing slowed and her throat felt scorched, but in a good way. She felt as if she could conquer anything now. She could be normal. Normal was good.

She pulled her cell phone out of her hoodie pocket and thumbed it on, scrolling through the contacts list.

"Hey," she said after a few seconds. When she heard Stephen's voice, she smiled. "I heard you tried to steal my job. I do believe I owe you a drink. Can you come over tonight?"

SEVEN

I t disgusted her that she had a "jail outfit." But Karen had been through this so many times with Travis, she actually did have a pair of loose jeans and a crew neck sweater that she considered her jail ensemble. There were rules about what you could wear into a jail, even as a visitor, and she didn't want to have to think about what those were every time she went in. She didn't want to think about her son being the type of person inhabiting a place where women couldn't be free to just dress however they saw fit.

Not to mention, the first time she'd worn it there—his first assault, that time on a convenience store clerk who'd suggested Travis buy the box of crackers he'd been eating near the restrooms—she'd been so upset, it was an outfit forever marked with hopelessness and parental guilt. She'd not known, back then, how quickly she'd become accustomed to visiting her son in jail. She'd never have guessed.

She'd told herself the last time—drugs—that she was done coming back. That if he should get himself in another predicament, he was on his own. She'd even considered getting rid of the jail outfit altogether. But Kendall's last phone call had been disturbing.

"Well, it's not good, Mom," she'd said. "They're calling it assault and battery for now, but the stupid guy is, like, not waking up, or at least that's what his skanky wife is saying. She probably just has him faking it so they can, like, sue or something." She'd laughed, as if this were some silly lark. "Like we have anything they can sue for. Anyway, so they're really going hard after Travis this time. That's why they set that ridiculous bail."

Yes, Karen knew what a sore subject bail was going to be. She hadn't planned to pay it anyway. She'd gone through her savings, twice, to bail Travis out over the years. She'd second mortgaged her home. She'd racked up credit card debt. And what good did it do? Just more bail to be paid a few years or, twice, a few months later. Fortunately, this time they'd set it beyond her financial reach, so she didn't even have to pretend she'd come through. There was some amount of freedom in being broke, even if it was just freedom from her son's debts. And God knew Travis and Kendall didn't have two pennies to rub together, so Travis was out of luck. "I'm sorry I couldn't pay that," she said.

"It's fine, whatever," Kendall had said, but Karen could hear the sour notes beneath the words. "But first they set that bail, and now they're saying they're going to go for maximum sentence on the assault charge, and that's if this guy doesn't really go and die. Travis is in a bad place right now. Like, mentally."

"I'm sure he is." Karen examined the corner behind her bedroom door. She could see dust buildup there.

"No, I mean I think he might do something."

"He can't do anything. He's in jail," Karen said. "And if he's smart, he'll stop doing things. What he needs to do is clean up his act and get a job so he can take care of his son, but if you can get him to understand that, you're doing better than I, and more power to you."

"Mom. You aren't getting it." Again, Karen could hear something sour beneath her words—something accusatory. "I mean, I think he's going to do something *to himself.*"

Karen sat forward. "Like what? Did he say something to you?"

There was a pause. "Not *exactly.* Oh, I'm getting another call. I've got to go."

And then she'd disconnected. And had gone silent for two days. Gamey. So freaking gamey. Sick and gamey and her son deserved better, Karen had ranted to Antoinette the next day at lunch, even though she knew in her heart that he didn't. What good woman would attach herself to a man like Travis? No, she was doomed to a lifetime of sick and gamey, because that was what her son deserved, and that was what he had given her. Payment for a lifetime of devotion.

So many times, Karen had thought about Travis dying.

Being shot in a drug deal or killed in an adrenaline-fueled car wreck or beaten to death in a bar fight. She'd thought she'd come to terms with the possibility some time ago. He was clearly on a destructive path; where that took him, she would just have to accept. But hearing Kendall's prediction that he might do something to himself made it more real than ever before, the possibility that she might lose her son. And there was something about the suddenness of a car hitting a concrete pylon versus the slow torture of a depression-filled suicide. He was still her baby, even though he'd turned out so terribly wrong.

So after two days of waiting to hear from Kendall, she couldn't take it anymore. She'd found her jail outfit in the back of her closet, taken a PTO day, and headed down to the jail.

And now she tugged at the crew collar of her sweater uncomfortably, feeling a bead of sweat escape from under her bra strap and roll down her back, as she sat across from him, separated by a Plexiglas wall. He held the phone to his ear, but wasn't saying anything through it.

"Are you sure you're not going to do anything stupid?" Karen asked, for the third time, holding the mouthpiece of the phone away from her mouth. God knew how often they cleaned those things. It looked like never.

"Hell, no, I'm not going to ax myself because of that asshole," Travis spat. "I told you already."

She breathed as much a sigh of relief as possible, given where she was. It was impossible to ever be totally relieved with Travis, and she'd more than once considered parenting him to be something like sinking to the bottom of a pool and never coming up again, your lungs so full of air it was an aching desire in your chest just to let it out.

"Kendall had me worried," she said.

"Don't listen to that crazy bitch."

"Travis," Karen said. "That's the mother of your child."

He shook his head. "Yeah, I know. I'm just pissed off is all."

"Well, it's not her fault you're back in here." She knew better than to take it any further. Travis would simply shut down, shut her out. She'd learned that a long time ago. "So have they said anything about when your trial will be?"

"Naw, they're just yanking my chain all the time," he said. "They're probably waiting for that guy to die so they can send me away forever." He paused, scraping at something on the Formica with his thumb, his eyes turned squarely down, away from his mother. "Or worse," he added.

Karen had been steadfastly trying not to think of the "or worse" part of what could happen to her son if the man died. There were lots of things you could soothe your children out of, but "death penalty" was most decidedly not one of them. They didn't seek the death penalty for manslaughter, did they? "Well, we can just pray he wakes up soon," she said. "Surely there's progress we just haven't heard about."

Travis sighed, leaned back to cross one leg over the other, and put on an air of casualness that never quite reached realistic. "Whatever," he said.

Karen checked her watch—time was just about up, which was good, because she couldn't see where else this conversation could go, and she felt so very weary of this.

This worry, this pain, this vigilance. She just couldn't do it anymore. Maybe she should track down Doug, see if he was up for it. She took the first twenty-six years; let him have a crack at the next twenty-six.

She left the jail, crossing the street at a jog, her sweater draped damp and heavy over her. She'd told Travis goodbye, but hadn't cried. She hadn't even kissed her fingertips and pressed them to the glass as she'd always done in the past. She slid into her car feeling so very, very numb to it all.

And hot.

She aimed her car toward home, unsure what to do with herself. She hadn't needed to take the whole day off. Not really. Not for a quick jail visit. She never took days off, because she couldn't handle the guilt. She took hours off, here and there, for doctor appointments and haircuts and trips to the DMV, but whole days were reserved for illness, which she rarely succumbed to now that Travis was grown. She had no real idea how to take time off.

She cranked the air conditioner up to full blast, but it wasn't touching the heat that had been baked into the gray vinyl seats. Her sweater felt like it was melting into her at this point. Choking her. Shrinking around her armpits and biceps and neck. And she was thirsty.

She pulled into the next gas station parking lot she passed, nosing her car into a spot outside the front door. She got out and lunged for the door, nearly knocking into a person coming out.

"Sorry," she mumbled, and then realized she knew the man whom she'd almost run into.

"Karen! Hey!"

Marty Squire stood directly in front of her, clutching a fountain drink in a foam cup at his chest. He'd traded his usual fastidious dress code for something much more casual—a pair of faded blue jeans with a dime-sized hole fraying the front left pocket, a USC T-shirt, and a logoed baseball cap.

"You caught me playing hooky," he said, holding up his drink as if presenting evidence. He gave her a glance, undoubtedly wondering why she was dressed so outrageously matronly, and on such a warm fall day. The very thought of him asking questions made her ears ring with embarrassment.

"Yeah, me, too," she said. She tugged on her collar. She could feel sweat gluing her hair to her temples. "Just stopping in for a drink." She started to shove through the door, but was forced to take a step back as a young man came out of the store. Awkward, she waited for the man to go on his way, and then went on through, offering Marty a shy wave. "See you."

She bought two bottles of water, and surprised herself by downing one of them while standing right next to the counter, as busy people buzzed up to the register to pay for gas, cigarettes, sodas. The cold water calmed her, made her feel much better. Goose bumps even popped up on her forearms. She felt more settled about going home. She would put on some yoga pants, perhaps work in the yard a little. Or maybe pour herself a glass of wine and pop in a movie. Possibly take a nap. None of those things felt like something she should be doing on a Friday afternoon, but she was going to try to make herself relax. Stop thinking about Travis, stop thinking about Kendall, just stop thinking.

She was startled to see Marty still standing on the sidewalk, sipping his drink, when she came out. She hesitated, then plowed forward as if she hadn't seen him, hoping lack of eye contact would keep him from approaching her. It didn't work. He pushed away from the wall as she passed.

"Hey, Karen, I was wondering if I could ask you something," he said, forcing her to stop. She wasn't interested, but she didn't want to be rude. He was sort of cute with his hair poking out from under that cap, graying at the temples.

"Yeah?" She twisted open the bottle cap.

"I was just wondering if maybe we could do dinner sometime?" He held up his cup. "Since we've already had drinks together, I thought maybe we could, you know, take it to the next level. I want to show you that I'm not all about the sixty-nine-cent deals."

He was charming, and Karen had to work to resist smiling at him. But then the sun clawed in through the fabric of her sweater and she was reminded once again why it was that she was off today and able to run into Marty Squire at the convenience store in the first place. The last thing she needed to do was answer a bunch of questions about why she wasn't working. The last thing she wanted was to regale this handsome man with all her failures as a mother: her criminal son and his "crazy bitch" girlfriend and their illegitimate baby who they all knew didn't stand a chance in this world.

"I don't think so," she said. "But thank you for the invitation."

Quickly, before he could argue or ask questions, she moved to her car, pressing the unlock button as she walked so she wouldn't have to so much as hesitate to get inside. She purposely avoided looking at him as she pulled away.

Kendall was waiting for her, sitting on Karen's front porch, baby Marcus wiggling on her lap, reaching for a blade of fountain grass that flopped and swayed in his direction. Kendall looked bored and impatient, and tapped her cell phone screen with her free hand. She glanced up sharply when Karen pulled into the driveway, then pulled herself to standing, clutching the baby against her stomach as if she were holding a bag of dirty laundry, his chubby bare feet kicking the air.

"Hey, I wasn't expecting you, big man," Karen said, reaching for Marcus as she came out of the garage.

Kendall handed him over. "He's wet," she said. "I'm out of diapers."

Karen could feel how wet he was. Not only was his diaper squishy and full, it had begun to leak out onto his onesie as well. He smelled faintly of urine and spit-up, and Karen wondered how long it had been since he'd been bathed.

"Grammy's got some," she said, holding him above her face and talking in a baby voice. He brightened, showing all of his gums in a smile, and kicked harder. "Let's go get you dry, little mister."

She carried Marcus into the house, not noticing if Kendall was following her; not even caring, really.

"Did you see Travis, then, I guess?" Kendall asked, just as Karen dug a diaper out of a bag next to her dresser and laid the little guy on her bed. He immediately grabbed for his toes, cooing. Such a happy baby. He had no idea what life he'd been born into.

"Yes," she said.

"And?"

"And he was there."

Kendall stood impatiently next to Karen, making no move or offer to help change the baby's diaper. "Well, how was he?"

Karen sighed. "He isn't exactly throwing any parties, but he's fine. He's not going to do anything to himself, if that's what you're worried about."

Kendall moved around to the other side of the bed and flopped down on it. Karen was instantly glad she'd made the bed that morning—the idea of Kendall touching her sheets, even clothed, icked her out. "Well, I'm glad he's doing so great, because we're not," she said. She sat up and looked at Karen accusatorily. "We're out of money. I can't even buy diapers and soon I'll be out of formula, too."

"What happened to your assistance?" Karen asked. She taped the baby's diaper shut and snapped the crotch of his onesie, trying to ignore the dampness on the snaps. Marcus smiled at her again, reaching up toward her. She bent her face down to meet his belly and rubbed her nose in it.

"Travis didn't want us to be on welfare," Kendall said. "He threw away our card."

Karen jerked upright. "He what? You need that. You have this baby to think about. It's not a time to be proud."

"Don't tell me," Kendall spat. "It's your son, you know."

Don't remind me, Karen thought as she picked up the baby and snuggled him close. He was so warm and innocent and perfect. He had Travis's mouth, and Kendall's prominent chin, but everything else about him was his own. Maybe there was hope for him after all. "How much do you need?" she asked.

As soon as three hundred dollars exchanged hands, Kendall began to act antsy to leave, looking at her phone over and over again, checking the time. She bounced her leg and chewed her thumb to shreds while Karen sat on the floor with Marcus, tickling him until he giggled, playing peekaboo. After only fifteen or twenty minutes, Kendall stood.

"We should probably go," she said.

"Already?" Karen scooped Marcus off the floor and cradled him, pressing her free hand to his slobbery little cheek.

"Yeah, I should get to the store before he, like, poops or something." But there was something in the distracted tone of her voice that made Karen doubt very much that Kendall was planning to spend that money on baby things. Her heart sank. "We'll try to come back this weekend," she said. "I might have a thing to go to, but I'll call."

"Okay," Karen said softly. "Sure. Okay." And she let go when Kendall reached for Marcus, grabbing him out of her arms with about as much tenderness and care as if she were plucking a weed. She watched as Kendall stepped into her sandals and hefted the baby off to her car. She listened to his cries as she bent into the backseat, buckling him in. She tried to remind herself that all babies cry when they're being put into something confining—a coat, a diaper, a car seat—and his cries did not mean that he was unhappy, or heading to an unhappy home environment. She tried to remind herself that she'd see him again soon, that she could be his safe place to go to, that she could save him even if she couldn't save Travis.

But as she held her hand in a wave that wasn't returned and Kendall roared out of the driveway, grating music pounding and pouring through the metal car doors so loudly Karen could see the windows jiggle with the drumbeat, she couldn't help feeling even more hopeless than she'd felt upon leaving the jail earlier that day.

She couldn't help feeling as frightened as she had the day of the bus wreck.

The car gone, Karen turned and went back inside, shutting the front door and shucking off her sweater and tossing it on the entryway floor. She went into her spare room and pulled up her laptop. Sitting in her jeans and bra, she typed in a name and hit Search.

Maddie Routh's address was the first to pop up.

EIGHT

Melinda drove them to the older side of Caldwell—past prewar houses with falling-down sheds and the park with its splash fountains and past moms pushing strollers with one hand while holding leashes connected to panting terriers in the other—and pulled up to a tiny house about half a block away from the junior high school, a stately brick building that had once been the high school before the city had outgrown it.

The house was white with black shutters, cute landscaping dotting the front yard, but looking ignored, a ceramic toad knocked over onto its side in a small patch of weeds. A faded summer wreath clung to the door, shrouded by the shadow of a screen. It was the kind of house a Realtor would refer to as a "starter house," perfect for a young couple trying to scrape together enough of a history to add to their future. The perfect house for a young couple like Michael and Maddie Routh.

"Is that it?" Karen asked, peering through the windshield.

"It's the address," Joanna responded from the backseat.

Melinda paused, idling, and held on to the steering wheel. She didn't know what to do next—ease up to the curb? Pull into the driveway? Simply slink away? They'd decided, after Karen greeted them that morning with an address scrawled onto a halved sheet of notebook paper, to come here. But they hadn't even thought to discuss what they would do once they arrived. Melinda supposed she was thinking it would become clear once they saw the house, but the inspiration she'd been hoping for had never arrived.

"Do you think she's home?" Joanna asked, leaning forward so her face was even with Melinda's shoulder.

"There's one way to find out," Karen said.

"Should we?" Melinda asked, still not budging from her spot. "I mean, I know this was my idea, but are we invading her privacy by doing this?"

"We talked about this, remember?" Joanna said.

Melinda did remember. Karen had dropped the piece of notebook paper into the middle of the table and they'd all stared at it, each wondering aloud whether even having it was invading the Routh family's privacy.

"It's public information," Joanna had said. "Anyone can find anyone online now. You just have to accept it."

"But this is more than finding it," Melinda had argued. "This is coming to her home."

"Well, we're not busting the door down," Karen had snapped, and then, when a silence fell over the table, clasped her hands together and apologized. "I'm sorry. It's not you. My son is having some troubles and I'm worried. It's making me crabby."

"Everything okay?" Joanna had asked.

"What kind of troubles?" Melinda had asked at the same time, and then blanched at her own nosiness. Were they those kinds of friends already? She wasn't sure if she knew.

Karen had taken a long sip of her coffee before answering, the small, plain hoop earrings jiggling in her lobes with the motion. "He got into a fight. Got himself tossed in jail. Definitely not the first time, but definitely the worst time. And his girlfriend is playing games with me—trying to get money, acting like she's going to run and take my grandson with her. It's a mess. It's been a mess for quite a while now."

"Oh," Joanna had said. "I'm sorry to hear that."

"Thanks," Karen answered, and then seemed to visibly gather herself. She tapped the paper on the table. "But let's concentrate on this for now. I say we visit. I need a distraction."

"Agreed," Joanna said. "And if she doesn't want us there, we'll leave. Just like we discussed before."

"You're right," Melinda had said. "There's nothing invasive about stopping by to see if someone's okay."

But now that they were sitting in front of Maddie Routh's house, a basket of flowers wilting on the backseat of Melinda's car, she wasn't so sure it wasn't invasive after all. The house was so buttoned-up. So dead-looking.

"Looks like she might be at work," Melinda said.

"It's Sunday," Joanna reminded her.

"She could be working on a Sunday. Or at church. Or visiting his grave. Or any number of things. The house looks empty is all I'm saying."

"Well, again, there's only one way to find out," Karen said. "Park the car and we'll go up. Come on."

And before Melinda could argue any more, Karen opened the passenger door of the little Toyota and stepped out into the street.

"Park," she repeated before closing the door.

Melinda watched as Karen strode to the curb and waited. She glanced at Joanna in the rearview mirror. Joanna caught her eye, shrugged, and picked up the flowers.

"What do we have to be nervous about?" she asked. "We're just wishing the poor girl well."

If only, Melinda thought, because it had dawned on her that what they were doing was much more than that. They were snooping. They were hoping to assuage their own feelings of guilt. They wanted the widow to answer the door with smiles and bright eyes and tell them that it was all okay, that she'd moved on without him. But one look at the front of the house told Melinda that smiles and reassurance were not going to be what they found at Maddie Routh's house. Not at all.

But that baby. You have to know about the baby.

Slowly, she pulled up alongside the curb—the driveway being too familiar and easy for her taste—and turned off the ignition. Joanna popped open her door and got out, leaving Melinda with the lingering scent of flowers and a sick feeling in the pit of her stomach.

Melinda took a deep breath. *Here goes nothing,* she said to herself, and then joined the others.

"Do you think she'll remember us?" Joanna asked as they walked up what seemed to Melinda to be a million-mile-long sidewalk.

"Probably not," Karen said. "It was such chaos."

"And she was in shock," Melinda added. "You wouldn't believe what the brain will just wipe away when someone is in shock. We see it all the time. Some people will forget details like where they were driving to, or who they were talking on the phone with. Others will swear they have no recollection of the entire day. Hours gone."

"Something tells me she will remember the day," Joanna said. The tissue paper around the flowers crinkled against her shirt, leaving a green stain.

They climbed the two porch steps and stood shoulder to shoulder on the porch. They stared at the front door, motionless. A small dog yapped in a nearby backyard.

"Well, we can't just stand here," Joanna said at last. "We'll look like we're up to something." She shifted the flowers into one hand, leaned forward, and pressed the doorbell.

The yapping continued, but otherwise, there was no sound, no movement.

"I guess she's not here," Melinda said. "Should we just leave the flowers?"

"We didn't write a note," Karen said. "Won't she wonder where they came from?"

"Probably not," said Joanna. "She probably gets flowers and casseroles and stuff all the time."

"I don't know," Karen said. "It's been a couple months. Most people stop checking in on someone after a few weeks. Just the way it is. Life moves on."

"Boy, don't I know it?" Joanna muttered.

"Huh?"

"Nothing," she said. She bent and placed the flowers by the front door, but just as she straightened again, the door rattled and then opened up. A gaunt woman appeared on the other side of the screen.

At first Melinda was sure they'd gotten the address wrong. It was another Michael and Maddie Routh at this address. How likely was that in a town as small as Caldwell?

"Can I help you?" the woman asked, and it was her voice that jarred Melinda back to the day of the crash. It was definitely the same woman—Melinda would recognize that voice anywhere—but she looked like what could best be described as a shell of the girl who had been Maddie Routh. Her eyes were swollen and slitted, as if from sleep and crying. Her skin was ruddy and mottled and dull, beset with a paleness that seemed to creep to the surface from within, rather than being the result of not getting enough light.

But more than that was how thin she was, her face sunken around her mouth—what would be smile lines on an ordinary person were deep crevices on her. Her arms looked vulnerable, as if anything could break them, and she fairly swam in a pair of filthy pajama pants and an old T-shirt. She was wearing one sock, the other foot bare. Half of her hair was pulled up into a loose, ratty ponytail; the other half hung listlessly down her cheek.

"Can I help you?" the woman repeated tiredly.

"Maddie Routh?" Joanna asked, and Melinda was thankful that one of them had found a voice, even if it was filled with surprise and intimidation.

"Yeah."

"I'm Joanna Chambers. This is Karen and Melinda. Um. You probably don't remember us."

It was a pointless observation. Anyone could see that the woman didn't remember them. She shook her head. "I'm sorry, I'm not interested," she said, and started to back away from the door.

"Wait," Joanna said. She bent to pick up the flowers and held them out to Maddie, who gazed at them, but made no move to take them. "We brought you these."

Maddie's eyes narrowed. "Why? You know, it really doesn't matter. I've thrown away so many flowers. I don't want to be rude, but you really should just take them with you. I can't keep up with it all. I just want to be left alone."

Joanna glanced over her shoulder at Melinda, her eyes seeming to beg for backup. Melinda stepped forward, trying to kick into professional mode. What would she say if she were standing here in her uniform? If she'd come to check up on someone whose accident they'd worked—something she'd never done before.

"We were on the scene," she said. She cleared her throat. "The accident in September?"

Maddie Routh's eyes seemed to cloud over. "Oh," she said. She studied each of them, but rather than register them with relief or excitement or gratitude, she looked nervous, half-panicked, even. "I don't really remember any specifics about that day. Is there . . . why . . . do you . . . ?"

"We just wanted to check on you," Karen said. Her voice was much steadier than either Joanna's or Melinda's. She sounded like a concerned mother. "We've been thinking about you and Michael and . . ."

But she trailed off, and Melinda's eyes immediately dropped to Maddie's belly, but the dirty T-shirt was too big to see any shape on the tiny woman. It dawned on Melinda that the T-shirt looked like a man's T-shirt. It probably belonged to Michael.

Maddie seemed to mull over what Karen had said for quite some time. Then she pushed open the door a little wider and backed up. "You can come in," she said, although not warmly.

They filed in after her, stepping into a dank and dark house that smelled stale and slightly meaty. Papers, mail, were scattered across the dusty tables. A stained blanket that was draped over the couch grazed the floor. Drinking glasses in various states of emptiness lined an end table.

Maddie picked up the blanket and tossed it into a heap

on the floor next to the table, then sat on the edge of the sofa. Joanna followed her lead, sitting next to her. Karen moved a stack of papers off an easy chair and slid into it. Melinda stood in the doorway, unsure what to do with herself.

"Sorry, I haven't cleaned much lately," Maddie said. She balled up the hem of her T-shirt, kneading the fabric in her fist.

"That's fine," Karen said. "We aren't here to check up on your housekeeping skills."

"Why are you here?" Maddie said quickly. "I don't really remember that day, so if you're looking for information or something, I probably can't help you."

"That's very normal," Melinda said, hating how she sounded so clinical. Not at all what they'd come here for.

"We're not looking for anything," Karen said. "We just wanted to check in on you. See how you were doing."

"It was a terrible accident," Joanna added,

Maddie turned on her, her eyes suddenly ablaze. "Yes, I remember that much," she snapped.

Joanna looked stricken. "I didn't mean . . . ," she stammered.

"I know exactly what you meant," Maddie said. "It didn't knock my brains out, as much as it tried." She reached up and touched a spot on the side of her head, and for the first time Melinda noticed a small shaved spot there, stubbles of hair growing back, where there had undoubtedly been stitches.

There was a beat of uncomfortable silence, which Melinda interrupted. "I think she just meant that because you were in such a terrible accident, we wanted to check on you."

"To see how you were getting through everything," Karen added.

Maddie let out a low, sardonic chuckle, watching her own hands as they twisted her T-shirt into angry wrinkles. "How I'm getting through everything," she muttered.

Melinda and Joanna exchanged glances, and Melinda wondered if Joanna was thinking what she was thinking—that this was a mistake. That it was worse than not being remembered. They were not wanted. Maddie Routh seemed to be angry that they were even there. Melinda tried to convey with her eyes that maybe they should leave, but Joanna didn't seem to catch the subtle message.

"I'm not," Maddie said suddenly, dropping her hands to either side of her on the couch. "I'm not getting through anything. Look around you. The house is falling apart. I'm falling apart. Everything is falling apart and I don't even care." She leveled her eyes at Melinda. "Michael was my life. And now he's gone and I watched him die, and I don't care what happens with the rest of my life now. Except I'm forced to." Her hands clawed their way back to her midsection, only now instead of twisting her T-shirt into knots she ground two fists into her belly. "I'm not making it through, but I'm forced to come out the other end."

"The baby," Karen said softly.

"Yeah. The baby," Maddie repeated. "The baby is the whole reason we were waiting at that stoplight that day. The baby is the reason neither of us saw that school bus coming. The baby is alive, but its father is dead. What kind of sense does that make?"

"I'm so sorry," Joanna said, and Melinda could see that Joanna had tears in her eyes.

"Me, too," Maddie said. "Because without Michael, I don't even know if I want it anymore." She closed her eyes and dipped her head forward. "The bundle of joy," she whispered, and gave another of those chuckles, a tear slipping out from under one of her eyelids.

Joanna reached over and tried patting Maddie's shoulder, but Maddie shrugged her off, and Joanna jerked back. "Sorry," she repeated. "I was just . . ."

"Yeah, you were just," Maddie said. She looked around the room at each of them. "You were all *just*." She stood. "Everyone is *just*, and nobody is actually helping." She closed her eyes, took a breath, opened them again, visibly steadying herself. "Look, I appreciate you all stopping by. But I'm not the best company right now. There's really nothing more you can do for me." She stood, walked briskly to the front door, and opened it.

It took a second or two for the rest of them to catch on, but after a couple of awkward glances, they got up and followed her, spilling out onto the porch.

Karen was last out the door. "I'm so sorry for your loss," she said softly, touching Maddie Routh on the elbow on her way past. "If you need anything, you can find me at the Tea Rose Diner most mornings."

"Just pretend I died," Maddie responded. "I do it all the time. I wish I had."

"The offer stands," Karen responded. "Come on," she said to Melinda and Joanna as she walked past, the wood of her pumps clacking on the sidewalk with purpose.

"I never expected all that," Joanna said when they got into the car. "I mean, I think I expected her to be confused about why we were there, but I didn't expect all of that."

"She's very angry," Karen added. "It's normal. We came at the wrong time."

"To put it mildly," Joanna said. "I'm a little worried about that baby."

"Me, too," Karen said. "I could see her being nervous about raising a child alone, or sad about the baby not ever knowing its father, but I didn't think she'd be so . . . against having it at all."

"Right?" Joanna said.

"I actually think I get it," Melinda said. And she did. A part of her really understood where Maddie Routh was coming from.

"But it's not the baby's fault that its father is dead," Joanna said. "It's nobody's fault, really."

"That's exactly the point," Melinda said. "How do you bring a baby into a world where people end up dead and it's nobody's fault?" She pulled into the diner parking lot and shifted the car into park. She didn't realize until she felt Karen's hand on top of her own that she was trembling.

"You okay?" Karen asked.

Melinda thought about that morning. Paul had been chattering away, so hopeful after their second meeting at the fertility clinic. He'd been like a kid waiting for Christmas. The guilt had eaten her up, so much so that she almost tossed her pill into the toilet, flushed it away.

Yet, in the end, she didn't. She'd stood in the shower and sobbed as she chewed.

"I don't know," she told Karen, sitting in her car in the Tea Rose parking lot. "I thought I was, but now I'm not sure that I am."

And for the first time, she told someone. The marathon lovemaking. The guilt-inducing doctor visits. The pills in the bottom of her tampon box.

She told Karen and Joanna everything.

NINE

Joanna couldn't remember ever being this nervous. Not for any audition, not for any rehearsal, not for any opening night performance.

She stood in her kitchen, her knees shaking as she went over the checklist again. Dinner: saucy white chicken enchiladas, check. Movie: *The Fabulous Baker Boys*, double check. Confidence: not a check, not even close.

Joanna bent to the narrow cabinet that sat between the stove and the wall. Her mother had proclaimed it a perfect place to store cookie sheets, but Stephen had always called it her Fun Time Cabinet, because all Joanna kept in there was booze. She fumbled around inside until she found a dusty bottle of whiskey. It had been left in her apartment at the end of one particularly rowdy LaEats staff party. She didn't like whiskey. Didn't like how boneless it made her feel. Pliable. Careless. But she needed a little bonelessness right now, a little pliability. What she wouldn't give to be without a care for just a few minutes.

She poured a hefty dollop into a juice glass and shot it, swallowing over and over afterward to keep her gag reflex from sending it right back up her esophagus. It burned, made her eyes water, but it also felt good the way it hit so hard. She poured, and shot, another.

Her mind tried to drift to Sutton, time and again. Sutton in her Adelaide costume, the dusk highlighting the smoothness of her skin underneath all the stage makeup. Sutton laughing, tucking a strand of hair behind her ear while she popped a green grape into her mouth. Sutton asking if she, Joanna, was okay, real worry behind her words. Joanna's gut thumped with every image, and with the whiskey rolling around in her belly, it was instantly harder to push those thoughts—which seemed to come more frequently after she'd called Stephen and set up this night—away.

She started to pour herself a third shot but was interrupted by a knock at the door. She quickly screwed the cap onto the whiskey bottle and shoved it back into the Fun Time Cabinet, then rinsed out her glass, and her mouth, with water.

"Sangria," Stephen said, holding up an enormous jug of red wine, as soon as Joanna opened the door. "Well, it will be if you have Sprite to mix it with," he added. "We are going to class this wine up."

Joanna felt herself smile, and she was filled with a warmth that she was certain wasn't all from the whiskey. It came from deep inside her. "I've missed you so much," she said. She hadn't realized how true that was until she'd seen him again.

"I thought you were dead," he said, scooting through the door. "I watched the news every night to see if they said anything about your secret life as a hooker and how that led to your great demise in a seedy motel in Northeast."

Joanna laughed out loud. "My shame is out," she said. "And you have a very active imagination."

He stopped next to her, looking deep into her eyes. Her heart thumped into hyperspeed, and all images of Sutton were wiped out of her mind entirely. "I'm exceedingly glad you're not stuffed into a barrel right now," he said.

He bent to kiss her cheek, but Joanna surprised herself and turned her mouth to his. The kiss landed, soft and quick. Stephen jerked back.

"Wow," he said. "You should go missing more often if this is the result. And this is terrible timing, but I've got to put this down. My forefinger has gone numb." He held up the jug, and then went into the kitchen with it.

"About that, the missing thing," Joanna said, shutting the door.

"I'll forgive you someday," he called. "The good news is I got rich off of double tips while you were gone, so now I can afford to take you on a roaring tour of the city via the fabulous metro bus." He poked his head around the corner. "You want yours over ice? Since we're going classy."

"Yeah," she said. She leaned back against the door. This. This felt good. Having Stephen back felt so good. She'd missed him. Maybe that was all she'd needed—a break, to figure things out. She'd gotten confused, but the answer had been in front of her all the time. She wasn't gay. She was just curious. But in the end, her love belonged here. With a man. With *this* man.

"It smells great in here," he said, coming back into the living room, holding two glasses. Joanna took one and clinked it against his. "Pizza pockets have come a long way, from the smell of things."

"That's because I actually cooked for you," Joanna said. She took a swallow of her wine, which went down smooth and easy and joined the whiskey to fill her with warmth and happiness. "And we have Michelle Pfeiffer in the house," she added, setting her glass down on the coffee table and picking up the DVD case. She waved it in front of him.

"Feelings is not parsley!" Stephen cried. One of their shared favorite quotes from the movie.

"It's less than parsley," Joanna countered, as she always did, the Susie Diamond to his Frank Baker. They had a history, Stephen and Joanna. Relationships depended on history. How could she have not seen that before?

He put the case back down on the coffee table and picked up his glass again. "I say we eat, drink, and be fabulous," he said, lifting his glass and then taking a sip.

"In a second," Joanna said. She pulled the glass out of his hand and set it on the table. "I really want to apologize."

"It's nothing," Stephen said. "I'm sorry Leese didn't keep your job open for you."

"Not just that," Joanna said, and she found her eyes suddenly filling with tears. She wished briefly that she hadn't drunk the whiskey. She wasn't sloppy, but she was afraid she would never be able to convey all the things she was thinking and feeling. "I mean, I am sorry to leave you in the lurch like that, yes. But I'm also sorry about disappearing on you. And about the night with the wine."

His head rolled back. "Oh, God, don't bring that up. I was such an asshole."

She grabbed his wrists, pulled. "No. No, you weren't. You were being honest, and I . . . I was confused, is all. But I'm not anymore."

He stopped pulling away. "What do you mean?"

Without thinking, Joanna did what she knew was the right thing to do. The only thing to be done. The only way out of this confusion and this hiding. She leaned into him and pressed her lips on his.

At first he was unmoving, stiff, and Joanna was bowled over by a sinking feeling that she'd made another mistake. That he didn't want her anymore and that she'd just made a fool of herself again. It had been over a month—what if he had a girlfriend now?

But when their lips parted, Stephen tipped his chin down and gazed at her warily. "Are you sure?" he whispered.

She nodded. "This is the way it's supposed to be," she said.

It seemed like it was only moments before they were in

her bedroom. So fast Joanna wasn't sure she could entirely recall how they'd gotten there. There had been such urgency—such tugging and pulling and breathing words into each other's mouths. It had been gymnastic and feverish, and Joanna was as caught up in it as she'd ever been. She wanted this. She wanted him.

They fumbled their way to her bed, attached as if their lips fused together while their hands removed clothing and explored.

And then, just as they reached her bed, Stephen got still. He put his hands on each side of her head and stared into her face as if he were trying to memorize it. She could feel him breaching the distance between them, pressing into her thigh.

"I've wanted this for so long," he whispered.

Joanna tipped her head up, parted her lips, and closed her eyes.

And as she fell backward beneath him, the images she'd been keeping at bay ever since calling him flooded her. Sutton, blushing in her Adelaide costume. Sutton, giggling as Joanna tucked a piece of hair behind her ear, feeding her a grape with her own mouth. Sutton's lips pressed against her. Sutton in her arms, skin creamy and warm as milk.

As Stephen shuddered and cried out against her, Joanna's eyes flew open. She gulped and gulped, flooded with guilt and shame and disappointment.

TEN

Karen stood in the lobby by a row of spill-proofed couches for a solid ten minutes before she could gather enough courage to approach the information desk. She figured the elderly lady sitting there would never give her the information she needed, and even though she'd promised herself she'd come up with a plan by the time she got to the hospital, she still hadn't.

But she didn't intend to spend her entire Saturday standing in a forever-flowing river of hospital bustle. The weather had finally cooled a bit. She could smell the coming winter in the air. Neighbors were putting decorative hay bales and cornstalks in their yards, and soon the kids would be donning costumes for trick-or-treating. She wondered briefly if Kendall would bother to dress up Marcus—if she'd bring him to

Karen's house, disguised as Batman or a pirate—or if she'd be too into herself to worry about something as boring as Halloween. Karen needed to pull some weeds, to mow her lawn, to prune the smoke tree before it dropped leaves into her gutters. She probably needed to clean her gutters, too. She'd been lucky the cold weather had held off as long as it had.

So why she was standing in the hospital, unmoving, when she had so much to do was beyond her. She knew only that when it came to "had to do's," this errand was at the top of the list.

Quietly, she ducked into the hospital chapel, a bare, cream-colored box that seemed afraid to commit to any actual representation of a god. *BYOF*, Karen thought. *Bring Your Own Faith.*

There was a stand of candles in red cups next to the front door, along with a metal locked box. Karen rooted through her purse, tucked a dollar through the slot on the top of the box, and grabbed a match.

"Curt MacDonald, I don't know you, but I'm praying for you," she said as she lit the match and touched it to a candlewick. "I'm praying like crazy."

She had learned the name of her son's victim only the night before. Kendall had somehow ferreted it out of someone—Karen honestly didn't want to know whom or how—and had even managed to discover in which hospital Mr. MacDonald was recovering. It should have frightened her, the reach of Kendall's manipulative prowess, but at the moment she could only muster gratitude over finally knowing something.

Having his name somehow made the whole thing more personal to Karen. She'd called Antoinette in tears, and Antoinette had been the one to talk her into visiting him today.

"Oh, sure, just show up at the hospital. Hi, Mr. MacDonald, my son's the one who almost beat you to death. I thought you'd like to have a face to go with the shittiest mother who ever lived. Can I get you some ice chips?"

"No," Antoinette had said. "You go and say a few prayers by his bedside. You tell his family how sorry you are and you make yourself feel a hell of a lot better. And you are not the shittiest mother who ever lived. The fact that you haven't disowned Travis yet means you have more patience than I would have. He's a grown man. He has to take blame for himself. This is about you living with what happened. And praying that Curt MacDonald lives through it, too. For all of your sakes."

"You're probably right," Karen had said. *And maybe the court will look on Travis more leniently if I've been to visit his victim*, she thought. But she would never articulate those words to anyone. She had the feeling that nobody would understand how she could possibly still be thinking of her son right now. She didn't entirely understand it herself.

"By the way, I ran into Marty Squire on the way to the parking garage tonight," Antoinette had told her.

"Ugh, not now. I don't want to hear about it," Karen whined. Why was this man suddenly everywhere?

"Oh, come on, Karen. He's so cute. And he's really, really into you. You want to hear what he said?"

"No."

"Yes, you do."

"I'll tell you what. If Curt MacDonald wakes up, I'll let you tell me all about it."

Antoinette had chuckled into the receiver. "Then if you don't get to that hospital and start praying, I will. I will not rest until I hear sloppy details about what Marty Squire wears under those suits of his."

"Gross."

"Oh, honey," Antoinette had said on a sigh. "It's so sad that you think sex is gross."

Now, kneeling in the chapel, watching the candle she'd just lit flicker in an unfelt breeze, Karen knew that Antoinette had been right about coming here, and it had nothing to do with Marty Squire. Her being at the hospital wouldn't help Curt MacDonald wake up, but it couldn't hurt. And maybe it would ease her guilt a little.

She tipped her eyes up toward the ceiling, which had a water stain right in the center. At least, she hoped it was a water stain. In a hospital, how could you ever be certain? She closed her eyes, licked her lips, clasped her hands together, and prayed for the life of a man she'd never met, and prayed for the soul of her son, whom she no longer believed in.

When she was done, she took a deep breath and marched to the information desk, hoping she looked more confident than she felt.

"May I help you?" the woman at the front desk—Beatrice, her name tag read—asked, fanning a novel out over her lap to keep her page.

"Yes, I need to visit someone," Karen said. "Curt Mac-Donald?"

The woman consulted a printout, running her gnarled finger down a list of names until she came to the right one. She found it, and peered up at Karen through thick bifocals.

"He's in the tower. Room 502. Go all the way to the end of that hall and take the elevators up to the fifth floor. You should be able to find him from there."

Karen blinked. It was really that easy? She'd expected to be grilled about whether she was family, maybe had been even a little concerned that, given how the man got his injuries, Curt MacDonald would be under some sort of protective custody. She'd expected the police to be worried that Travis, or one of his henchmen, would come finish the job to keep Curt MacDonald from talking if he should ever wake up. She supposed Travis didn't look like the kind of guy who could afford henchmen, and the police knew it.

She probably needed to stop watching so many crime dramas on TV.

"Thank you," Karen said. The elderly lady smiled and nodded, her hands already reaching for the paperback in her lap before Karen even walked away from the desk.

She headed toward the hallway that the lady had pointed down, ducking into the gift shop on the way. She didn't know if Curt MacDonald was into flowers, but it couldn't hurt, right? Although after she bought them, she fretted about whom he'd tell his family and friends they were from. If he even knew.

God, this was so stupid.

Stupid, but necessary.

She chose a mostly yellow bouquet, thinking the color was vibrant and might stimulate thoughts of waking up, getting out of bed, heading outside. Of course, he'd first have to open his eyes to see them.

Twice, she set the bouquet on top of trash cans in the hallway, with thoughts of abandoning it. But twice she'd picked it up again, slowly making her way down the long corridor that would take her to "the tower," which sounded medieval and torturous and deadly. Filled with trapped heroes and damsels in distress. A place where villains kept their victims locked away from the rest of the world. The image somehow fit Travis. She pictured her son, with his widow's peak and his pointy eyebrows, his face red and angry from fighting, foam caught in the corners of his mouth, as he stood over a drunk and enraged Curt MacDonald. She'd never seen Travis get into a fight, but the way she imagined it was indeed very villainous.

She was alone on the elevator, which meant that it was not nearly as long a ride as she wished it would've been. She felt her fingers begin to go cold around the vase she was holding. Dread began filling her, like water filling a bathtub—first shallowly shimmering in the very recesses of her, but quickly building upon itself until she was sure she would drown in it.

Suddenly, a thought occurred to her. Would Marty Squire be working so hard to get into her life if he knew her life included visiting the deathbeds of her son's victims? And why the hell would she be thinking of Marty Squire at a time like this anyway? She shook him away.

The elevator doors opened, and Karen paused for so long, they began to close again. She briefly considered letting them go and just sitting cross-legged in the corner of the elevator car, pushing no buttons, going nowhere until someone else summoned the elevator. She would be surprised by which floor she ended up on. Perhaps the maternity ward, where she could look at the babies in the nursery and fantasize that she was starting over. Maybe with a do-over, she'd get it right.

But just as the doors began to close, a nurse stepped over the threshold, making them bounce back.

"You getting off here?" she asked. "This is five."

Karen found herself nodding, and then stepping through the doors, which promptly shut behind her, abandoning her in the brightly lit, beeping hallway. She stood just outside the elevator, so glad she had the vase to clutch.

"Can I help you?" another nurse asked, from behind a large desk in the center of the unit. She was young, intense, giving the sense that she had other, much more urgent things to do than babysit some loon who'd just spilled out of the elevator onto her floor.

"Curt MacDonald," Karen said, her voice feeling rough and small. She cleared her throat a few times, chasing away the nothing that was lodged there. "I think he's in 502?"

The nurse nodded and pointed down the hallway with a pen. "Last room before the lounge."

Karen nodded and took a few steps, then turned to the nurse again. "Has there been any change?"

The nurse smiled—a bit condescendingly for Karen's taste—and tilted her head to one side. "And you are . . . ?"

"His aunt," Karen lied, shocked to hear the words tumble out of her mouth so easily. Was it really this simple to completely violate someone's privacy?

The nurse didn't look convinced. "You're welcome to see him," she said on another condescending smile. "I can ask the family if they'd like me to share updates with you."

"No, no," Karen said. "I'll just drop these off." She held up the flowers, for the first time actually wanting to get to Curt MacDonald's room. She needed to at least see him before the hospital kicked her out.

Her shoes clicked loudly on the polished tile as she made her way to room 502. When she pushed open the door, which had been hanging half-ajar, she was surprised to see a very young woman—barely more than a teenager, really sitting in a chair across from the foot of Curt's bed. The woman had been leaning forward, craning toward the door, surely tipped off to Karen's arrival by the sound of her shoes.

"Oh," Karen said, stopping short.

The woman smiled warmly. "Hello," she said. "Come on in. It's just me in here. Sandra went to grab some lunch."

Karen stepped inside the room. She had no idea who Sandra was, but it seemed like a good idea to pretend that she did.

"Still sleeping," the woman said. She smiled again, gesturing toward the form in the bed.

Karen finally turned to face him, her breath catching in her throat. She set the flowers on a nearby windowsill, hoping the movement would keep her from showing her shock too much.

Curt MacDonald was young. Impossibly young. For some reason, throughout all of this, Karen had imagined an older man, a haggard drunk who'd been dodging bar fights for decades. She'd imagined a ruddy alcoholic face, lined and spotted hands with tobacco-tarnished fingers. Someone who spent a lifetime looking for trouble.

Instead, she was faced with a man who looked no older than Travis himself, only softer, pinker. This boy looked like he'd never stepped foot in a bar. Had he not been lined with mostly healed scars, he would have had the perfection of youth.

"We thought maybe today would be the day. It's our anniversary," said the young woman, and when Karen turned to her, she realized that the girl belonged with a boy this age. The girl shrugged. "Not wedding anniversary, of course. That's still upcoming." She held up her left hand and wiggled her ring finger, which was bejeweled with a glittering solitaire. "It's the anniversary of the first time he asked me out. Three years—can you believe it?"

Karen shook her head. "Happy anniversary," she croaked.

"Thank you," the girl said, and smiled, showing off deep dimples and a brilliant whitening job. She was really beautiful. Way too beautiful to be sitting at her fiancée's hospital bedside. She should be out in the world, choosing bridesmaids' dresses and squabbling over whom to put on the guest list and whether she wanted fondant or buttercream for her wedding cake. "I'm sure he's celebrating, even if he can't say it. Sandra's having a much harder time with it than I am. I know my Curt. He's coming back." She gave Karen a curious look, then stood and offered her hand. "I'm sorry, I don't think we've officially met. I'm Katy."

Karen took her hand and held on to it. It was so warm. "Karen," she said.

"You look like the MacDonald side. Are you Craig's sister?"

"Uh, no, I'm . . . from a different side," Karen said, as if there were multiples "sides" of a family to choose from. "You're engaged to Curt?"

Katy nodded, her face clouding over only momentarily before she pasted another hopeful grin onto it. "Technically, we were supposed to get married the weekend that this happened. He was at his bachelor party that night." She took a few steps forward and picked up his hand, squeezed it between her palms. She let out a soft breath of affectionate laughter. "That's the funny thing. He never goes to bars. He doesn't like to drink. But his friend Amos insisted, and he went along because that's the kind of guy he is. Always pleasing other people. They tested his blood alcohol when they brought him in and it didn't even register. He had been drinking soda all night. Leave it to my Curt to be the designated driver at his own bachelor party."

Karen felt a lump form in her throat. This was all so

wrong. Where was the grizzled drug addict who'd baited her son into a bar brawl? Where was the man who deserved this?

"Have there been any changes?" she squeaked out through what felt like a packed throat.

Katy's smile turned sad and she tilted her head to one side, studying Curt's face. She reached up and stroked his cheek with the back of one finger. "Not really," she said. "He's made a few movements here and there, and we thought maybe he was waking up, but the doctors say those are involuntary movements and there haven't been any real changes. We're hopeful, though. Curt's a fighter. He won't give up and neither will we."

"No, of course, you can't," Karen said.

"I just wish I could understand why, you know?" Katy said. She'd slipped her hand out of Curt's and laid his gently across his chest. She crossed her arms, bunching up as if she was cold. "His friends all swear he wasn't doing anything wrong. Said he bumped into the other guy's barstool or something. Amos says he had his hands up and kept telling the guy he didn't want any trouble. I just wish I could figure out why the guy couldn't have just left him alone. Sandra said Curt has never been in a fistfight his whole life. He didn't know how to fight. It just seems so . . ." She shrugged.

"Senseless," Karen supplied for her, and Katy nodded.

"Yeah. That's how I know he's going to come back to me. There's no way this is how he's going to go out. It's just not possible."

But anything was possible, and Karen knew that. If it was possible that her son had done this—this!—to the young man lying in front of her, a man who hadn't been drinking, a man who didn't want any trouble, then it was possible that Curt MacDonald would never wake up from his bachelor party. Unjust and unfair, definitely. But impossible? No.

There was a bustling sound in the hallway, and the door was pushed open. Karen and Katy both turned as a woman came into the room, carrying a plastic sack.

"Oh, she's back," Katy said, her smile returning.

Karen didn't know who "she" was, but she guessed her to be Sandra, the one who'd stepped out. And from the haggard look on Sandra's face, the matte pallor of her skin, the dark circles under her eyes, Karen guessed that Sandra was Curt's mother. She was certain of it. Only a mother could look so ill at her son's hospital bed.

"I brought you a sandwich," the woman said, holding the plastic bag out. Katy took it. "Cafeteria was busy today. I should have gone out. No changes?"

Katy shook her head. "Not yet."

The woman gave Curt a quick once-over and dropped her purse onto the chair Katy had been occupying when Karen had arrived. Only then did she seem to really notice that Karen was standing there. "Hi," she said.

"Hi," Karen responded, taking an involuntary step back from the bed, as if the woman would be able to sniff out that she was an intruder—someone who didn't belong by Curt's bedside.

"I'm sorry," the woman said. "I guess I've forgotten who you are. You'll have to forgive me. It's been a trying few weeks."

"Of course," Karen said, her entire body going electric. Now that she was face-to-face with the other mother, she was hit with the enormity of what her being there at all would mean. How could she have shown up there? How could she have thought it would be the right thing to do? How could Antoinette have set her up for this? She wanted to escape, to run out of the room with no explanation. Surely they would be better off to forever wonder who the strange woman had been who'd visited Curt than to know that she had been the person who'd raised the man who'd beaten Curt nearly to death.

The woman tipped her head forward, as if she was straining to hear Karen speak, her eyebrows jotting up into her hairline.

"I'm Karen," Karen said, offering her hand, but then thinking better of it and letting it drop to her side.

The woman shook her head uncomprehendingly. "I'm sorry. You worked with Curt?"

Karen realized how easy it would be to just nod, pretend that this was exactly how she knew Curt. But that was not why she was here, and while she was, at the moment, a swirl of confusion and guilt and grief, she still felt that to come here and lie would somehow only make her feel worse about this horrible situation.

"Uh, no," she said, her voice shaky. "I actually . . . um . . ." She shifted her weight, felt tears spring to her eyes, as if they'd been waiting for the right moment to appear. "My son is Travis Freeman," she finally blurted, feeling as if the words had been ripped out of her on the sinew of an enormous painful scab.

It took a moment for the name to register with the woman. Her eyes darted to the floor as she searched for how she knew Travis Freeman. But then Karen could see it dawn on her. Her head snapped up, a red blotch instantaneously appearing on her neck, as if Karen had slapped her. "Travis Freeman," she said dully.

Karen nodded. "I came to"—*say "apologize," say "apologize," say "apologize"*—"to pray for your son's recovery," she said instead. "I prayed. In the chapel. And I brought him flowers." She gestured toward the windowsill.

The woman gazed at the flowers and then turned slowly back toward Karen. "You came to pray for my son's recovery," she said, and Karen wished she would say something else, something new, stop just repeating Karen's words.

Karen nodded.

The woman's face split into a grin, but unlike the brilliant grin that had been on Katy's face, this one looked bruised and fragile. She nodded, as if listening to an amusing tale that nobody else could hear. "You should be praying for your own son," she finally said. "My son doesn't need your prayers. He is a good person who never hurt anyone in his life. Save your prayers for the monster that you raised. I know about him. Repeat offender." She said these last two words with such venom, Karen actually backed up

a step. "This is a game to him. People's lives are meaning-
less. He needs your prayers so much more than my Curt."

"It's not," Karen had been saying. "It's not a game." But
her voice was soft and uncertain. "He is sorry." She didn't
know why she was saying this. Travis had been anything
but sorry when she last saw him. She was protecting him
again. It was so easy to say your son needed tough love, but
much harder to believe it when his enemies were standing
right in front of you.

"Yes, he is," the woman said. "A very sorry human being. You should leave. You have no business being here."

"I came to apologize," Karen said, but it was clearly too
late. Her voice came out whiny, plaintive, like she was bar-
tering with this woman for an extra cookie or a later bed-
time.

"And you did," the woman said. "Thank you for that."

Karen backed toward the door. "I'm sorry," she practically whispered, wishing the woman had been yelling, had
been giving her reason to be angry. Instead, the woman
had been so confident, so resolute. It served only to make
Karen feel defeated. "I'm sorry," she said again, then turned
and left the room.

"You okay?" she heard Katy ask as she walked away
from Curt MacDonald's doorway.

"That took a lot of nerve," the woman said.

And then Katy's voice, faint and fading as Karen moved
toward the elevator: "Don't worry, they'll put him away for
a long time this time. You heard them say . . ."

The elevator doors slid open and Karen stepped inside on numb legs. She couldn't blame them. Who could? She would want Curt MacDonald to be put away forever if it were Travis in that bed. She would think Curt MacDonald was a monster. She would want justice.

She felt so sorry, so guilty. Travis had taken a boy from his mother, a young man from his future wife. Travis had done this, and she had raised Travis alone. She had never foreseen the man the sweet little boy with the dimpled chin would become. She had never suspected he would be this man she now called her son. She was ignorant. She was negligent.

But she was still his mother. And she wanted to shield him from Curt MacDonald's mother.

And old habits died hard. Or maybe old protectors never stopped protecting. Or maybe she was stupid or crazy, but Karen still had some nugget of hope inside her that Travis could be saved somehow. That time behind bars would only make him worse, would only take him further down the path he was on. If Curt MacDonald was going to be lost, what sense would it make to lose Travis, too? Why not salvage one young life if it was at all possible? Besides, she had created this monster—it was up to her to fix him. And if she was going to undo the mistakes she'd obviously made in raising him, how could she possibly do it if he was locked up?

She pulled her phone out of her purse and thumbed through the contacts list until she found the one she was looking for. Alone in the elevator, she pressed TALK and waited through the few rings that would take her to the voice mail she wanted.

"Hello, Mr. Sidwell? This is Karen Freeman, down in Human Resources. I'm wondering if you might have a moment to chat sometime this week? My son is having some legal troubles, and I need advice. . . ."

ELEVEN

I t had been an extremely rough day. First a call on a child choking. The mother had managed to dislodge the chunk of hot dog that had wedged itself in her toddler's throat just moments before Melinda and Jason had arrived, but both mother and child were nearly hysterical, shaking with tears and adrenaline even as they took his vitals and reassured her he was fine. Melinda had finally suggested the mother take the child to urgent care to have him checked out by a doctor, which had calmed the mother, but had only set off another wave of wailing from the child.

Jason was in a bad mood after that. Melinda didn't love it when she had to work with him. He was moody and un-predictable, given to melancholy calls with his whiny wife, which he always took on speaker.

I hate this job, Jason. You need a new job. I can't raise the kids by myself all the time without you, Jason. You agreed when Sara was born, Jason.

On and on the woman went, her tune never changing from day to day. The calls only reinforced Melinda's own child problems. She always wondered if it would be Paul someday making those calls, demanding she give up the career she'd worked so hard to establish herself in. They couldn't have a child—why didn't Paul see that? Her career wasn't amenable to it. Jason was proof of that every single day.

They weren't even back to the station yet after the choking call before they got another call. A child had a seizure during a school assembly, terrifying her teachers and other students. Melinda felt on display as she walked through the school, all the kids staring from their classroom doors and desks and the cafeteria. She felt sorry for the little girl as they escorted her out of the school. How humiliated the little girl must have felt, being the center of such attention. Kids had horribly long memories. They would forever recall her as the girl who'd shaken on the floor of the gymnasium during the magazine-sale assembly. How would her mother stand knowing that her daughter not only had this medical problem but would likely be a pariah because of it? The thought made Melinda so sad she felt she might burst into tears.

"What's your problem, Crocker?" Jason had grumbled when they got back in the truck, addressing her by her last name only—something else she disliked about him.

"What?"

"You've been bitchy all day. What's the deal?"

Melinda had rolled her eyes as she swiveled to pull her seat belt around herself. "That's rich," she mumbled.

"Huh?"

"I said there's nothing wrong. What's wrong with you?"

"Nothing. I'm not the one with the problem."

"Whatever."

That was pretty much the extent of any conversation Melinda had ever had with Jason. She checked her watch, hoping her shift was almost over.

There had been one more call before she finally got to go home. A car accident that was probably more suicide than accident. A man—a doctor, one of the officers had told them—had driven his truck directly into the concrete abutment of a bridge. His death had most likely been instantaneous, but it gutted Melinda just the same. As she peered in through the wrecked window at the man's lifeless body, all she could see was the memory of blood draining from Michael Routh's pale face. All she could hear were the frantic cries of Maddie Routh, intermingled with the sobs of the children who were still straggling out of the tipped bus. All she could feel was the anxiety of lives being forever changed. *Please, kids, don't come over here. Stay with your teacher. Stay with your bus. You don't want to see this.*

By the time she nosed her car into the driveway, she was bone tired, emotionally wrung out, unsure how she'd be able to ever make herself get up and put on her uniform again in the morning.

Paul's car was in the garage. Immediately, guilt and anxiety washed over her, while at the same time she couldn't wait to get inside and fall into his arms. Let him take the day away from her. They'd have dinner. He'd encourage her to talk about her workday. His voice would soothe her. He would give her a little shoulder rub and remind her that what she did made her a hero to some people. He'd curl up around her in bed under the blue glow of late-night talk shows. Most likely, he would make love to her, and she'd go through the motions, wishing she could have a glass of wine to help alleviate what she was feeling. She wanted to enjoy his body against hers again, but she was always too tense to even feel him these days.

"I'm home," she called, tossing her car keys on the kitchen counter. She shucked her shoes right there by the kitchen table, a habit that annoyed him but that she couldn't seem to shake no matter how hard she tried. "What's for dinner? I'm starving." She continued to shed items—her lunch bag, her purse—as she walked through the living room. The bedroom light was on, and she could hear Paul's dresser drawer squeak open. She unbuckled her belt and let it hang, untucked her shirt, let out a breath. "Very long day today—had to work with Jason. Did you know he looks angry even when he chews? He has this vein that pops out in the middle of his forehead and his nostrils flare out. The dude is eating a sandwich, and . . ."

Melinda had rounded the corner into the bedroom, her hand still twisted up into the back of her hair, trying to loose an elastic from her ponytail. She stopped when she saw her husband, sitting on the edge of the bed, rifling through his dresser drawer, a duffel bag open on the bed.

"What's going on?" she asked, and, when he didn't respond, prompted, "Paul? Is something wrong?"

Paul had found the shirt he was searching for, and held it crumpled in his fist. He shut the drawer with a thud and tossed the shirt into the duffel.

"Paul?" Melinda prompted again, stepping toward him. "What are you doing?"

He stood to face her, and Melinda's stomach dropped. Something was very, very wrong. Her husband didn't often look like this. The last time she'd seen this expression on his face, his brother had gone off on a drunken rampage and had shoved their aging father into a wall. This look meant only one thing. He was pissed.

"Do you have anything you want to talk about, Melinda?" he asked. His voice was like a stranger's.

She shook her head. "What . . . ?"

"You sure you don't want to tell me anything?"

She felt a jolt of adrenaline rush through her, causing her limbs to instantly go icy. Her ears rang with her heartbeat. He knew. Somehow, he knew. She could feel his knowledge hovering in the air between them.

"No," she said. "I don't know what you're talking about, Paul."

"Well, let me give you a hint," he said. He reached up onto his dresser and pulled down a blue plastic envelope that she knew all too well. She could see the foil tags peek out of the bottom from where she'd popped the pills through their blisters. "Look familiar?" He tossed the packet onto the bed. It lay there, half-used, between the two of them, damning evidence.

"How did you find them?" Melinda asked, at once sick and angry. Knowing she had no right to feel angry, but feeling it just the same. "Were you going through my things?"

"No, I wasn't going through your things. Stupid me, I would never think you had anything to hide from me. Why would I look through your things?" He placed his hands on his hips. "I was looking for the Tylenol because my colossally shitty day gave me a killer headache. Congratulations, by the way. You sure know how to drive a headache away."

"You thought you'd find Tylenol in my tampons?" she asked, knowing it was a mistake to let annoyance seep into her voice. She felt a great need to defend herself, to deflect his anger. Maybe if he'd done something wrong, too, she would look less wrong. It was stupid and childish, and she knew it, but she couldn't help herself.

"I accidentally knocked the box out of the cabinet and the lid opened up," he said. He picked up the pill packet and shook it. "Does it matter how I found them? The date on the prescription is this month. And I guess your reaction is all I need to hear to know that the date is accurate."

Melinda didn't respond. She didn't know how. A million responses were milling through her brain, muddled and chaotic, and no one thought could break through.

"Why?" he asked. "I mean, we've been to the fertility

clinic, for God's sake. You cried, Melinda. You sat in that office and cried. I consoled you."

Just hearing about how she'd cried made helpless tears spring to Melinda's eyes. They'd been real tears in that fertility clinic office. But he would never believe that. He would think the tears were part of her cover-up.

"I cried because I didn't know how to tell you," she said. "I felt so guilty."

"Tell me what? That you were making family planning decisions for both of us without letting me in on it? That you were lying to me? Is that what you didn't know how to tell me? Seriously, Melinda, it should be really easy. You had about a billion chances to just say, 'Hey, Paul, maybe we should talk about the fact that I never got off of my birth control pills before you go and make a fool of yourself and waste a shitload of money with a bunch of fertility testing.' You'd think you could at least manage that much." He sank onto the bed and propped his elbows on his knees, resting his forehead in his hands.

"I'm sorry," she said. "It didn't seem that easy. You were so . . . excited."

"Oh, well, forgive me for being excited to start a family with you," he said. "Yeah. I was. I thought we both were. I was excited for us, Melinda. Not for me. I never saw this as being about one of us. Unlike you, I guess."

She walked to the side of the bed, where he was, and reached out to touch the back of his head. He jerked away from her touch, and she shrank back a few steps. She had known he would be upset, but she had never expected him to shut her out so completely.

"I'm sorry," she repeated. "You have no idea how much it was eating me up. Every day I felt so guilty."

"But you took it every day anyway. You should have been feeling guilty. Lying to your husband should make you feel guilty."

She nodded. "I'm just not ready to have kids."

He dropped his hands. "So were you planning on ever clueing me in on when you'd be ready? Since this is all about you."

"That's the thing," she said. "I don't know if I'll ever be ready."

He gazed at her, bewilderment in his eyes and in the helpless way his hands hung between his knees. "You said you wanted kids. We talked about this before we ever got engaged."

"I did want them. And I do, in theory. It's just . . . every time I think about having my own kids now, I just . . . I can't. All I can think about is the drowning call we went on that one summer, and the time that kid lost half his leg under his dad's lawn mower, and all the car accidents. I can't do it, Paul. Every time I look at our baby, I'll just be waiting for catastrophe to strike."

"So you're just going to have no children rather than take a chance that something bad might happen to one?" he asked. "Bad things happen, Melinda. You can't stop them. Does what you're saying actually seem rational to you?"

She shrugged. She honestly hadn't thought it all the way through to that end before. Was that what she was doing? Was she willing to never hold her own child in her arms because she'd seen so many moms' arms be emptied? Was the pain of the *maybe* worse than the pain of never having her own baby? "I don't know," she said simply.

"You don't know."

She shook her head. "And that's why I had to take the pills, Paul. Because I don't know, which tells me I'm not ready. And I don't know if I'll ever be ready. I want to be, but I can't make any promises. Not right now."

"The problem wasn't you taking the pills. It was you taking them without telling me. This isn't a game, Melinda. It's our life. These are decisions we're supposed to make together, even if it means you have to have a conversation with me that you don't want to have. Don't I at least deserve that much?"

He did, and she knew he did. From the very beginning, she knew he deserved that much. That was what the guilt was about—not about keeping herself from getting pregnant, but about hiding her fears from him.

He pulled himself up from the bed and leaned over to grab his duffel. "Can I ask you something?" She watched as he zipped his duffel. "Are you having an affair?"

"What?"

He shouldered the duffel. "Do you need the pills because you're screwing around and you don't want to take the chance that you'll get pregnant and not know who the father is?"

She touched her collarbone with her fingertips. "I can't believe you would even ask me that."

"Well, we'll just add it to the list of unbelievable things today," he said. "Are you?"

"Of course I'm not," she spat.

He stared at her for what seemed an uncomfortably long time, and then edged his way around the bed and around her.

"Where are you going?" she asked, following him, her heart pounding anew.

"The gym," he said. "And then to Anthony's. I'm going to stay with him for a few days."

"Your brother lives in Des Moines," she said, pointing out the obvious about Anthony.

"The drive will give me time to think," he said over his shoulder.

"When will you be back?"

"I don't know, a few days, a few weeks. I'll call." He plucked his car keys out of the key bowl on the table next to the front door, then veered through the living room, where he picked up a book he'd left by the couch.

She followed him through the living room and into the kitchen. "Paul, wait," she said, suddenly feeling desperate and panicky. "Don't go. We can talk."

He whirled on her just as he reached the door to the garage. His eyes were wide, mocking. "So now we can talk? I think it's a little late for that, don't you?"

"Come on, Paul. Don't be like that," she whispered. Her hands were shaking.

"Be like what? Hurt?" he asked. "Don't you understand? You changed huge things about our relationship, and you never even bothered to tell me. Wouldn't you be hurt if I'd done this to you?" And when she had no answer for that, he opened the garage door and disappeared through it. "I'll call," he said over his shoulder. "Don't forget to take your pill in the morning."

He slammed the door behind him. Melinda didn't move. She heard the rumble of the garage door opener and the whoosh of Paul's Explorer starting up. She listened as her husband backed out of the garage and shut the door behind him. After the hum of the opener stopped, she stayed in that same spot and listened to the silence.

This. Was this less pain than the possibility of being a victim?

She honestly didn't know at this point.

She closed her eyes and was flooded with the image of that mangled little red car on the lawn of the Tea Rose Diner, adrenaline and Maddie Routh's cracking voice drowning out the cries of the children just feet away, next to their ruined school bus.

Help him! Help Michael! He's dying!

And Karen, so calm, like she bathed in strangers' blood every day.

I'm holding his head, honey, see? We'll get him some help. Sir? Sir, help is on the way.

Joanna, knocking the shattered glass away from the rear windshield, trying to climb into the car, just as she'd done at the bus moments before.

I can maybe reach the seat-belt buckles from back here. Hang on, I'm trying. I'm coming up.

And Melinda, sinking into a professional calm as she, too, fumbled to press the release button on the seat belt, trying to blot out the shrieking of the young upside-down woman.

Okay, we're gonna get you out. Can you lean over? I just need to try to get the seat belt dislodged so I can get you out of there.

And the image Melinda would never forget, not as long as she lived, no matter how many accident scenes or tragedies she worked. Maddie Routh's terrified eyes, bulging and shocked, and the way her hands shook around a pregnancy test stick, which she held up for Melinda to see. Maddie's voice suddenly losing its shriek and instead going low and pleading.

Please. We're having a baby. He can't die.

But he did.

He did.

TWELVE

Joanna was first into their booth at the Tea Rose. She checked the time on her phone. Everyone was late. Melinda's job meant she came and went when she could, but tardiness was unlike Karen. When Joanna had talked to her on the phone the night before, she hadn't said anything about being late. She'd only relayed that Melinda's husband had left her, that they should all try to meet for coffee in the morning, because Melinda sounded bad.

"Can I get you something while you wait?" Sheila asked, setting a coffee carafe on the table and turning over Joanna's cup. She poured the first one, while sliding a tiny creamer pitcher across the table at the same time.

"How about a grapefruit?" Joanna asked. She was still trying to get used to this eating-healthy nonsense. She really wanted sausage and bacon and the kind of hash browns that were crispy on one side and buttery and soft on the other. But she was trying to eat more healthily for Stephen. Okay, not really *for Stephen.* Just for the distraction. Telling herself that she wanted to look good for her man somehow kept her mind off Sutton. In theory. It was a theory she was still working out.

She and Stephen had been official for two weeks now. They'd made love exactly six times. And every time, she found herself unable to blot Sutton out of her mind while with him. She couldn't climax without thinking about Sutton's cherry lips, a realization that both terrified and excited her. She'd resorted to faking, and while she knew women faked all the time, it still broke her heart to know that she was faking it with Stephen. He'd be crushed if he knew.

She loved him. Really loved him. Heart-skip-a-beat, butterflies-in-the-belly love. And, it was weird, but she was attracted to him, too. But she felt strange when he touched her—as if she were doing something wrong. Her body responded to his fingers, but still she dreamed of Sutton, even while she so desperately didn't want to.

Everything seemed to have gotten more complicated than before. How was that even possible?

She'd taken to texting and calling Karen on a daily basis. She felt an older-sister connection to her. She'd told her about Stephen, but she'd fantasized about telling her everything. Instead, they'd ended up talking mostly about Karen's son, who Joanna guessed Karen thought was plain old no good, but no way would a mother say that out loud.

As if summoned, Karen came through the door and headed straight for their booth. She looked distracted, maybe even frazzled, her hair flattened on one side and her shirt slightly wrinkled.

"Hey, sorry I'm late," she said, scooting into her side of the booth. "I had a phone conference with my boss. Now my son's lawyer. So awkward."

"I just got here anyway," Joanna said. "Did the guy wake up yet?"

Karen turned over her coffee cup and filled it in one swift motion. She shook her head. "Not yet. At least not that we've heard. Not that we'd be first on their list of people to notify, you know? Maybe there'll be a miracle today."

"Miracle Monday," Joanna said, smiling. It was something Sutton had said when they'd both found out they'd gotten parts in *Guys and Dolls.* Joanna hadn't known Sutton yet at that point, but the tiny brunette had already caught her eye, with her ivory knit beret and her torn denim mini-skirt. She'd seemed so professional and perfect. Born for the stage. And sexy as hell. Joanna's face burned at the thought. Where the hell was that grapefruit?

"I like the sound of that," Karen said. She regarded Joanna over her cup. "You're looking awfully pink cheeked this morning. Someone had a good weekend, I guess."

Joanna chuckled. "I must have." She touched one cheek. "I didn't realize."

Karen sipped her coffee and grinned, her lipstick imprinted on the side of her mug. "It's a glow. Love will do that to you."

Immediately, Joanna's smile vanished. Love. She hated the word. She didn't know what it meant anymore.

"Not that I would know," Karen added, echoing Joanna's thoughts.

"Speaking of, is that guy still bothering you?"

Karen grimaced. "I wouldn't really say 'bothering.' More like being relentless. And yes. He just happened to be having lunch outside our building every day this week. Who does that in wind like this? It's cold outside."

"But he's hot on the inside," Joanna teased. "Just kidding," she said when she saw Karen's face. "You're right. It's weird. Maybe you should get a restraining order."

Karen set down her cup and waved her hand. "He's harmless. He just wants to get a drink. I'm thinking of giving in, just to make him go away."

"I'm pretty sure that the best way to make a guy go away is not to go on a date with him," Joanna said. "But then again I'm not exactly an expert on guys," she mumbled.

Karen squinted at her. "Everything okay?"

"Yeah. I'm just saying I've only had one boyfriend. That hardly makes me an expert. How is Melinda?"

"Oh." Karen swiveled in the booth to peer at the door. "She should be here by now. She didn't sound good this morning."

Sheila brought Joanna's grapefruit. Joanna stared at it for a second, wishing it would magically sprout into a plateful of French toast. This was stupid—as if eating right would make her suddenly stop being so confused. She reached over and grabbed a handful of sugar packets, ripped them all open at once, and dumped them over the top of the fruit. She doubted it would do any good, but anything would be better than eating it plain.

"I wouldn't guess she would sound too good. So what happened? Why did Paul leave?"

Karen shrugged. "She didn't say. Just that he's gone, and that she thought she'd hear from him by now, but she hadn't. Maybe we should check on her."

"I don't think that'll be necessary." Joanna pointed out the window, where they saw a disheveled Melinda climb out of her car. Squinting angrily out into the grayish sky, she headed toward them, the wind whipping her hair back away from her forehead, which was creased with annoyance. She was in her uniform, but it was rumpled and untucked.

"Hey, there," Karen said as Melinda slid into the booth next to her. "How are you?"

"Next question," Melinda grumped. "It's flipping cold out there."

"Winter is here, I'm afraid," Karen said. She filled Melinda's coffee cup, and then upended the rest of the carafe into Joanna's cup. "Can you believe next week is Thanksgiving?"

Joanna's stomach cramped up on the bite of grapefruit she'd just swallowed. Yes, she knew Thanksgiving was coming. She had been a mess of nerves about it for days. Stephen had brought it up, how his parents would love to see her, would be so excited to spend the holidays with her. She still hadn't had more than the very barest of conversations with her own parents since she came out of hiding back in October. The thought of schmoozing up Mr. and Mrs. Heartland America made her skin go cold and clammy. Would her . . . problem . . . be obvious to them? Would they take one look at her and know that her lips had touched Alyria's? Would they hear her ambivalence in every word she spoke? She could envision his mother, standing at the end of the Thanksgiving table, pointing at her accusingly. *This girl is an impostor!*

"I don't have anything to be thankful for right now," Melinda said, taking a long gulp of coffee that burned Joanna's throat just to watch.

"What happened?" Joanna asked, glad for the distraction. This grapefruit wasn't working.

Sheila came to the table with another carafe of coffee. "Breakfast?" she asked, and Melinda shook her head.

"Coffee's about all my stomach can handle these days," she said. "Thanks, Sheila. I don't know if I can even talk about it this morning. It's all so surreal. Every morning, I wake up expecting him to be right there, and—"

"That's strange," Sheila interrupted. Joanna glanced at the waitress, who was staring out the window.

They all turned to follow her gaze.

Joanna sucked in a breath.

"Oh," Karen said.

"What on earth?" Sheila said.

"That's Maddie Routh," Melinda said. "Isn't it?"

Joanna barely recognized her, but yes, it did appear to be Maddie Routh, who was sitting behind the steering wheel of a car she'd just parked half onto the walkway. The car leaned as the front passenger-side tire rested a full four inches above the others.

"I think so," she said.

"What is she doing here? I wonder," Karen said. She'd reached into her purse and grabbed her phone in her fist, something Joanna had noticed she had a habit of doing anytime she was nervous.

They watched in silence as Maddie sat in the car, slumped forward so that her forehead rested on the steering wheel. She seemed to be rocking back and forth, and when she sat up again, she wiped her eyes with a balled-up tissue. She rested her head sideways on the driver's-side window and splayed a hand over the window as if she were reaching out to something. She appeared to be talking to herself. Talking and crying.

After a few moments, her door popped open, and a leg dropped out, but still she sat there for the longest time, half in and half out of the skewed car.

"Do you think we should go out there?" Joanna asked.

Karen shook her head. "She didn't seem to really want anything to do with us, remember?"

"But she's upset," Joanna said. She pushed her barely touched grapefruit away. "Maybe she needs something."

"No, I agree with Karen," Melinda said. "Let's wait for her to come in. See if she comes over here. If so, great. If not, we leave her alone."

But Joanna didn't know if she could just leave Maddie Routh alone. She was still haunted by a feeling of not having done enough for her. She'd been so intent on getting the children out—the little boy with the blood on the front of his white shirt. It had come from his nose—no big deal— but he was so frightened. So shattered. She'd barely had time to even register what had happened with Maddie and Michael Routh. One minute she'd been grabbing that boy by the armpits and pulling him through the window, telling him everything was fine, and the next she'd been slicing her own hands and knees climbing through the rear windshield of a smashed red car.

She hadn't realized at the time she'd been climbing into a car with a dead man. She hadn't realized she'd been witnessing a widowing right in that very moment. Would she have still crawled inside the car had she known these things? She wasn't sure.

Maddie Routh had been so panic-stricken. She'd been losing the love of her life and she'd known it.

The night before that crash, the night with Stephen and the wine and the kiss, Joanna had lost her best friend. She'd given up on love. She'd given up on happiness and life and all the things that came with the freedom to love whomever your heart selected.

In a way, she saw them as the same, Maddie and her. They were both alone, loveless. But at the same time she was jealous of Maddie Routh, because Maddie had felt the love before losing it, and Joanna never had.

And she knew, though she would not admit it to herself, that she would not feel it with Stephen. Not really. No matter how many grapefruits she ate, or how many times she made love to him while thinking of someone else.

"Who is Maddie Routh?" Sheila asked.

"The one whose husband died in that wreck back in September," Melinda said.

"Oh." Sheila set the empty carafe she'd been holding onto the table, totally absorbed in what they were all seeing out at the curb.

Maddie Routh's leg pulled back into the car, and the door shut again. But just as soon as it had, it reopened, and this time she pulled her whole body out of the car and stood, the wind pushing her shirt against her belly, which was still not noticeably pregnant, but had a roundness that someone in the know might recognize.

She stood, her eyes closed against the wind, her mouth still working around words that none of the ladies inside the diner could hear. They all continued to stare, no one breathing a word, as she took an unsteady step forward, and then another, wobbling up the walkway toward the doors.

"She doesn't have a jacket on in that wind," Karen observed.

"She doesn't have any shoes on, either," Sheila said. "Her feet must be freezing."

"I think we should do something," Joanna said, scooting toward the edge of the booth. Though she wasn't sure what she thought they should do.

"She's really not supposed to come in here with no shoes on," Sheila said.

But no sooner had she said that than Maddie Routh veered off the walkway, her bare feet disappearing into the crunchy browned grass, dormant for the season. The discolored divots had even blended in with the rest of the dying lawn.

And that was right where Maddie Routh was headed.

Step by shaky step, she made her way through the lawn until her toes rested in one of the dips in the ground. She was now right outside the window where they were sitting. Had the glass not been between them, Joanna might have been able to lean over and touch her. Maddie had stopped talking, and only stared at her toes as they wriggled in the grass, the cuffs of her jeans frayed and filthy.

Joanna couldn't help herself. She reached out and knocked lightly on the glass. Karen darted a look at her, but Maddie Routh didn't even seem to hear the sound at all. Instead of responding to Joanna's knock, she sank to her knees in the center of the biggest divot, running her hands over the tops of the grass blades, just as Joanna had done on her first trip back to the diner after the crash. A serene look cascaded over Maddie Routh's face—her lids heavy and at half-mast, the angry creases wiped clean from her forehead.

"I'm going out there," Joanna said.

"Maybe we should," Melinda agreed.

"Okay," Karen said.

They slid out of the booth and past Sheila, who was holding the carafe again and heading toward the kitchen, watching over her shoulder as they filed toward the door.

Joanna gasped as the wind blew down the front of her

shirt as soon as she opened the door. She remembered how hot the *Guys and Dolls* practices had been at first, all of their makeup melting and gathering in pools in the creases of their faces. She remembered one of the rehearsals, when Sutton had come up behind her and pressed an ice cube to the back of her neck.

You looked hot, Sutton had said, with a smirk, as Joanna gasped, every inch of her body instantly rising into goose bumps. Sutton had rubbed the cube in circles on Joanna's neck for a few seconds before tucking it into her mouth and walking away.

It was easily one of the sexiest moments of Joanna's life.

She hated thinking about it now. Thinking about it led to thinking about where Sutton might be performing now that the outdoor theater season was over. Which would lead to thoughts that maybe she should find out, drop by a rehearsal, see how things were going. Which would lead to thoughts that no amount of grapefruit could wipe out.

Instead of thinking about those things, she pressed forward into the wind and the noise of the morning rush hour traffic, both of which seemed to have picked up considerably since she'd arrived at the Tea Rose. She absently held the door for Melinda, who held it for Karen, and the three of them gathered along the walkway, facing the divots.

Maddie Routh was lying down in the biggest one now. Curled up with her arms pressed into her stomach, her cheek erased by the grass that had been shaded by her husband's blood months before. She wasn't crying. She wasn't talking. If anything, she looked as though she might be sleeping.

Joanna went to her first, crouched down next to her, hugging her own knees. "Maddie?" she asked softly. "Hello?"

At first, Maddie seemed not to have heard her, but then she slowly opened her eyes and blinked at the overcast sky.

"Hey," Joanna said. "Maybe you should come inside. This wind is pretty cold."

Maddie only stared, and then closed her eyes again, pressing her cheek harder into the grass. She loosened one of her arms from her belly and stretched it across the grass as if she was hugging it.

"Maddie?" Melinda had joined Joanna, though she'd remained standing. "Let's go inside and pour you a cup of coffee."

"I don't drink coffee," Maddie Routh said dreamily. "Michael drank loads of it. I can't even stand the smell of it now." She moved her arm back to her belly. "Can't stand the smell of most things now. Thanks to this."

Joanna eased onto her bottom, her arms still hugging her bent legs. The long skirt that she'd worn that day was too thin for winter. She'd known that it was out of season when she'd put it on, but she'd never guessed she'd be sitting outside in it. She reached out to touch Maddie Routh's hair, which looked cleaner than it had before, but was still greasy and tangled.

"Can we do anything to help?" she asked.

Maddie Routh blinked, picked at the grass. "I hate it here," she said.

"Yeah, I can understand that," Joanna said. "It must be really hard to visit."

"I don't," Maddie Routh said. "I have avoided coming past this corner ever since it happened. I have never driven by even one time. Can you believe that? I will drive miles out of my way so that I don't have to drive by this spot in the middle of the city."

"Sure, we can believe it," Karen said. She crouched, too, a movement that was a little awkward in her work skirt and pumps. "I think we all would avoid it."

"But you don't," Maddie Routh said. "Why are you here?"

The three ladies glanced at one another, and Joanna was sure that what was passing between them at that moment was a question. *Why exactly are we here?* they seemed to say.

"We're worried about you," Joanna said. "Remember when we visited you at your house?"

Maddie Routh chuckled, a frightening sound that made chills travel the length of Joanna's spine.

"Worried about someone you don't even know," she said, as if this were a marvel.

"And about the baby," Karen said. "How are things going with the baby?"

Maddie Routh's face clouded. She closed her eyes and pushed her arms into her belly even harder, splitting herself in half. Joanna noticed how thin her waist really had gotten. Even thinner than the last time they had seen her.

"I would make the world's worst mother," she said.

"No, you wouldn't," Melinda said. "Trust me on that."
Joanna glanced at Melinda, who seemed to have sprouted

tears in the corners of her eyes. But then again maybe it was the wind. Melinda caught Joanna's curious look and answered it with a look of her own. "What? I've seen a lot of shitty mothers in my line of work. You wouldn't even be close to the world's worst."

Maddie Routh sat up, and then stood, towering over Joanna. Karen stood with her, smoothing her skirt over her thighs as she straightened.

"No, Michael would have been a great father, but I would be a terrible mother. I don't want this anymore, don't you see? I don't want to have to keep driving around town to avoid this corner, and I don't want this dent in the grass and I don't want . . ." She tugged at the hem of her shirt with two fists. "I don't want this baby."

The three ladies went silent, alarmed.

"Things will look better with time," Karen said. "When the baby is born."

Maddie turned in a slow circle, her head tilted up toward the sky. If she'd heard Karen, she made no indication of such. She turned her palms up, pressed her shoulders back, her chest out. A lazy smile spread across her face.

Again, the ladies exchanged alarmed glances. Joanna shivered in her thin dress, and hugged her knees tighter.

Melinda reached out for Maddie Routh's elbow. "Listen, I think we should all go inside. We can talk in there where it's warm."

But Maddie kept turning, gently pulling her arm free of Melinda's grasp.

"Come on, Maddie, let's go in," Karen added.

Maddie stopped and faced Melinda and Karen. "You don't even know me," she said, the grin still in place, giving her a creepy look, especially from Joanna's viewpoint below. "And you won't miss me. So you should just go inside and stop worrying. Stop thinking about me at all. I'm already gone."

Karen's mouth opened around words that didn't come out.

"I'm going to call the police," Melinda muttered, pulling her phone out of her uniform pocket.

Maddie reached out and rested her hand over Melinda's, clutching down on her fingers so that they wrapped around the phone, useless. "Thank you," she said, peering into Melinda's eyes intensely. "Thank you for saving me and for trying to save him. You were a hero." She let go of Melinda's hand and gazed at Karen, and then Joanna. "You are all heroes, and you should be really proud about it. I'm sorry I didn't tell you that before."

She began walking back to her car, a slow, dreamy gait so different from the uneven one she'd walked with when she'd first arrived.

"That was weird," Karen whispered as soon as she got out of earshot. "Do you think she should be driving?"

"She's definitely off," Joanna said, pulling herself up to standing. "She almost seemed drugged."

"Surely not, with the baby," Karen said.

"But she said herself that she doesn't want that baby," Melinda argued, in a voice that was, in Joanna's opinion, a little too loud. Almost as if she wanted Maddie Routh to hear her. Almost as if the baby was somehow a sore point for her and she was tired of arguing about it. "Besides, I've seen pregnant moms do worse."

"Maybe we should go after her," Joanna said.

"We don't have any right," Karen said. "As much as we want her to be, she is not tied to us in any way if she doesn't want to be. She's probably right—we need to stop worrying about her. We're not wanted."

"But if she's on some sort of drugs, we can't just let her get behind the wheel of that c—" Melinda stopped short, her eyes growing wide, her hands flying up over her mouth.

Joanna and Karen turned just in time to see Maddie Routh abruptly turn toward the highway, still dense with rush hour traffic, and break into a sprint.

"Maddie! Stop!" Joanna shouted.

"She's going to get hit!" Karen said.

Without saying another word, the three women sprang into motion, each running across the lawn of the Tea Rose Diner, trying to catch Maddie Routh.

THIRTEEN

Karen found herself sitting in a waiting room in a different wing of the same hospital where she'd visited Curt MacDonald not long before. The coffee was terrible, and her work clothes were rucked beyond all repair. The heels of her pumps wore matching clumps of claylike mud and grass from her little impromptu jog after Maddie. She'd nearly rolled an ankle trying to catch the woman. There was a run in her brand-new black stockings. There was a grass stain on her skirt, just above the knee.

They'd caught her in time. Melinda was wicked fast in her work boots. She'd gotten there first, but Maddie Routh had fought her, slapped at her and clawed at her face. Kicked at her. Joanna had reached them next and wrapped herself around Maddie Routh's shoulders, all the while shouting, "The baby! Be careful of the baby!"

Karen wasn't surprised to be the last one to reach her. Nor was she surprised when she stumbled at the last minute, falling up against Melinda, whose knees buckled and brought the whole mess of them down. Cars honked as the women worked to subdue Maddie Routh while not really touching her at all.

"Leave me alone! Let me go!" Maddie kept screaming, and Karen had a moment of feeling embarrassed and self-conscious as cars slowed and one even stopped, a man jumping out and rushing to them.

"Hey! Hey!" he yelled, but nobody except Karen was listening.

The struggle didn't last long. Maddie Routh had succumbed to ragged sobbing into the gravel and dirt by the side of the road, with Joanna breathlessly shushing her and rubbing her back. Melinda knelt and called the police. The man stood around awkwardly for a few moments, before getting back in his car and leaving without a word. Karen couldn't blame him for wanting to be gone before the police arrived. She imagined the last thing a decent guy on his way to work wanted to get embroiled in was a tussle among four women.

God, *on his way to work*. Where Karen should have been long ago. She definitely did not need to show poor performance at work right now. Not when Mr. Sidwell was already doing her a serious favor. She needed to get up off this hospital chair and get herself to the office before half the day was gone. There was really no need for her to still be sitting here.

They'd bandaged a couple of scrapes on Maddie Routh's cheek. They'd checked out the baby and everything looked fine. They were keeping her for a psych consult. They were going to share none of this with Karen, and why should they? Just because she was one of the three ladies who brought her in didn't mean she was wanted there. And, in fact, she knew she wasn't.

But Curt MacDonald was upstairs at that very moment. For some reason it was hard to leave the hospital knowing he was right above her. Knowing that she could possibly poke her head into 502 and see if there had been any progress. Knowing that there was a chance he might be alone and she could talk to him, pray with him. His fiancée and mother had to leave sometime, right? And if she could say something that would bring him back . . . God, she knew she was grasping.

Her phone beeped. It was a text from Melinda.

U still there?

Reluctantly, she texted back.

Yes.
Any news?
No.
You should leave. She will be fine. We can talk in the morning.

What about you? Karen texted. We didn't get to talk today.

Still no Paul, Melinda responded. But my problems don't matter right now.

Of course they do.

There was a long pause—so long that Karen figured Melinda must have gone out on a call—and she started to put her phone back into her purse. But just as she started to, it beeped again.

Go to work, Melinda texted. We will talk tomorrow.

She got to work just minutes before lunch. Antoinette was scanning a menu from the new Mexican restaurant two blocks down.

"You're here. Thank God. I thought I was going to have to eat burritos with Zeke from PR."

"The guy with all the dandruff? Why him?"

Antoinette waved her hand dismissively. "Long story, best told over virgin margs. Let's just say he might have won me in a little wager with Sal, the old bastard. But I can totally blow him off now that my friend in need is here. How is the girl? So weird what happened to you today, right?"

Karen felt the beginnings of a migraine start to push in on her temples. Maybe coming to work hadn't been such a great idea. She'd taken off her panty hose, but hadn't bothered with the dirt on her heels, and now her feet were sweating inside of them, making her feel dirty and tired.

Plus, skirts without hosiery were strictly against Sidwell Cain dress code.

She ducked into her office and picked up the messages their new intern had left on her desk. The first two were from the insurance company. The third stopped her cold.

> Caller: Kendall
> Contact: You know the number
> Message: Moving, needs money, see Mark before she goes

Karen flipped the piece of paper over a couple of times, looking for more information, as if the intern had run out of room and maybe had scrawled the rest of Kendall's message—the part that said she was just kidding; Marcus would be around always—on the back. But, of course, the cryptic message was all there was.

So Kendall was bailing after all. Of course she was. Why would Karen have thought anything else? Why on earth would she expect one of Travis's fly-by-night floozies to stick around through better or worse? To girls like Kendall, Travis was a good time and a paycheck, and when those things dried up, he was yesterday's news.

But what if Kendall moved far? How would Karen ever see the baby then? With Travis locked away and the baby gone, what else would she have to get up for in the morning? This shitty job? She slammed the messages down on her desk and rolled her chair out. She would call Kendall right now. Maybe make some threats. Grandparents' rights were a thing, weren't they? She could demand that Kendall not take that baby far, that she let him have visitation time with Grandma Karen. But just as she began to sit down, there was a knock at the door. Mr. Sidwell's head poked around the doorjamb.

"Oh, good, you're here," he said, barging on in, although Karen guessed you couldn't really consider it "barging" when a man walked into a room in an office building that he owned. Had she detected a hint of something under those words—*you're here?* An accusation of some sort? A hint that he was sorry he'd hired trash like her, maybe? God, she should never have gotten a boss involved in Travis's nonsense.

"There was an incident on the way to work this morning. Not mine," she added. "A woman tried to kill herself on Highway Thirty-two."

Mr. Sidwell half nodded, his disinterest in Karen's morning commute problems evident. He pinched the razor-sharp creases on the fronts of his pant legs and hitched them up as he sat in Karen's "visitor's chair," although the only visitor besides new hires that Karen ever had was Antoinette, and she usually sat on the corner of Karen's desk.

"We're going to plead down," he said. "I think we can get it down to drunk and disorderly."

Karen gaped. "I'm sorry?"

"Your son's priors aren't going to do him any favors, but I can pull a few strings, and I'm pretty sure we can plead down."

"I'm shocked," she said when she could finally find some

words. "If Curt MacDonald doesn't wake up? Drunk and disorderly won't really cover that, will it?"

He tossed his head side to side, as if he was mulling something over. "If it comes down to that, we'll handle it. We'll get witnesses that say the guy hit Travis first. We can definitely make a case that he was a loose cannon, out looking for a fight, that kind of thing."

Karen shook her head. "But he wasn't. He was at his bachelor party."

"Good, we'll use that. The guy was wasted, unstoppable. Travis feared for his life." He stood and pinched his trouser creases again, let the pants legs drop back down to rest on the tops of his shiny leather shoes. "Either way, I think we're good. Just thought you'd like to know the good news before I talk to your son." He showed a few teeth in what Karen guessed was supposed to be a grin, but looked a little more like hunger. "Our innocent man."

He was gone before Karen could even form the thought for her next argument—that Curt wasn't even drinking, that his blood alcohol level could attest to that. That he had been happy and getting married the next day and her son had been the aggressor.

She blew out a puff of air between pouched lips and leaned back in her chair.

"You ready to get your salsa on, Mama?" Antoinette asked, popping into Karen's office, her white tennis shoes gleaming against her navy tights. She checked her watch. "We've got fifty-five minutes. Although I think Sidwell should give us that extra five minutes that he took with his little impromptu meeting." She tilted her head to the side. "You okay?"

Karen opened one eye. "I'm great. Travis is going to get away with murder."

Antoinette gasped. "The guy died?"

"No, but if he does, *our innocent man* is still golden." Karen started to kick off her pumps, but thought better of it. As much as she wanted out of those shoes, the thought of stuffing her sweaty feet into her tennis shoes sounded even worse. Instead, she just heaved herself up out of her chair and grabbed her coat and purse.

"Well, that's good news, right?" Antoinette said, dodging out of Karen's way as she pawed the light off.

"I guess," Karen said. "It just doesn't feel exactly good, you know? I met the guy's fiancée. He had a life."

They walked toward the stairs. "Travis has a life, too, though," Antoinette said.

Karen looked at her plainly. "I don't know if he does. He seems to have chosen otherwise."

"Aw, don't talk like that. He'll turn around."

"If you say so."

They walked the rest of the two flights without speaking, and when they emerged into the lobby, suddenly Karen didn't know exactly why she was even coming to lunch. She had no appetite. She didn't feel like Mexican food. She didn't even really feel like being around people. Not even Antoinette, which was definitely unusual. Usually Antoinette could be counted on to cheer her up. She'd never wanted to get away from her before.

The problem was, Antoinette would have no way of understanding. She had no children. She had no grandchild that she might never see again. She had no slut du jour calling her "Mom" and asking for money every few weeks.

She'd never held a man's last few drops of blood in her hands.

She'd never heard the cries of a new widow's pain.

She'd never watched a woman give up on life because everything she'd once lived for was now gone.

"Hey, look at that," Antoinette said, poking Karen's ribs with her elbow. "It's your boyfriend."

Sure enough, there he was, eating a sandwich in the courtyard, a paperback balanced on his crossed legs, a pair of earmuffs wrapped across his head. He looked ridiculous.

And suddenly Karen felt so very alone.

The wind was still blowing as hard as it had been that morning, and Karen hadn't bothered to button her coat. But she marched across the courtyard anyway, ignoring Antoinette's surprised yelps.

"Hi," she said when she'd finally gotten to him. She moved a piece of her windblown hair to be captured behind her ear.

Marty Squire looked up from his paperback, his sandwich paused in midair. "Oh, hey," he said. "I haven't seen you in a while. How are things?"

Even Karen had to admit, he looked sort of handsome in a puffy down hunter green jacket over his suit pants. Like a ski god.

"You're not married or anything, are you?" she asked cynically.

His eyebrows rose. "Nope. Divorced. No kids."

"Ever been in jail?"

He chuckled. "Haven't even been on a jury, which I try not to take personally. And I'm not a pedophile, if that was your next question."

"It was one of them," she admitted. "You're not going to discover tomorrow that you're actually gay?"

"Not planning on it. But tomorrow's a long way away," he said.

She took a short breath in and let it out again. The events of the morning were still crushing her, and she wasn't sure what she was meant to be doing, or where she would fit in the world even two days from now. But she knew she was tired of doing it all alone. And that Marty Squire had a nice behind and looked like a stable human being. She needed a stable human being in her life right now. And she wouldn't mind a nice behind to go with that stability.

"I'll go out with you," she said.

Again, he grinned. He'd set his sandwich down on the bench beside him and closed the paperback. "Shouldn't I ask you first? Or do I get a say in this?"

"If you don't want to . . . ," Karen said, momentarily burning with shame, sure she'd believed Antoinette's bullshit for too long. Maybe he was into Ant instead. Or someone else entirely. Or maybe the man just enjoyed a sandwich outdoors on a bone-chilling day.

"Oh, I definitely want to," he said.

The wind whipped at Karen's coat again. Antoinette

stepped forward. "I hate to interrupt this, but we will have to inhale our tacos if we don't get going."

"So?" Karen asked Marty.

"So what?"

"So are you going to ask or not? I have tacos to inhale."

Another thing she liked about Marty Squire: he looked at her as if she were charming and not a floundering middle-aged woman with a bad seed. "Would you like to go out with me sometime?" he asked.

"Yes. When?"

"Um . . . Friday night? LaEats? Around seven?"

She nodded. "Sounds fine."

"Well, I'm glad I live up to my reputation as 'fine,'" he said. He pulled out his phone. "Can I have your number?"

She held out her hand and he passed his phone to her. She quickly keyed her number into his contacts list and handed it back. "You can call for my address," she said. "And you can eat inside now. You've won."

She turned and joined Antoinette, who stood with her palms over her ears to shield them from the wind, a shocked expression on her face.

"You didn't tell me you were going to do that," she said as soon as they were out of Marty Squire's earshot.

"I didn't know I was going to," Karen said, walking so briskly, for a change Antoinette had to work to keep up. She felt oddly exhilarated and excited. Wary, but excited.

"That was crazy."

"Yet not the craziest thing I've done today," Karen said. "You wouldn't believe."

They reached the Mexican restaurant, which they could smell before they even opened the door. Karen's previously upset stomach growled.

"You two are going to make a really cute couple," Antoinette said, batting her eyes as she walked inside the restaurant.

Karen didn't answer. But she thought that weirder things had happened in this world.

FOURTEEN

"I 'm going to see her," Melinda said, before the other two had even sat down. She'd arrived early, looking very put together in her pressed and tucked uniform. Eager for the day to begin. The truth was, she was far from either of those things, but somewhere during her sleepless night—the likes of which there had been too many to count since Paul had gone—she had decided that it was time to stop pining and begin the process of moving on with her life. If that was what she was going to have to end up doing.

When Melinda was thirteen, she'd felt like the most unlovable creature on the face of the earth. She was small, but not in a cute way like some of the petite cheerleaders. She was boyish. She sat with her legs spread apart at the knees and walked with a side-to-side swing of the shoulders. She knew nothing about makeup—her mother didn't believe in it, and she was too afraid to sneak it the way Holly did—and wore her cousin's hand-me-downs, a decade out of fashion. Her arms naturally fell in a rounded way about three inches apart from her body when she moved. *Like a muscleman getting ready for a fight,* her grandma used to say.

No thirteen-year-old girl wanted to be a makeup-less muscleman.

Especially not a thirteen-year-old who was desperately in love with Mitch Duvell, the blond-haired, blue-eyed, handsome soccer player with whom all the girls were in love. Mitch sat next to Melinda in science class. They were lab partners, and he was always really nice to her. And for about three months, she believed that maybe he really did like her. Maybe he could see the girliness underneath the plain face and the bruiser gait. She had her friend Jackie ask him if he liked her.

He'd laughed. Had thrown his head back and laughed out loud. Melinda had been waiting around the corner by the vending machines, so she didn't see it happening, but she heard. She definitely heard, and she burned with shame and turned and ran out of the school before Jackie could even find her and relay the message. She knew what the message was.

And two days later she saw Mitch Duvell holding hands with adorable Amber Crane, who wore ruffled short skirts and had a fake tan.

For the rest of that year, Melinda didn't even bother to

make eye contact with anyone, much less find another boy to like. She was certain that she would be alone forever. That no boy existed who would ever love her for who she was. And she knew that no matter how much she might want to, she couldn't change.

And now, all these years later, her husband gone more days than Melinda cared to count, with no word, she felt like that thirteen-year-old all over again. Unloved. Unlovable. Forever alone.

Might as well be good at the one thing I'm good at, she thought. *Might as well put on the uniform and go save lives.*

And so she did, though in her heart she prayed that tonight would be the night that Paul would finally call. Or come home. They would work this out. They would figure out what to do next to save their marriage.

She was hopeful. Terrified, but hopeful.

And she needed to see Maddie Routh. She couldn't explain why, but touching base with Maddie was what she needed more than anything. Knowing that Maddie was okay would somehow let her know that she would be okay, too.

She'd texted both Karen and Joanna and told them she would be at the diner—an unnecessary formality at this point, as they were all at the diner most days, what sometimes felt to Melinda like three people clinging to a life raft, each hoping that she would not be the first to slide into the water. Or die of thirst. Or be eaten by a shark. Especially not the shark. They all seemed to have their own sharks circling the raft.

But now that they were finally here, she realized she

had wanted to tell them only that she was planning to visit Maddie Routh, something she could have told them easily via text. But she supposed she had sort of hoped that they would want to go with her.

"I'm going to see her," she said, before they had even had a chance to sit down.

"Who?" Joanna asked as she slid into her side of the booth.

Melinda got up to let Karen in. "Maddie Routh. I'm going to see her today."

"At the hospital? Are they just going to let you walk in and see her?" Joanna asked.

"They might," Karen said. "They let me walk right up to see Curt MacDonald that one time."

Melinda shook her head. "She's not there anymore. They kept her for the requisite seventy-two hours and sent her on her way."

"Oh, that's right, I forgot you have an in at the hospital," Joanna said. "So they let her go?"

"Yes, and there's no way she's ready to be on her own again already, but there's not really anything they can do. All she has to do is convince them she's not a danger to herself or others, and they have to let her go."

"I don't think she would be able to convince me," Karen said. "Not after the scene here four days ago."

"Me, either," Melinda said. "That's why I'm going to see her. You want to come?"

Karen shook her head. "I can't. I have to get to work. And I have . . . plans . . . tonight."

"That sounds loaded," Joanna said, leaning across the table.

Karen seemed to blanch at the thought. "I'm going out with that guy I've been telling you about."

"The stalker?" Joanna asked, her eyes wide.

"I don't think he's a stalker, really," Karen said. "I think he's just tenacious."

"So are rapists," Joanna said. "Are you sure about this? You should be careful."

"He's not a rapist," Karen said. "He's an accountant."

"Accountants can be rapists, too," Melinda said. "It's not like rape is job-specific. Is he really a stalker?" She realized she'd been so into her own problems, she'd only been barely listening to Karen's and Joanna's.

"No," Karen said, a little loudly. "He's a guy who works in my building. He's been pursuing me for a while, and I finally said yes. I'm tired of being alone."

Sheila appeared at the table with her coffeepot. "What'n it going to be today, ladies?" she asked.

Karen glanced at her cell phone. "Can I have my coffee to go today? Sorry," she said, looking from Joanna to Melinda. "I can't stay. I really do have to get to work. My son's girlfriend is moving, or maybe already moved—I don't know—and I'm wanting to meet with Travis's lawyer to see what sort of options I have to see my grandson. Probably none."

"We'll all take our coffees to go, then," Joanna told Sheila. "And can you add a slice of Boston cream pie to mine? Actually, make it two."

"What happened to the grapefruit?" Karen asked.

Joanna made a pained face. "It's too gross. Besides, it's a pie kind of day, if you know what I mean."

"Uh-oh. Trouble with Stephen?" Melinda asked.

"Stephen is wonderful," was all Joanna said, but she didn't look as dreamy-eyed about it as she used to.

Sheila disappeared and came back a few minutes later with their coffees, and a bag for Joanna.

"You coming with me, Joanna?" Melinda asked.

"Not this time," Joanna said. She opened her bag and peered inside. Then she reached in and pulled out a foam container. "On second thought, I don't want to wait for my pie." She opened the clamshell and dug inside the bag for the plastic fork. "Tell Maddie I hope she's doing better, though," she said around a mouthful of chocolate and cream.

Right away, Melinda recognized the car Maddie had been driving. It was parked in her driveway, blocked in by a newer car behind it. It was the kind of car an older person would have—white, shining in the afternoon sun, windows reflective and clean, nothing but an umbrella on the floorboard.

Melinda walked past it, peering inside curiously, on her way to the front door. She was past any feeling of invasion when it came to Maddie Routh at this point. She'd saved her life twice. She was part of this woman's history now. She was part of her future, too, and she intended to make sure Maddie Routh had one.

"Oh, no," the woman who opened the front door said,

resting her hand on her voluptuous chest. She was an older woman with frosted hair and wide-lensed glasses, with the unmistakable air of upper middle class about her. Her nails were manicured with taupe polish; her tunic was spot free; her jeans were designer, but not stylish. She was larger than Maddie Routh—much larger, since Maddie had lost so much weight—but Melinda could see the resemblance just the same. "What's happened now? It isn't Brad, is it?"

"Brad? No, it's . . ." At first, Melinda was confused, but then she remembered that she was wearing her uniform. "I'm not here because of any sort of emergency. I'm on my way to work."

"Oh, thank goodness," the woman said. "I don't think I can take another tragedy. What can I do for you?"

"I'm here to see Maddie," Melinda said.

"She didn't say anything about a friend stopping by," the woman said, but she said it not accusatorily, but rather with a relieved smile. She reached one arm out toward Melinda. "Please, come in."

Melinda followed her inside, noticing right away how much cleaner it was than it had been the last time she'd been here. "I'm Helen, by the way. Maddie's mom. I've been staying to help out."

"Melinda," Melinda said as she backed onto the couch. Helen stayed standing. "I'm not really Maddie's friend. I mean, I'm not *not* her friend, either, if that makes sense. I'm . . . I was there. That day."

"Oh," Helen said, suddenly growing much more serious. She sank onto the couch, too, trapping her hands, flat, between her knees. "You're one of the ladies who had her taken to the hospital."

"Yes, I called the police," Melinda said. *I also kind of tackled her*, she thought, but didn't say aloud. You never knew who in this world was lawyer-happy. "And I was there the day of the crash, too."

"I had no idea," Helen said. She gazed at Melinda in awe. "My God, I need to thank you. You saved my little girl." Melinda thought she saw Helen's eyes get swimmy behind her giant glasses.

"No, I didn't do anything anyone else wouldn't do. It was instinct. I was just sorry we couldn't save her husband."

Helen scooted back in her seat and arranged a pillow to support her. "The family all misses Michael very much. It's been a rough few months around here, as I'm sure you can guess. We're all trying to help as much as we can, but it's impossible to take the pain away. And it's impossible to be with her twenty-four/seven. So we come, we visit. Half the time she throws us out. We make food she won't eat. We try to have conversations with her and she's just nasty to us. She's the worst to her father. He won't even come around anymore. It breaks his heart to see her this way. He can't handle it. We never thought she would suffer something like this, so none of us is really prepared to deal with it. No mother wants to think of their child as having to suffer in their lifetime. It's unreasonable to believe they won't, but it's just the way it is. Seeing your child in pain is just . . .

terrible. Michael's mother—wonderful woman—is in awful shape. She doesn't deserve this. Nobody does."

"I'm sorry for your loss," Melinda said, because she didn't know what else to say. Every word Helen spoke punched her in the heart. She wished, speaking of unreasonable, that Paul were there, so she could point to Helen and say, *See? See, this is exactly why I take those pills!*

"Thank you," Helen said. She reached up and touched the corners of her eyes under her glasses. "Well, I'm sure Maddie will be happy to see you. She's actually out on the back porch. Too cold for me, but she says she likes it this way. She says the cold makes her feel better. I'm just glad to see her get out of bed." She got up and headed toward another room that Melinda couldn't quite see from her vantage point; Melinda followed. "Now, don't take it personally if she's not much of a conversationalist," Helen warned. "She's not having the best day. I wish she would have stayed in that hospital."

You and me both, Melinda thought. She followed Helen through a sunny kitchen with a large sliding glass door. Through the door, she could see the top of Maddie's head poking above a patio chair back. She stepped outside.

It was still cold, but at least the wind had died down. One of those late November afternoons that were crisp and chilly, the brightness of the sun deceptive. Melinda sat in a patio chair on the other side of Maddie's.

Maddie was wrapped in a coat and a blanket, but they both had the appearance of having been placed over her, rather than put on. Her hands rested, gloveless, on top of the blanket. They were red and dry looking. Cold. Maddie made no motion to indicate that she realized she'd been joined by Melinda. She seemed to be staring out at nothing, not even blinking. Tears streaked down her cheeks, and Melinda guessed they were from the cold air more than anything.

"Hey," Melinda finally said, pulling her own coat closed around herself.

"What are you doing here?" Maddie asked, but in a monotone, and without tearing her eyes away from the nothing that she was looking at.

"I wanted to see if you were okay," Melinda said.

"Really." A statement, not a question.

"Yes," Melinda said. She cleared her throat. "Really."

"No, I'm not okay. I've been telling you that since the first time you invaded my privacy," Maddie said. Her voice was brittle, accusatory, but still lifeless. "What, do you take yourself for some kind of superhero, is that it? You a savior now?"

"No. I never took myself for anything. I'm just checking up on someone who I thought might need—"

"You just have to rescue the poor widow, don't you, Spidey?" Maddie asked, and even though she was being angry and snotty, Melinda couldn't help but smile. As long as Maddie Routh was fighting, she was living.

"I tackled you," Melinda said.

"I know you tackled me. I damn near bit my tongue off."

"But you're okay?"

Maddie finally turned to Melinda then—head only, the rest of her body still stiff and frozen. "No, I've already told you that."

"I mean, you're not hurt? The baby's not hurt?"

Maddie rolled her eyes and went back to her original position. "The baby is fine, unfortunately," she said. "And, unfortunately, so am I. Although I do present some challenges for my doctors, who are pretty sure I need every antidepressant, antianxiety, antipsychotic, anti-me medicine ever made."

"They're probably right. You were trying to kill yourself. That's not okay. You need meds."

She shook her head. "If I'm going to be forced to live this life and have this baby, I'm not going to take any chances with it. I'm alone here. I can't raise a kid with problems on top of that."

"Stepping out into the middle of rush hour traffic is a hell of a chance, don't you think? There are meds that are perfectly safe during pregnancy. A lot safer than depression."

"No."

Melinda leaned forward so she could better see Maddie's face, not that it had changed any. "Maddie, you can't just go on like this."

"I said no. Michael wouldn't have wanted it."

"Yes, he would have wanted you to be safe. He would have wanted your baby to be safe."

Maddie sprang out of her chair so quickly, Melinda actually jumped. The blanket that had been covering Maddie shucked off, and it was then that Melinda could see that

Maddie had been wearing only underwear with her coat. She was barefoot as well.

"How would you know what Michael would have wanted?" she screamed. Melinda could see Helen's form appear at the sliding glass door. "You didn't know him. Not for one second. He was already dead before you even got to the car, wasn't he?"

A memory pressed in on Melinda, of Michael Routh as he had been when she'd arrived at the car. She'd been standing on the passenger side—miles away from him, it seemed—and had been so fixed on getting Maddie out, she'd barely noticed him. But she noticed the blood. She noticed the way she could hear it fall in heavy droplets— *pat pat pat*—against the cloth roof liner. She noticed the sounds that were coming from him—rattling, gasping sounds, and then a final gurgle that she knew from experience was a very bad sound.

She should have been over there. She should have been on Michael's side, helping him. She was the only one trained to do it. Karen had stood there and watched him die; Melinda might have been able to prevent it, if she'd been able to find where all the blood was coming from.

This was the first she was able to articulate, even to just herself, what had been bothering her since the crash. She was born to help, to fix, and yet she'd watched a man die while wasting her time trying to unbuckle the seat belt of someone who was sure to survive.

It was just more proof that something was wrong. She was all wrong. She was not fit to be a mother, or a wife, or even the woman sitting here lecturing Maddie Routh about depression. Maybe she was the one who needed help. Maybe she was the one who needed meds.

"He was, wasn't he?" Maddie repeated. Foamy spit had collected in the corners of her mouth, and her legs were shivering, but still she made no move to cover up. "Dead as the proverbial doornail."

"Yes," Melinda said. "He was gone." It was a lie, but it felt like a merciful one. If she didn't do anything to save him, the least she could do was save Maddie from the pain of knowing he suffered, even if for only a very short time.

"That's what I thought," Maddie said bitterly. "You didn't know him, so how could you possibly know what he would have wanted for me and our baby? And what does it matter now anyway? He's not here. I'm stuck with this all by myself, so I might as well make the decisions and I say no. I don't want to be drugged up. I don't want to feel better."

"Why wouldn't you want to feel better?"

"Because I don't deserve to. It's unfair. I deserve to feel like this."

"You don't deserve that," Melinda said, standing. "Don't say that. You've been through so much."

"I deserve to be dead!" Maddie shrieked.

Helen opened the sliding door and stepped out, looking concerned. "Maddie, you should put that blanket back on," she said in a pleading voice. Unsure. Melinda added this to her list of the potential atrocities of motherhood—moments when your child doesn't die, but desperately wants to.

Maddie stared at Melinda for so long she started to feel

uncomfortable, and then Maddie slowly bent and picked up the blanket. She wrapped it around herself loosely, most of one leg still bare to the cold November air.

"What do you want from me? What do I have to do to make you leave me alone?" she asked.

Melinda thought about it. She licked her lips. "Live," she said. "You have to live."

Maddie loosed a quick snort of laughter. "If that's what you call this," she said, "then great. I'm living. You can leave now."

Melinda pulled her own jacket tighter around herself and started toward the door.

"You've done your good deed," she heard from behind her back. She stopped, but didn't turn. And, when Maddie Routh didn't follow it up with anything else, she moved on.

If it was such a good deed, why was she leaving feeling so bad?

FIFTEEN

Joanna hadn't expected it to feel so good to come home on Thanksgiving Day.

She'd been avoiding her parents for so long, she was almost afraid to come around. But her mom had become overwrought when Joanna had made noises like she might not make it on Turkey Day, and so she'd given in.

It had been the opposite of what she'd feared. It had been warm and accepting and the food had been delicious. Her aunt Francis had plied her with glass after glass of wine and had asked her zero questions about her life. Her mother had been so happy to see her, she didn't say a word about the months she'd been MIA.

And, of course, they'd all loved Stephen, who was charming and kind and brought her mother a fall bouquet—

rust-colored sunflowers and orange spray roses. He had helped Joanna's father carve the turkey and had washed the pots and pans after dinner and was stunningly, annoyingly perfect.

They'd been making it to Sunday dinners ever since.

And now here Joanna was, seated at her mother's table on a Thursday afternoon, just days away from Christmas, picking at a beautiful chicken salad that her mother had "thrown together" out of leftovers, feeling her gut twist with dread and guilt.

Feeling the *Venus in Fur* ticket she'd been given earlier that day practically burning through her pocket and into her hip.

"So how is Stephen?" Joanna's mom asked, curling herself into a kitchen chair the way she curled into every chair—legs folded into pretzel-like contortions, house slippers dangling at odd angles.

"Fine," Joanna answered. She didn't want to talk about Stephen. She felt too wretched to talk about him.

"Just fine?" her mother asked. "Is something wrong?"

Joanna felt twelve again, her mother joining her for an after-school snack and a manipulative grilling session, where Joanna began by feeling like she was just answering her mother's innocent questions but ended feeling as if she'd betrayed all her friends by spilling their juiciest secrets. Her mother was a master of wheedling information out of people.

"Not really," Joanna answered. She speared a piece of chicken and poked it into her mouth. It tasted like the refrigerator—she'd always hated the flavor of leftover chicken. "Everything's fine."

The truth was, they'd been fighting. Well, not Stephen. It was nearly impossible to get Stephen to fight over anything. More like Joanna had been picking fights. Had been picking at him, pointing out his every flaw, and even some that she'd conjured just to have something to pick at. She'd begun to see their relationship as something of an old scab—dangling and dangerous, ready to be ripped away. Yet she couldn't quite pinpoint what was wrong with it.

He was kind and generous and they had so much in common. They were still the best friends they'd always been, and in some ways, Joanna felt as if nobody would ever know her as deeply as Stephen did.

But there was something absent. She missed Sutton. Her confusion grew clearer every day. Stephen could never fully give her what she wanted. They were destined to always be at a polite distance that only she could feel. She'd begun to regret coming on to him. She'd begun to resent herself for having done it. So cliché. So tired.

"Not really? Everything's fine?" her mother repeated. "Well, that doesn't sound great. What's wrong? Did he cheat?" Joanna put her fork down impatiently. "Did you cheat?"

"No, Mom, nobody has cheated on anyone. There's nothing wrong."

Her mother continued to eat, shoveling in chicken as if there were nothing awkward between them, but Joanna couldn't make herself eat any more. She pushed her chair away from the table miserably, stretched her legs out in front of her.

"Joanna, you know I can tell when there's something wrong with you. I'm your mother."

"I just don't want to talk about it," Joanna said, thinking, *More like*, can't *talk about it*. "It's fine. We're fine."

Her mother folded up the cloth napkin that had been in her lap and daintily—a little superiorly, Joanna thought—laid it on the table next to her plate. "You know what I noticed the last time you two were here?" she asked.

Joanna didn't answer, but flicked her eyes upward, impatient, nervous. Vanda Jordan, the leading lady in *Venus in Fur*, was said to carry the play. Desperate, coarse, charming, sexy, bold. She would spend some of her time onstage stripped to lingerie. She would seduce her opposite—a character named Thomas Novachek. *Kiss my foot*, she was meant to say at one point, flinging aside her filmy white gown to reveal a black leather high-heeled boot. Joanna had learned, through Rhyan Singleton, another of the Hot Box girls, that Sutton had scored the role of Vanda. And Rhyan had given Joanna a ticket. Having the ticket in her pocket made her breath feel shallow.

Was this what her mother had seen the last time she and Stephen were there?

"Do you know?" her mother prompted.

Joanna shrugged, morphing, as she always did when her mother started to irritate her, into an insolent preteen. "No idea. I had spinach in my teeth?"

"Don't be obtuse, Joanna May. I saw Stephen pining

over you with hearts in his eyeballs. You could have or-
dered him to lick the bottom of your shoe and he would
have bent to his knee." *Kiss my foot!* "He is in love with you,
Joanna." Her mother leaned forward and poked the table
with a fingernail. "I can see it plain as day. But I don't see
hearts in your eyes, honey. I see something else."

Joanna lifted her eyes to meet her mother's, daring her
to see, begging her to. *Please,* she thought, *please tell me that
you see in me what I do. Please make me say it out loud. Or,
better, say it for me.*

"What do you see?" she finally asked, through numb lips.

Her mother shook her head, biting her lower lip, thinking. "I don't know," she said. "Fear, maybe? Reluctance? Are
you afraid of falling in love? Or just afraid of falling in love
with him?"

Joanna felt tears spring to her eyes. It was not what
she'd hoped her mother would say, yet the woman was sur-
prisingly close.

"Mom, it's not love," she said. "We've only been together a couple months."

"Maybe it's not for you," her mom said, picking up and
unfolding her napkin, spreading it neatly across her lap.
She grabbed her fork and began eating again. "But I can
see it in him. You mark my words." She pointed at Joanna's
plate with her fork. "Eat something. You're getting so thin."

"I've been eating healthy," Joanna said. She caught a
knowing look from her mother. "Not for him," she added,
"so don't get excited." *He couldn't be farther from the reason,*
she added internally.

"Well, I don't see what could possibly be wrong with him. Why wouldn't you want to fall in love with such a sweet guy? What am I missing?"

Again, Joanna thought of the ticket in her pocket, of the beret resting on Sutton's head, of the way the makeup tubes and vials pressed against her hip as she fell under the weight of Alyria in the dressing room.

"You're not missing anything," Joanna said. "He's my best friend. I love him."

All true statements. Yet her mother chewed her chicken salad slowly, squinting at Joanna with her head tilted to one side, unconvinced.

The set of *Venus in Fur* was stark. Whitewashed brick walls all around, a singular desk off to one side—messy, covered with papers and foam coffee cups. A writer's desk. Along the back wall, two chairs, empty, waiting for auditions that would never happen. In center stage, a tattered chaise lounge—the only prop necessary for the audition of the play.

Nothing sexy here, yet Joanna couldn't help but feel the tingle of anticipation. Somewhere backstage was Sutton. Somewhere existed black leather thigh-high boots that were meant to be zipped over her silky legs—*kiss my foot!*—and somewhere in the hushed excitement of the darkened backstage area, Sutton's shoulders glittered with lotion and makeup. No, nothing sexy about the unadorned stage as it was now; the sexiness was in what Joanna knew lay ahead.

She sank into her folding chair, watching the couples

stream in, and tried to block out her mother's words from earlier in the day. She had been unable to tell whether the woman could see what was really going on or whether she actually thought Joanna was being obstinate about Stephen, afraid to love him for some unknown reason. She'd sat there miserably, pushing the chicken salad around on her plate and listening as her mother hopped from topic to topic—Aunt Irene's colonoscopy, cousin Samara's new baby, her father's new golfing habit—gingerly, as if avoiding something. But damned if Joanna could figure out what topic was being avoided exactly.

By the time she'd left the house, she'd already been well into berating herself for her inability to tell even her own mother the truth. If anyone deserved to know, shouldn't it be the woman who'd raised her? Didn't she believe in her mother's unconditional love? She supposed that was the worst part about being confused—you didn't want to find out how many unconditional loves had conditions that you couldn't live up to after all.

She honestly didn't know what would happen with Stephen. She loved him. She did. And she still felt something when they made love. But it was a hollow something. Or maybe she was so messed up in the head that she didn't even know what real love felt like anymore. Maybe she'd worked on closing herself down for so long, she'd forgotten how to open up again.

She couldn't imagine ever breaking up with Stephen. She needed him for too many things. She would miss him terribly. She would probably want to die without him.

Wasn't that love?

Yet the idea of never breaking up with him made her chest ache. And when she sat in the audience at the tiny Trimbull Theater, watching all the happy couples filing in, she felt so isolated. Stephen would have come with her. He loved the theater—it was one of the millions of interests they shared. In fact, he would probably be hurt to find out that she'd gone without him. So why hadn't she brought him? Why wasn't she walking in with her fingers looped through his?

She knew why. She just hated admitting it.

The lights dimmed and the play started, and immediately all thoughts went out of Joanna's head. It was the intoxication of the theater itself along with the adrenaline of finally seeing Sutton again.

The actor playing Thomas Novachek was short, dark-haired, stocky. Not very attractive, Joanna was happy to see. He had an intensity around his eyebrows, something that bespoke a perfectionism that would make him a horrible leading man to play off. He would be the kind who would passive-aggressively toss barbs at you after a rehearsal because you'd run over his line or stood in his light or any of a million other imagined infractions. The kind of leading man who had a reputation. The kind that everyone mocked at after-performance parties over beers and glasses of Crown and Coke.

Thomas Novachek stormed the stage and bemoaned not being able to find the right actress to play the role of Wanda von Dunayev, when suddenly there she was, bursting into the room like a thunderclap. Sutton Harris as Vanda Jordan—disheveled, pushy, loud. Dear God, she was perfect.

Joanna closed her eyes and just listened for a moment. The sound of Sutton's voice both calmed and exhilarated her. She longed to be on the stage with them. Scratch that— she longed to be on the stage *instead* of that persnickety leading man. Wouldn't that turn *Venus in Fur*, with its breathy BDSM undertones, on its head?

She opened her eyes and slipped into Sutton's voice, letting it carry her, float her above the theater. She felt in that moment the same way she did when mesmerized by Stephen's touch. The same feeling of caress, the same feeling of guilt, the same feeling of being torn in two.

Sutton was amazing. Sultry and funny and breathtaking. The audience rode the play through her—laughing and nodding their heads and holding their breath. The play could have gone on forever and still it would have felt like only moments to Joanna. She was the first to jump to her feet for curtain call. She could tell by the extra crook in one corner of Sutton's mouth that she had seen her.

When the curtain fell, Joanna was unsure what to do. Go along with the tide, let herself be carried out of the theater on the chatter of all those happy couples, or stick around, hope to find her way back to the makeup room?

In the end, it hadn't been up to her. Sutton popped through the curtain before the audience had even cleared out. She trotted down the stage steps and made her way over to Joanna.

"I didn't know you were coming," she said. "What'd you think?"

"So good," Joanna said. "Really, you were amazing."

Sutton clasped her hands in front of her belly and hopped on her toes, like an excited child. "Really? Thank you. It means so much coming from you."

"I knew you would be, though. That's why I came." *Well, not entirely why,* a tiny voice inside Joanna's mind corrected, but she shoved that voice aside.

"We miss you," Sutton said. "Theo is backstage. I should get him."

"No, no," Joanna said. "I have to get going pretty soon anyway."

Sutton's face fell. "I was sort of hoping you'd come out with us tonight," she said. "I'd love to have drinks with you." She reached out and brushed Joanna's arms with her fingers as she said this, sending spikes of pleasure and nostalgia through Joanna. A fantasy of sitting at a high-top table, toasting Vanda Jordan—*kiss my foot!*—shuddered through her before she could shut it down. Stephen would be coming home from work. He would be waiting for her to call. Maybe even waiting in her apartment, the "guest bedroom" that only he had ever slept in a mere formality at this point.

"I wish I could," she said. "Maybe next time. How long is this running?"

"Through the holidays," Sutton said. "Come January, it's all *Seussical* up in here. I haven't auditioned. I think I would rather die. Oh, but hey, I heard that the downtown playhouse will be auditioning for *Les Mis* in January. Can you imagine?" She broke into soft song, her voice so beautiful and clear, even when unrehearsed, that Joanna's arms were blanketed in goose bumps. "Don't you fret, Monsieur Marius. . . ." She giggled, covering her mouth with one hand.

"Éponine?" Joanna said. "I'd have had you pegged for Cosette."

"Are you kidding? You're the waify, big-eyed blonde. Look at your lips like little bows. Cosette was made for you." She clamped her hand over Joanna's forearm. "Try out with me."

"Nobody's going to want me after what happened with *Guys and Dolls*."

"They won't know. We won't tell them."

"Word gets around. You know that," Joanna said, finding herself near tears over this revelation. Until this point, she had considered herself not going back to theater *yet*. It hadn't occurred to her that she might never get the chance to. It had always been her choice. Now it was a matter of burned bridges. "But I'll come see you, Cosette. And I'll come see Vanda again, I promise."

Sutton bit her lip in an adorably disappointed posture. "Okay," she said. "You sure you won't go out with us tonight? Theo and I will treat."

"I wish I could, but my b—" For some reason, she couldn't finish the word "boyfriend." Not to Sutton. Finishing the word might mean the end of a fantasy that she wasn't ready to let go of yet. "But I have to get home," she finished instead.

"Next time, I won't let you off the hook," Sutton said, and she leaned forward and brushed a kiss on Joanna's cheek. Joanna burned with desire, and then, when Sutton pulled away, with shame. She glanced quickly around to see if anyone had seen it.

"Deal," she said. "Enjoy your after-party."

"Not without you," Sutton said, but she was already making her way toward the stage, hopping up the stage steps like they weren't even there.

Joanna started up the aisle toward the door, where she could still hear the murmurings of the crowd. All those couples discussing what they'd seen. All so happy. She checked the time. Stephen would be expecting her to call any minute now.

Her thoughts took her to Maddie Routh. Her love for Michael had been so certain, so complete.

But look where that had gotten her.

Joanna wasn't sure whose fate was worse.

SIXTEEN

New Year's Eve had never been Karen's favorite holiday. She'd always lumped it in with Valentine's Day and Mother's Day bullshit holidays that looked great in TV commercials, but had no place for women like her. She wasn't a big drinker. She wasn't a dater at all. She wasn't the get-blind-and-kiss-the-first-fool-you-see-at-midnight type. What was the point?

But she'd put off Marty Squire one too many times, and she'd begun to see a weariness growing inside him. She'd have thought she'd welcome that weariness, would hope that he'd give up, but for some reason it made her nervous instead. Nervous that he might stop asking.

They'd gone out exactly three times since that day she accepted his invitation in the courtyard at her office. All three dates had been fun, something that had surprised Karen to no end. She'd have thought herself too old for fun. Or at least too jaded.

Their first date, he'd shown up groomed within an inch of his life, carrying flowers and a lopsided grin. He'd taken her to dinner and a movie. Standard, yet something she'd never been treated to before. She felt awkward allowing him to pay her way, but after a while she began to get used to it. She could almost hear her grandmother scolding her in the back of her mind, telling her to let him treat her like a lady should be treated. Her grandmother had been tough, but her biggest supporter in this world. Her grandmother would have liked overly groomed Marty Squire.

On their second date, the week after Thanksgiving, they had driven through one of those Christmas in the Park light shows. Karen hadn't done that since Travis was a toddler—she'd never quite understood the fascination with choking on exhaust and wasting gasoline so you could see a light-up polar bear or baby seal with a Christmas bow on its head. But Marty Squire had bought them both hot chocolates and had somehow procured an entire box of warm chocolate chip cookies. They'd chatted while inching their car in line up to the front gate. Karen had learned that Marty Squire wanted to be a history teacher but ended up in the family accounting business instead. She'd also learned that he'd studied opera in college, but wasn't very good, and that he played on a recreational kickball team in the fall. Karen told him about Travis— nervous, but figuring there was no way around the subject—and about her job at Sidwell Cain. She'd told him about her brother, Gary, who was a stuntman in California (not ever working for anyone famous, though), and how she rarely talked to him because they had nothing in common. They both joked about Antoinette and how they felt she should be in the backseat, bossing them around on what to say next.

And then they'd passed through the gate, Marty had opened the thermos of chocolate and the box of cookies, and the car had been flooded with warmth and memories that nearly bowled Karen over. He turned up the radio, which was tuned to the local station that played the music that went along with the choreographed lights. And it was in that moment, biting into her first cookie, watching a fountain of green and red and gold sprout in front of her, that Karen finally understood what made these lights wonderful.

Their third date had been to a hockey game. He'd put his arm around the back of her chair. The closeness gave her a lump in her throat that sank to her stomach and eventually made her nauseated. They'd left the game early, and she'd escaped into her house before he could so much as get out of the driver's seat of his car.

That had been three weeks ago. They hadn't spoken since. Karen honestly didn't know what to say.

He'd texted her on Christmas Eve.

I'm sorry if I did something to upset you. I'd like to see you again.

Maybe after the holidays. I'm busy with my grandson, she'd responded. It was a lie. Marcus was long gone, as far as she could tell. Kendall had taken the last five thousand dollars she'd given her and split, vaguely mentioning something about Connecticut, where her family was, spouting off something about sending her their address when they got settled. But that had been before Thanksgiving. On Christmas Day, Karen had tried calling Kendall, had wanted to send Marcus a gift. There had been no answer. Girlfriend du Jour and Baby du Jour were ghosts.

It was sad and pathetic, and Christmas Day was sad and pathetic. She didn't want to visit her son in jail on Christmas Day. But she really had no one else to spend the holiday with. After trying to call Gary twice and getting a voice mail both times, she'd finally given in and texted Marty.

Merry Christmas. When can I see you again?

He'd responded right away.

What are you doing NYE?

And now, here she was, waiting for him to pick her up, a mixture of giddiness and anxiety that threatened to bring that lump back into her stomach again. She'd made a promise to herself that she would have fun. She would be open-minded. Maybe New Year's Eve celebrations would be like Christmas in the Park for her. Something she'd never understood because she'd never had anyone to share it with, but would enjoy now that she did.

She paced back and forth between her bedroom and the living room, second-guessing every possible choice that she'd made. Were her shoes too high? Was her dress too dowdy? Should she be wearing jeans instead? Maybe he had something more casual in mind? God, why didn't she ask him what he had in mind?

Just when she'd almost talked herself into changing into her pajamas and telling him she was sick when he got there, the doorbell rang. Too late for choices now. Time to go.

Marty Squire looked gorgeous in a silvery gray suit and an electric blue tie. He stood clutching a shiny red bag in one hand. He held it out when she opened the door.

"Merry Christmas," he said.

"Christmas is over," she answered.

"You look amazing."

She took the bag. "You shouldn't have. I didn't get you anything."

"I didn't do it because I wanted something in return," he said. "Just open it."

"Come on in." She stepped out of the doorway. "It's cold out there."

She led him into her house, which felt scandalous, even though she knew it wasn't. She'd been so wary of bringing anyone into Travis's home, it had felt shocking to have a man inside. What a joke. As if her sheltering Travis from any semblance of an unsavory adult life had saved him. She sat down on her couch and set the gift in her lap. Slowly, she pulled out the tissue paper and looked inside.

"Shoes?" she asked, pulling out a shoe box. She opened it, revealing a gleaming pair of sneakers inside. "No, it really is shoes."

"I noticed that you like to wear them when you walk to lunch. I was hoping that this would prompt you to walk to lots more lunches. With me."

She smiled. She couldn't help it. It was a sweet, if clumsy, gesture. "Most men would opt for perfume or chocolates," she said, admiring the sneakers. They were very nice. Nicer than the ones she had been wearing at the office.

"I didn't want to move too fast," he said. "You seem to like to take it very slowly. I wanted something that would show you that I'm great with slow, but that I'm still hoping to be in the race."

She laughed out loud. "There is no race. Hasn't been for twenty-six years. You're the only participant."

He mock-wiped his brow as he sank onto the couch next to her. "Whew. That's a relief. I'm a terrible runner."

"You wouldn't be if you had shoes like these," she said. She peered at the inside of the shoe. "They're the right size, too. Should I be concerned that you know my shoe size and we've only been out on three dates? You haven't been going through my things while I'm at work or something, have you?"

"I'm just a really good guesser," he said. "Anyway, Merry Christmas, Karen Freeman."

She smiled. "Thank you. And Merry Christmas to you, Marty Squire."

There was a moment of awkward silence between them, which Karen used to stuff the shoes back into their gift bag.

"Do you like Mexican food?" Marty asked when she was finished. "I've booked us for a party at Abuelita Margarita. They're having quite the fiesta from what I understand. Limited tickets. Mexican fusion bar. Cocktails. Bring your own champagne. Do you drink champagne?"

"I haven't in years," Karen said, reaching for her coat, which hung on a hook by the front door. She was glad she'd stuck with the dress. "But I love a good enchilada."

Abuelita's was packed. Karen could hardly believe it was a private party. The dance floor was shoulder to shoulder and the buffet had a never-ending line wrapped around it. She lost count how many times the girls from the back had to come out with fresh pans of tamales, beans, and rice.

"Sorry there were no enchiladas," Marty said, or shouted, really, as the music was so loud the table thrummed under their silverware.

"Are you kidding?" Karen shouted back. "The food is amazing." And it was. She imagined a legion of grannies in the back, hand rolling the tamales, which were dense and perfect and swimming in cheese and chili sauce. She'd already had two and was considering having another go through the buffet line. She wasn't sure, though, if that would be poor dating form. She'd always been able to eat whatever she wanted, with little to no weight consequences, and so had retained her teenage eating habits. Four tamales seemed like nothing, even with the beans and rice and tortillas with cheese dip and salsa.

"I owe you some enchiladas, though," he said.

"You do not."

He leveled his eyes at her—so light blue they were almost gray, and ringed with dark lashes. "It gives me an excuse to take you out again."

She took it wrong. "You need an excuse?"

"More like I need insurance. If I owe you something, you can't say no. Can I borrow ten dollars?"

Karen was taken aback, holding her fork in the air above her plate, Billy Idol's "White Wedding" pounding through her head—they'd busted out the retro tunes on the dance floor now. She had a fleeting moment of being certain that she had been right to be wary—obviously Mr. Marty Squire was going to turn out to be a big zero. But then a mischievous grin spread across his face, disarming her.

"A joke," he said. "Just a joke."

And then she got it. It seeped in slowly. He was flirting, and she was too dense to see it. *Lighten up, Mom,* she could almost hear Travis saying. One of his favorite lines. She laughed, scraping some cheese sauce off her plate with the side of her fork. "Well, then, I guess since you owe me . . ."

"Terrible, this ball and chain on my ankle," he joked, and they both laughed. "Can I get you a drink?"

"No, thank you," Karen said automatically, but then found herself nodding instead. "Actually, why the heck not? It's New Year's Eve. We should live a little."

Marty bought them both something fizzy and pink. The carbonation made her nose tickle, and the booze warmed her belly. She was glad after just a few sips that she hadn't gone back for another plate at the buffet. She was full and happy and when she clinked her glass against Marty's, she secretly wished for more nights like these.

"Do you want to dance?" he asked after they'd drained their glasses.

Karen wrinkled her nose. "I never have."

Marty Squire raised his eyebrows in surprise. "Never?"

She shook her head.

"Nobody's ever taken you dancing before?"

She ran her finger around the rim of her empty glass, feeling embarrassed and self-conscious. "Not since high school. I was all about raising Travis." She shrugged. "There wasn't time for any of that. He's been a handful since he was about twelve."

More like eleven, if she let herself admit it. That was the first time she had police on her doorstep, a contrite Travis standing in front of them. He'd been caught spray-painting obscene pictures on the side of the elementary school. She'd been mortified, of course, but had chalked it up to young male shenanigans. Nothing to take too seriously. But then the drugs had come along a year later and she was forced to admit that Travis wasn't into shenanigans. He was into serious troublemaking, and she was in over her head.

But at least twelve was a preteen. Eleven was still a child. Admitting, even to herself, that her sweet little boy had been trouble since he was a child felt too raw, too damning. Too hopeless.

"Would you like to?" Marty asked, seemingly unfazed

by her confession about her rotten son. He held a hand palm-up across the table. "Dance?"

Reluctantly, she took it. "As long as you don't laugh at me."

"Never," he said.

They took the dance floor just as the song transitioned to something slow and in Spanish. It had the weighty rhythmic sensuality that Karen thought all Latino songs had. Drumbeats that made your hips move of their own volition. Pulses that beat through your body, made an arch form in the small of your back without your even realizing it.

Marty Squire pulled her in close, one hand wrapped around her, the other clutching hers out to the side. Very traditional, but he stood closer than she expected. She could feel the contours of his chest and stomach brush up against hers.

"Ready?" he asked. He was so close she could smell the cilantro on his breath, making her tuck her own lips in self-consciously. She nodded. "I must warn you. I am an accomplished ballroom dancer."

"Really?" she barked.

He grinned and shook his head. "Everything I know about dancing came from my grandmother. She used to put on records and pour herself a juice glass full of whiskey and make me dance with her when I was a kid. Everything I know is probably either old-fashioned or completely wrong."

But when he moved, it felt right. Karen found herself following the flow of his legs easily, letting him lead her with his arms, his shoulders, his hips. A couple times she felt herself brush up against him full-bodied and the rush nearly took her breath away. Her brain kept trying to send frantic SOSs—*Not ready for this! Not ready!*—but the fizzy drink she'd had helped keep the internal noise to a minimum. She found herself closing her eyes and just . . . enjoying.

They danced through three songs and then got thirsty again. Back at the table, they sat side by side, leaning their shoulders into each other as talk turned personal. What was Karen's childhood like? What happened between Marty and his ex-wife? Where did each of them want to be in ten years? By the bottom of her third fizzy glass, Karen was feeling fine, so fine that she almost didn't bother to answer her phone when it lit up the inside of her purse.

But it was Kendall.

Karen excused herself and stepped outside into the cold, but much quieter, vestibule.

"Mom? It's me." Karen thought she could hear a party going on in the background, though she couldn't be sure that she wasn't just hearing her own party spilling over into the microphone of her phone.

"Yes, hello," Karen said. "I've been wondering about you. Is everything okay? It's not the baby, is it?"

"No," Kendall said. Her tone was sour, and Karen could almost visualize the pout on the girl's face. It was too predictable. She heard a crash of breaking glass, followed by laughter. She was sure that had come from Kendall's end of the phone, not hers. Nobody had broken anything at Abuelita's. "Marcus is fine. But listen, so things haven't really worked out here like I thought they would."

"Where is 'here'?" Karen asked, trying to keep the sour

tone out of her own voice, but having a hard time, given that she still had no idea where in the world her own grandson lived now.

"I think we're going to come home, I guess."

"Home here? From where? Where are you?"

"It's a long story," Kendall said. "It doesn't matter anymore. It didn't work out, so we're coming back."

Karen leaned against the cold window that faced the outside. The windows were foggy, streams of condensation dripping down into their frames. She wondered if her dress was getting wet, but at the moment didn't care. The cold was refreshing and was clearing her head a little. "Have you talked to Travis?" she asked.

Kendall laughed into the phone. Far in the distance, Karen could hear what sounded like a baby crying. Dear God, where did Kendall have her grandson? "Now is not a good time for that," she said. "I can't come home to him anyway. Not with him locked up all the time. Besides, we got evicted from that apartment, so it's not like we can just go back to living there."

"Evicted? I gave you rent money to cover it."

"Well, it got used," Kendall said, irritation sliding through the phone.

Got used, Karen thought. *Right.* Got used for God knew what, but she knew not for the baby. "So where do you plan to go?" Karen asked. She bit her tongue before she did something dumb like offer to let them stay at her house. Yes, it would be wonderful to have Marcus under her roof, but she couldn't exactly trust that Kendall wouldn't steal her blind. If she was going to make an offer like that, it would have to be when she was completely sober, when she'd had some time to think about what precisely she was offering. Why, oh why, did she decide to drink? After all these years?

She also couldn't guarantee that Kendall wouldn't up and leave Marcus with her. Was she ready to start over again at forty-six years old? Without warning, a memory of Maddie Routh gripping the positive pregnancy test strip pushed itself into her mind. She closed her eyes against it.

"I just need some money, Mom," Kendall said, and Karen burned with anger over the use of the word "Mom." Kendall pulled it out artfully, whenever she thought it would buy her something she was after. Thinking that Karen was stupid enough or gullible enough or desperate enough to believe that the girl had any sort of actual affection for her.

"Money?" Karen repeated. "I gave you money to get to where you are now. What happened to it?"

"It got me out here. But now I'm out, and I need more. So I can come back." Kendall said this last sentence plaintively, so false it made Karen's skin crawl. She was being played. Even she could see that much.

"I don't have it," she said.

"What do you mean you don't have it?" Kendall barked into the phone. "I need it to get back."

"I'm out," Karen said. "I'm a single mom. I'm not made of money."

"That's bullshit," Kendall spat. "Travis told me how

much money you have. It's just been the two of you all these years. It's not like you had to pay college tuition or anything. You're loaded."

"I don't know what Travis told you," Karen said. She could hear her own voice ratcheting up. "But I'm all tapped out. I don't have anything to give you."

"Don't you even care about Marcus getting home?"

"Of course I care," Karen said. She swallowed before speaking the next words. "But I can't help this time. You'll have to do it yourself."

"Fine," Kendall said. "You know, I guess I never expected you to turn your back on family."

But you're not my family, Karen wanted to shout. *You're my son's Tramp of the Hour. He's probably already got the next you lined up for when he's let out of jail.* She blinked, shocked to even hear herself think this about her son, even if it was true.

"Of course I'm not going to turn my back on Mar—," Karen began, but Kendall had cut her off. Karen stared at her phone screen and, when it didn't light up again, murmured, "Happy New Year, Kendall," and stuffed it back into her purse.

Marty was working on a piece of cake when she got back to the table. A piece waited for her at the seat next to him, but her mood had been dampened. She sat in her original seat across from him again. The air felt cloying, full of sweat and spices.

"Everything okay?" he asked.

Karen sighed, pulled the paper plate toward her, and began picking at the cake listlessly. "My son's girlfriend. Wanting money again."

"Ah." He tucked another bite into his mouth.

"You sure you want to get involved with a woman like me?" Karen asked, dragging her fork to make tracks through the icing.

Marty stifled a smile. "A woman like what?"

"A hot mess," Karen said. "Well, I'm not a hot mess. But I come equipped with one. I've obviously failed. Look at my son's life, and it keeps spilling over into mine. Don't you wonder what's wrong with me?"

Marty speared a piece of cake and held it across the table. It shivered on the end of his fork, inches from her mouth. "Not even a little bit," he said.

Karen tried to stare him down—tried to see the lie, or at least the little niggle of fear behind his confidence—but after a moment couldn't help but let his smile become contagious. She bit the cake off his fork, licking the icing off her lips.

"Fifty seconds!" a woman yelled, plowing through the crowd, carrying a bottle of champagne in each hand. "Fifty seconds!"

The music stopped and the DJ took up the count, as Marty tore the foil off the bottle of champagne he'd brought. Karen found herself drawn to her feet and pulled into the crowd, feeling Marty's arm snake around her waist as they reached ten . . . nine . . . eight. . . . She allowed herself to lean into him. Six . . . five . . . four . . . The crowd frenzied tighter, pushing her closer and closer, and she didn't fight it. Instead, she turned to face him.

"Three, two, one! Happy New Year!" Karen shouted, unable to hear her own voice over the cheering of the crowd and the sudden explosion of music.

Marty popped the cork and a fountain of champagne bubbled out of the bottle. He held it away, but they were too closed in and a streak of foam smeared down the front of Karen's dress. She didn't mind. She threw her head back to laugh.

And didn't pull away when she felt Marty Squire's mouth on her own.

"Happy New Year, hot mess," he said.

"Happy New Year," Karen answered, and kissed him again.

It would be morning before she found the text that Kendall had sent at 12:07:

I need $1,000 to get home or u will never see Marcus again. Think it through.

SEVENTEEN

When Paul finally came home, there was nothing but silence. For days. It wasn't a grudge sort of silence, but rather the sort of silence where neither of them knew what to say. It seemed like too much water had gone under the bridge. She'd lied; he'd left angry. He'd stayed gone two months, rather than two nights. She'd spent the holidays alone, in an empty house. What was there to talk about? How did you even begin a conversation about that?

Melinda tried not to think about it. She worked extra shifts when she could. She arrived at the diner before everyone else and left after they'd gone. And when she was out of other options, she visited her sister, Holly.

Melinda and Holly had always been close. Best friends

as well as sisters. But after Holly had her third child, she'd had less and less time to hang out with her sister. This meant that Melinda always had to visit Holly at her house, where there was a minefield of toys and constant mayhem and frequent interruptions. It was agonizing, the jealousy that Melinda felt.

Once Melinda had begun secretly taking the birth control pills, she rarely visited—only if she was needed for babysitting, which was heart-filling and gutting all at once—and eventually she just stopped visiting altogether, despite her sister's phone calls.

When Melinda pulled into her sister's driveway after Paul had been home for a week, it was the first time she'd been there since the day Holly had been called to jury duty and Melinda had been called back to the Tea Rose Diner. She'd been conveniently "working" throughout the holidays, mailing her gifts to the family. She couldn't face them without Paul. She didn't want to have to explain.

Holly stood in the door, a displeased look on her face. "Well, look who's gracing me with her company today," she said.

"Just let me in, Hols. You know you will, and the quicker you do it, the quicker I can apologize," Melinda said, and then, when her sister didn't budge, pulled out a brown paper sack. "I brought brownies from Lotta Chocolotta. Your favorite."

Holly gazed at the sack, then rolled her eyes and turned and disappeared into the depths of the house—as close to an invitation as Melinda was going to get. Melinda knew where to go, though. Straight back to the kitchen, where Holly was already filling the coffeemaker with water.

"So to what do I owe this special treat?" Holly asked.

"I'm sorry, Sis," Melinda said, sliding onto a barstool. She plucked two napkins out of the napkin holder on the bar and laid them out, then set a brownie on each. "Really, I didn't mean to ignore you."

"Where have you been? Mom says she hasn't heard from you, either."

"Well, that's not exactly unusual."

"True," Holly said, pouring coffee grounds into the coffeemaker and pushing the brew button. "I was always the suck-up."

"Yes, you were. How is Mom, anyway?"

Holly leaned over the bar and picked up her brownie. She studied it before pinching off a tiny piece and tucking it into her mouth.

Mitchell, Holly's oldest, bounded into the room. "Ooh, yum! Can I have one?"

"Aunt Melinda brought them for me," Holly answered.

"Please?" he begged, clasping his hands together as if he was praying.

"No," she snapped. "Aren't you even going to say hi to Aunt Melinda, Mr. Rude?"

"Hi," Mitchell said sullenly.

"Don't worry, I brought enough for everyone," Melinda said. She pulled out a brownie and handed it over the bar. Holly sighed and threw her arms into the air, but Melinda knew she wouldn't really get mad. Holly liked it that Melinda spoiled her kids when she came around. She'd have expected nothing less.

"Anyway, Mom?" Melinda asked, once Mitchell had left.

Holly shrugged, then picked another corner off her brownie and ate it. "She's wondering what's going on with you. She said she heard that Paul left."

"Where did she hear that?" Melinda asked.

"God, I don't know. Where does Mom hear half the crap she hears? From the Old Lady Brigade."

Melinda paused. It had gotten around. Of course it had. Had she really expected it not to? "Well, it was true," she said. She didn't need to look up to know Holly's reaction. She could sense the shock in the air. "But he's back now."

"What? When did that happen?"

"Back in November," Melinda said.

"November?" Holly repeated, in a voice so loud, another kid popped into the room. Holly handed that kid a brownie without being asked, or even looking to see whom she handed it to. "What the hell, Linds? You're just now telling me this?"

Melinda shrugged, playing with the handle of her coffee mug. She wasn't hungry for brownies anymore, but a good slug of coffee sounded so good it made her mouth water. As if she could sense this—and she probably could; Holly had always been a very intuitive sister—Holly grabbed the pot out from under the gurgling coffeemaker and filled Melinda's cup.

"What happened?" she asked, filling her own as well.

She grabbed a container of vanilla caramel creamer—both sisters' favorite—and laid out two spoons in front of them. Melinda was glad of the distraction of fixing up her coffee. "Why didn't you tell me?"

"I was embarrassed," Melinda said. "And I think a little depressed. Maybe I still am, actually. It's been hard. Do you remember that bus crash?"

"Of course."

"I've been really worried about the woman who survived. The one in the car. She's pregnant, and she's a disaster. But every time I come near her, she tells me to get out of her life."

"What do you mean, every time you come near her? You're coming near her? Why?"

Melinda stirred the coffee. The alarm in her sister's voice drove home what Maddie Routh had been saying all these months: she had no place in her life. Saving her from a crash did not give her access to the woman's life if she didn't want her in there.

So why couldn't she stay away?

Because she couldn't stop thinking about her.

Holly shook her head, her brow furrowed. "Wait a minute. I'm confused. What does this have to do with Paul leaving you?"

"It doesn't. Not really. But in a way it does, too. It's because of all the tragedy out there, you know? Because this woman exists, and her baby exists, that's what it has to do with Paul leaving."

"You're not making any sense, Linds," Holly said. She

took another wary bite of brownie. "Should I be worried about you?"

"No," Melinda said. "But how do you do it?"

"Do what?"

"How do you ever let your kids out of your arms? How do you put them in a car every day? How do you not go insane with worry that they will have to be scraped off of a highway, or pulled from the bottom of a lake, or their brains hosed off of a bathroom floor someday?"

Holly looked stricken. "Jesus. That's a real cheery thought. What the hell is wrong with you?"

Question of the hour, Melinda thought. "I'm sorry."

Holly set her brownie back down on the napkin. "Why would you even say such a thing? Is this why Paul left you? Are you going crazy? This is a real question, Linds. If you're losing your shit, I need to warn Mom and Dad and host an . . . intervention or something."

"I'm not going crazy," Melinda said, but she was doubtful. Maybe this was what the beginning of crazy looked like. Maybe crazy started as irrational fear, and was followed by lying, and then inserting yourself into someone else's life when you weren't wanted. Maybe crazy drove husbands away and made them come back silent. Maybe crazy made you hide from your family over the holidays. Maybe crazy had you imagining the violent deaths of your nieces and nephews when talking to their mother. "Maybe I am," she muttered.

Holly took a sip of her coffee. "Did something happen?"

Her eyes grew big over the top of her mug. "You didn't cheat on him, did you?"

At that, Melinda burst into tears. "I lied to him," she cried. "I felt so guilty, but I did it anyway. Holly, I'm going to lose him, and I'm going to lose Maddie Routh, and I can't explain why the thought of losing them hurts equally, but it does."

Holly hurried around the counter and folded Melinda into her arms, shushing her. "It'll be okay," she said. "It'll be okay."

But hadn't Melinda said the same thing to Maddie Routh that day of the crash? Hadn't she consoled her similarly? And now Maddie Routh was a skeleton, sunk into herself and her misery.

Melinda hoped her sister wasn't lying as baldly as she had on that day.

EIGHTEEN

Sutton made an amazing Éponine. Tough, street-smart, boyish, but somehow fragile and gentle beneath. The way she pined for Marius was tragic and lovely. Her voice was reedy, would carry the audience to the point of breaking, but never fall over the edge. No one ever doubted her loyalty to the one she loved.

Joanna watched every performance the first week, telling Stephen that she was working doubles in her new job at Café Fellowship. He trusted her completely, never doubted her for a second. She'd earned that, or at least that was what he believed.

Not that she had done anything to betray him. Sutton never even knew she was in the audience. Never knew that she had her every line, every lyric, every move, memorized.

Second Chance Friends

Never knew that the patchy beret she wore as Éponine brought back memories of the first time they'd met, and that those memories buoyed Joanna through the rest of the evening.

By the time she got home, Stephen would be waiting for her with a glass of wine and a movie cued up, but instead she would eagerly fall into bed with him, thinking, *Beret, beret, beret.*

But tonight when she came home, Stephen was waiting not with a glass of wine but with something else.

"Hey," she said, dropping her keys on the kitchen table. She untied her apron, which stank of the catfish special, and dropped it on top of the keys. She didn't feel like washing it tonight. She was too tired, too full of watching Éponine's death—"A Little Fall of Rain" so wrenching, not an eye in the audience was dry—too wrung out to think about domesticity. She would have to stink for one more day. She kicked off her shoes under the table and sprang her hair from its pony tail.

It was only then that she noticed something different.

Stephen wasn't in his usual waiter-wear: white button-down, open to reveal a T-shirt underneath, and black work trousers. He was in jeans and a rugby shirt, green and yellow, perfect for his dark hair and olive complexion. He looked gorgeous and clean. She could smell the cologne across the room.

He was holding a glass, but it was a champagne glass, and the neck of a bottle poked out from the top of an ice bucket, rather than the usual wine box taking up half the coffee table.

Joanna noticed candles as well. Every candle she had

was lit, and a few more had been brought in. The lights were turned low, and the TV was off.

"Champagne?" she asked. "Are we celebrating something?"

"I hope to be in a few minutes," Stephen said, leaning over and kissing her neck. "How was your day?"

"Long," she lied. "I thought my last table would never leave. Catfish brings out the dedicated eaters."

He chuckled, still nuzzling her neck. Goose bumps rose on her arms. "Yes, it does," he said.

She backed away a step. "Didn't you work tonight?"

"I called in," he said. "I had some things to take care of. No big deal. We've been pretty dead. No catfish at LaEats."

"What kind of things?" Joanna asked. She still hadn't taken the champagne glass, and Stephen set them both on the coffee table. He looked nervous, tortured. "What's going on?"

He grabbed both of her hands in his and pulled her toward the couch, sat her down, and then sat next to her.

"It's our four-month anniversary," he said.

"Right," she said. He'd reminded her that morning with a text.

"And four months doesn't really sound like all that long, but it seems like it's been so much longer. You know what I mean?"

She nodded. "We've been friends for four years—that's probably why. You're not getting bored already, are you?" She wasn't sure whether an affirmative answer here would be a good thing or a bad thing.

"Of course not," he said. "Actually, quite the opposite. I loved meeting your family over the holidays. And I loved having you meet mine. They adore you, by the way."

Joanna smiled. "My mom would date you herself if she could get away with it," she said.

"Anyway, do you remember the infamous *While You Were Sleeping* wine night?"

How could she forget? Stephen was fond of bringing up that night every chance he got. How he'd put it all out there for her, and how she'd jilted him. Left him with lips pouched and heart in hand. She nodded.

"You remember what we were talking about before I admitted liking you?"

"Secret crushes," she said, feeling like her mouth was barely opening. He knew. He had to know. Her secret crush on Sutton was not so secret, and he knew. God, was he about to do something really stupid like ask her to have a threesome or some awful bullshit?

"Secret *marriage* fantasies," he corrected. "So even though four months doesn't sound like that long, I've been thinking about this since before that night way back then."

Joanna's mouth went dry as she realized what this was really about. It wasn't the *secret* part that he was focused on tonight. It was the *marriage* part. Her legs tensed, as if to run. But instead she sat still, mute, wide-eyed, as her best friend lowered himself to one knee next to the couch.

Details were lost on Joanna. She didn't know if Stephen gazed deeply into her eyes or if his hands shook as he reached into his pocket. She only half heard the words that were coming out of his mouth—*known for a long time . . . meant to be together . . . best moments of my life*—but all she could really hear was a terrible ringing in her ears.

An hour before, she'd been so lost in *Les Misérables* that she had temporarily forgotten that Stephen existed. That was bad, right? You didn't marry someone whose existence slipped your mind in deep moments, did you? Or maybe those were the people you were supposed to marry—the ones who were so deeply embedded in your life, you could let them go and still be able to come back to them later.

Insanely, Joanna's mind turned to her mother in that moment. She would be beaming, wringing her hands together happily, mentally planning Christmases with her grandchildren. She would be so happy. Floating for days. She would get miles of bragging out of it. Everyone she knew would hear all about Joanna's romantic proposal from her best friend, who just happened to be the most amazing man. *With good teeth*, she could hear her mother say. *You know how important dental hygiene is.*

Next thing she knew, Stephen was holding out a black velvet box, which he opened to expose a sparkling solitaire. Not too garish, but enough to show importance—just what she would expect from Stephen. She could hear her breath whistle in and out of her skull. Her hands were coated with sweat.

She realized when she finally glanced at him that he was waiting with an expectant look on his face, which must have meant he'd asked the question and she hadn't heard it.

But it had been a mistake to look at him, she realized. Her heart melted at the sight of him. She loved him so much. He was the last person in the world that she would want to see hurt, even if by her. She'd been so destroyed the last time she'd hurt him. She'd had to disappear for a month. If she said no now, she just might have to disappear forever.

The thought blurred everything for her. She loved Stephen, but she also loved Sutton. She knew that much. She'd never allowed herself to love a woman before, so she didn't know if what she was feeling for Stephen was *love* love, or just best-friend love. She didn't know how to find out.

And in that instant, she was struck with the knowledge that whether she accepted Stephen's proposal was not a matter of her own happiness. Perhaps it never was, and never could have been. She had an obligation to him, to her mom, even to Alyria, from whose advances she'd run away. This was not about Joanna being true to herself, even if she didn't know who Joanna herself was. This was about expectations.

She let out a gasp, which Stephen might have taken to be one of surprise, of elation, but was really just a realization that she had been holding her breath for a few beats, and in that gasp were tears and laughter and all the things that the proposed-to are supposed to release at that exact moment. It was picture-perfect, really, Joanna's reaction. Stephen relaxed, smiled deeply, as she nodded. His fingers fumbled out the ring, which he slid onto her finger—a perfect fit, of course—and then he wrapped her in his arms, going for a hug first instead of a kiss, which Joanna thought strangely platonic for the occasion, but she didn't mind. She was too busy trying to stay upright, trying to wrap her head around what she had just done.

She'd just accepted a marriage proposal.

From a man.

The die had been cast, to use an old, tired expression. Like it or not, Joanna had resolved her confusion. She'd made her decision.

He had bought dinner. Fancy dinner. A risk, Joanna thought—what if her answer hadn't been cause for celebration? They ate and sipped champagne and sat tangled together on the couch that would forever hold a memory for them. They decided to spring the news on their friends and parents later. They wanted to enjoy being the only ones who knew for a while.

"When?" he asked, picking up her hand and inspecting the ring for the hundredth time. "God, you have beautiful hands."

"I don't know," she said. "Do you have a date in mind?"

He laid his head on her shoulder. "Tomorrow."

She laughed hollowly, something tugging at her deep down. Not tomorrow. Far from tomorrow. She needed time. "I'm talented, but I don't think I can put together a wedding in one day."

"I bet you could," he said, picking up her hand again and kissing it. "How about June?"

Joanna did the math. It was February; that would leave them four months. "I don't know. June is so cliché," she said. "December?"

He wrinkled his nose. "Then our special day would always be competing with Christmas," he said.

"What about next April?"

He pulled away, took her in. "You're making it farther and farther away." He turned, gathering his knees up on the couch next to her, and took both of her hands in his. "Listen, I don't care when it is. I really don't. I just want to marry you. But I really, really don't want to wait that long." He kissed her hands in between each word of the last sentence.

Her heart melted. He really was so good to her. "Okay," she said. "October. Fall. It will be beautiful with the leaves and everything."

He mulled it over. "Yeah," he said. "Fall. I think I like that. An outdoor wedding?"

"No way. The weather."

"Good point. How about the little chapel up at the college?"

"That's fine."

"God, I can't wait," he said, and he lunged up against her, tipping her back onto the couch. "I love you, future Mrs. Wilkinson. Have I mentioned that?" He kissed her.

"Maybe once or twice," she said, giggling, between kisses.

"Once or twice, huh? Then I'm about five trillion behind schedule. I love you. I love you. I love you." He worked his way down the side of her face, down her neck, into the collar of her shirt. Joanna let herself be carried away in his kisses, in the dreamy image of the perfect fall wedding, in the life with her best friend.

And, later, when she pulled up memories of Éponine, a lifetime of wedded bliss with Stephen, dotted with the occasional fantasy about Sutton, seemed totally doable.

Three hours later, Joanna woke in a panic. Stephen had left sometime around midnight, kissing her so many times at the door, her chin felt chapped. He'd wanted to spend the night, but had an early morning interview at a bank. *I'm getting a legit job for us, Joanna*, he'd said. *I'll go back to school if I need to.*

Now, lying in bed alone, the base of her neck ringed with cold sweat, Joanna tried to imagine Stephen heading to work in a tie and a polished pair of shoes, coming home at five, ready for a home-cooked dinner made by his loving wife. She tried to imagine herself in that role—carrying a cookie sheet to the front door or planting azaleas in the front lawn or dusting a piece of furniture they'd found together "antiquing." She tried to imagine not going to Sutton's shows.

The champagne and steak sat disagreeably in her stomach, and she rushed to the bathroom and crouched over the toilet. She made retching noises and strained until her nose ran, but nothing came up.

She sat on the tile floor in her underwear, staring at her twinkling diamond through terrified eyes.

After some time, Joanna went back to bed, but sleep wouldn't come. The bed felt too hot, the room too cold, and there was no such thing as a comfortable position. It seemed like daylight was lifetimes away. She couldn't stay there.

Second Chance Friends

. . .

The Tea Rose Diner was never very busy during the overnight hours, but that didn't stop Annie from keeping it open. The lore was that her mother, who had owned it before her, had closed the Tea Rose only one time, on a Tuesday night when Annie's sister, Betty, had the croup. They said that Leonard Franklin, a regular nightly patron up until the day he dropped dead at ninety-six years old, had waited outside on a bench by the front door all night, unsure what to do with himself without his coffee and late-night pancakes. Annie's mother had vowed, then and there, that the Tea Rose would never close again, and even though Annie had no Leonard Franklins to speak of, and only the rarest witching-hour customer, she kept it open out of loyalty, often working the overnight shift herself.

This night was no different. There was only one patron in the Tea Rose when Joanna arrived at 4:13 a.m. A homeless woman, hunkered over a cup of coffee in a back booth.

"Can I get you something?" Annie asked when Joanna slid onto a stool at the bar. Had Sheila been working, she might have said, *Hey, Joanna, you still going grapefruit or are you eating like a normal person today?* But Annie didn't know Joanna like Sheila did, and the bleary hour of the morning made it unlikely that she would memorize anything about her now.

"Coffee," Joanna said, her voice late-night scratchy. "And Boston cream pie, please. Two slices."

Annie nodded and bustled away. Joanna could hear the rumble of a dishwasher running somewhere in the back, the hum of the pie case, which Annie opened to scoop out two slices of Boston cream pie. It was quiet. Peaceful. Just as it had been the morning she had come here to disappear five months before. Until.

Annie came back with the pie and the coffeepot. She turned over a mug in front of Joanna and poured. "Late-night snack or early breakfast?" she asked.

"More like therapy," Joanna said. "So a little of both?"

"I think you're not the only one needing some therapy tonight," Annie said. She tipped her orange curls toward the woman in the back booth. "Been here for hours. She's probably had four pots of coffee herself, and I haven't seen her get up to pee once. She's crying it all out, as far as I can see."

Joanna turned and tried to unassumingly peer at the lady. She was nearly doubled over the table, writing in a notebook, her arm curled protectively around it, as if shielding it from the wandering eyes of a nosy crowd. Something about her looked familiar, but Joanna couldn't quite put her finger on it.

"Personally, I don't think she should be drinking all that caffeine," Annie said. "Not as big pregnant as she is."

Big pregnant.

It dawned on Joanna that she did know who the woman was. The blond, matted hair, the thin arms, the bedraggled look. Maddie Routh.

"Holy crap," Joanna breathed, and she was up and out of her seat before Annie could even ask what the problem was.

Joanna made her way to Maddie Routh's booth and slid into it without asking permission. At first, Maddie made no move to indicate that she had noticed Joanna's presence at all. Just kept writing in her notebook, leaned in close, her shoulders hunched, every so often stopping to wipe her beet red nose on the back of her hand. But after a few seconds, Joanna reached across the table and lightly laid her hand on Maddie's arm, stopping the pen. Maddie looked up, confusion turning to recognition, turning to weary acceptance.

"Did the other one send you?" she asked. Her nose was so clogged with tears it came out as *Did the otha wud sed you?*

"Other what?"

"The other one who's been following me around. The one who came to my house. The one who follows me to the grocery store. I saw her there, you know. She pretended she was looking at the Pop-Tarts, but she was watching me—I know it."

"Are you talking about Melinda?" Joanna asked. She knew that Melinda had felt a particular need to reach out to Maddie, had been talking about it for some time now, their obligation to make sure she was safe and okay. Had been the first to suggest it, now that she thought about it. Melinda had a particular connection to Maddie—one that she herself probably couldn't quite pinpoint. "No, she didn't send me."

Maddie Routh sniffed. "Great. There are two of you after me, then. How long until the third one starts?"

"I didn't come after you," Joanna said. "It's just coincidence. I couldn't sleep. I came for pie."

Maddie Routh stared pointedly at the table in front of Joanna. Joanna gestured toward the counter, where her pie and coffee still waited for her. She could see the steam swirling up from the coffee mug.

"What are you writing?" she asked.

Maddie looked down at the paper. "Names," she said. She moved her arm so Joanna could see. The paper was filled with words in columns, bunched in tiny writing, crammed together. Hundreds, it looked like. Maddie turned the page back and Joanna saw an identical page under it.

"For the baby?" Joanna asked.

"It has to have a name, right?" Maddie said. She leveled her bloodshot eyes at Joanna, and Joanna could have sworn she could swim in the depth of anguish there. "I've got to give it a name. Maybe if I give it a name . . ." She trailed off, but Joanna guessed she could finish the sentence. Maybe if Maddie could give her baby a name, she would start to want it.

"Can I see?" Joanna asked, holding her palm up for the notebook.

Maddie seemed to think it over, and then pushed it across the table. "Michael wanted to name it Max, boy or girl. Can you believe that? The three *M*s: Michael, Maddie, and Max. We argued over it. Twice. But it was mostly play argue. I mean, I didn't like it, but I would have gone with it if it was really important to him. I don't know if he knew that. Do you think he knew that?"

"I didn't know him," Joanna said. "But I'm sure he did. It seems like you guys were happy."

Maddie smiled a wobbly smile. "We were. So happy."

The wobble was contagious. Joanna wasn't sure whether she would have been able to sound so sure and convincing if someone would have asked the same of her and Stephen. Were they happy, or was she just pretending because it was easier to pretend to be happy when you were wearing some-one's engagement ring?

She glanced at her hand. She'd taken the ring off before going to the diner and slipped it into her jewelry box. She'd worn it only hours before taking it off the first time. Surely, this was a bad sign.

"I can't name it Max now," Maddie said. "Not without him here. Not with me telling him that I hated the idea."

"Sure," Joanna said. "I get it. You have some really nice ones here, though. I like Ruthie May. Very cute."

Maddie pulled the notebook back across the table and slung her arm over it protectively. "No. It won't work. None of these will work. Because all I can think about when I think of this baby is Max. It's supposed to be Max. It's sup-posed to be one of the three Ms, not the two Ms. There was never supposed to be only two Ms."

"Maybe if it's a boy, you should go with Michael," Jo-anna suggested. "And Michaelyn if it's a girl. Pay tribute to him, and then it really will be like three Ms."

Maddie squinted at her, not unkindly. "Why are you here?"

Now, that was the million-dollar question, wasn't it? Joanna thought. Why was she here exactly? She knew why—the Tea Rose was her hideout—but was she really ready to admit that?

"I got engaged tonight," she said. She curled her hand into a ball when Maddie's eyes darted toward her finger. "To my best friend."

Maddie's chest heaved a few times with deep breaths, but the anguish and anger seemed to have left her. "You are really lucky," she said. "Take my advice. Don't ever take your fiancé for granted. Live every single moment together like it's your last. You have no idea how many regrets your mind can dig up after the person you love has gone."

Joanna glanced over at her coffee and pie. She wished she'd brought it to the table with her. The distraction would be helpful.

Maddie tilted her head to the side. "You're not happy," she said with wonder.

"I'm happy," Joanna said.

"No, you're not. I can tell. Something's wrong. Don't you love him?"

"Of course I do. He's my best friend."

"That's not the same thing, though," Maddie said. She rested her head on her hand, propped up on one elbow. "When Michael proposed, I couldn't wait to tell the whole world. I showed everyone the ring. It was one of the best times of my life. But you're here, in the middle of the night, and I know that means you're not happy because I'm here in the middle of the night and I'm not happy."

"It's just a lot to take in all at once, I guess," Joanna said.

"Was it a surprise proposal?"

"Definitely." Joanna chuckled, patted her hand on the

tabletop a few times. "I was definitely surprised. I should get back to my coffee. Getting cold, I'm sure." She slid out of the booth and started back to the counter, but was stopped when Maddie reached out and grabbed her shirt-tail.

"Thank you for helping me with the baby names," she said.

"I didn't really help with anything."

Maddie let her hand drop. "Well, I'm not crying any-more, so you must have done something." She paused. "Lis-ten, I know you guys are trying to be there for me. And I'm sorry I'm so difficult to help. I'm trying to put my life back together, but it's hard when you don't really even want to have a life. I'd rather be with Michael than trying to gut this out alone, and that's a feeling that won't go away. I don't think the other chick understands that."

Joanna shook her head. "Probably not."

Maddie rolled her eyes. "But she's trying to comfort me. I can see that. I just don't always want to see it. I keep being mean to her, and then I feel bad, which only makes everything worse."

Joanna crouched back into the booth seat across from Maddie. "Are you getting help?"

"My mom's around. I sent her home tonight to get some rest and take care of my dad, but I really just wanted some time alone."

"To kill yourself?" Joanna asked.

Maddie's hands worried themselves along the spiral edge of her notebook. She shrugged. "I came here, didn't I?"

She had a point, although Joanna wondered if she was here only because it was a lot harder to fling yourself into traffic at three in the morning than it was during rush hour. "I'm glad you did," Joanna said softly.

"Why are you all so into making sure I survive, anyway?" Maddie asked.

"Because we were there," Joanna replied. "I can't really explain it. We weren't even friends before the crash. We'd never met before. Now we see each other every day and we text each other at night. Something happened that day to bind us all together. You, too."

"Maybe it was Michael," Maddie said, but she said it in a voice so low, Joanna could barely hear her, and when Joanna asked her to repeat herself, she shook her head. "Anyway. Your coffee."

"Yeah," Joanna said. She slid out of the booth again and headed toward the counter, where her coffee and pie still awaited her. Annie appeared within moments of her return.

"She okay, or should I be calling the cops?"

Joanna glanced back over at Maddie, who was bent over her notebook again, writing. "She's okay, I think," Joanna said. "For now, anyway."

But as she dug into her pie and nursed her coffee, she began to wonder how long Maddie Routh would stay okay.

NINETEEN

Her jail-visiting outfit made much more sense in February. The sweater, which had trapped heat in during the fall, did an okay job of keeping the cold out—but the wind's fingers found ways to claw through and dig into her skin, making her duck her chin into the cowl-neck and wrap her arms around herself, grabbing fabric in her fists and squeezing tight.

She'd never visited in the winter before and wasn't sure how coats worked in the jail. She didn't want to take hers off, or go for an extra pat down, so she just left it in her car and promised herself that she would walk fast. *Faster than the wind blows, Karen,* she thought, bent forward against the wind.

March was almost here. Surely it would bring better

weather. Blue skies and sunshine. A break from the bluster and blow. It was hard to believe that she'd almost gone a whole season without her son by her side. It was even harder to believe she'd gone all that time without her grandson.

Travis looked sickly, coming to the window. He'd lost weight. He'd had a bad haircut. He'd acquired a very crudely drawn tattoo that began on his neck and snaked its way up onto his cheek. He had a cut needling out from under one eyebrow and up his forehead. It looked as if it had been Steri-Stripped and was now healing into what would definitely be a permanent scar. Travis liked scars—always had. He thought they made him look tough.

Karen thought he looked like a thug. Before, she had always been visiting her baby boy in jail. Now she was visiting her thug son. He looked the part, which was a bad sign.

She sat across from him and picked up the phone.

"What happened to your eye?" she asked.

He reached up and touched the wound. Grinned. *Just the way you would expect a thug to do*, she thought. "Some asshole thought he was tougher than me," he said. "He's missing part of his tongue now."

Karen winced. "Travis, that kind of thing just makes it harder for Frank Sidwell to defend you. You know that, right? You have to keep your nose clean."

"The guy hit me first," he said, his shoulders rounding and his fingertips touching his chest. The innocent act— she'd seen it so many times. Once, she'd believed it. Those days were long, long gone. "What was I supposed to do? Let him kill me?"

"No, of course not," she said. "But you have to stay away from guys like that."

"Mom, this isn't recess at boarding school. There is no staying away from these guys if they want to get to you. That's just the way it works. I have to defend myself, or I'll be on the news next week. Did you come to lecture me or what? Because I don't need this right now."

"I'm not lecturing," Karen said, though it was hard not to get stuck on his words. She didn't realize until that moment that she'd been waiting a long time to see him on the news. Had been expecting it. Dreading, but in an inevitable sort of way. "I just wanted to check in with you. Have you talked to Kendall?"

He gave another wry smile, as if nothing was worth taking seriously anymore. How long had he been doing that? Longer than Karen wanted to admit. She remembered looking at that smirk of his as far back as junior high school, and wanting to shake him and scream at him. *Take things seriously! This is serious, dammit!*

"That bitch," he murmured. "Let me guess. She's asking for money."

No, in fact, she was asking for nothing. She was saying nothing. She wasn't around, as far as Karen could tell. After the New Year's Eve text, Karen had gotten radio silence. Kendall was making good on her threat, Karen supposed, trying not to kick herself for her decision. As much as she loved Marcus, and wanted to spend time with him, wanted him in her life, she knew that if she gave Kendall another dime, she would never get out from under the requests.

"I haven't heard from her," Karen said. "You either?"

"Fuck no. She's probably off fucking some other guy by now. God knows where Marcus is. Probably dead."

Karen pressed her hand over her heart. "Travis!" she exclaimed. "Don't say things like that. He's your son."

"In theory," he said.

"In reality," she countered. Though she supposed he could be right. With Kendall, you never really could tell, but Karen had taken that baby into her heart. She had imprinted him with family connection. She wasn't ready to let that go. Not yet. Maybe not ever.

"Well, I wouldn't count on hearing from her again," Travis said. "Did you give her money?"

"No, but she asked. More like demanded."

He sniffed. "Sounds like Kendall. So what have you heard from Sidwell lately? He gonna get me off pretty soon or what?"

"I talked to him this morning," she said. "He still feels confident we can get a plea deal, but he says you're not interested."

Travis leaned back in his chair and crossed one leg over the other. "Hell, no, I'm not interested in no plea deal. I take that deal and I'm gonna be sitting in here for even longer."

"But if you don't take the deal, you could be found guilty, and then what?"

"I ain't worried. I been found guilty lots of times and never stayed in here for long."

Karen swallowed. "Travis. This time is different. You're

a repeat offender. The family is going to press for a harsh penalty. This guy has been in a coma for months, Travis. He could die."

Travis scratched his neck uncomfortably, but still maintained that maddening air of nonchalance. "Yeah, whatever," he said. "Not my problem."

"Are you kidding me?" Karen started to stand up—her best lecturing position—but the phone cord wouldn't allow such generous movement, and she plopped down again. "It is your biggest problem. I don't think you understand what will happen to you if this guy dies, Travis. You will have murdered him."

"He asked for it."

Karen sat back in her chair, stunned, blinking. She remembered the biggest fight she'd ever had with her mother. It had been the day she'd found out she was pregnant. Her mother had cried, raged, accused her of stupidity. *You don't know the first thing about raising a child,* she had said. *You will make stupid mistakes. You will put this child at risk because you're just a child yourself.*

She'd disregarded her mother at the time. Hated her for those words, actually. She'd struck out alone, written off getting any help from the negative woman. If she couldn't believe in her own daughter, then she didn't deserve to have a daughter anymore.

But now, as she sat across from this frightening man, a filthy bulletproof window separating them, talking to him through a jail phone for the millionth time, hearing the callousness in his voice, the total disregard for human suffering, for feelings, for life, her mother's words had never rung truer.

She'd thought she'd known what she was doing, but that was what made her dangerous. She'd made stupid mistakes, and was so stupid herself, she couldn't even pinpoint them now. Was it the time she threw the fit at the day care for putting him in time-out after he'd retaliated against the little boy who'd flung a block at him? The boy had left a small mark on Travis's cheek, but Travis had bitten a chunk out of the boy's arm. Was it all those times she turned a blind eye when she knew he was doing something irresponsible, or illegal, or dangerous, just because harmony with her one and only son was more important to her than making sure he chose wisely? Was it doing everything she could to get him off the hook every time he was busted?

She'd spanked him. She'd grounded him. She'd lost her temper and screamed at him. But mostly, she'd loved him. She'd let him call the shots because things were just easier when he did.

She'd put her child at risk, just as her mother had predicted she'd do. But what was worse was that she'd put other people's children at risk at the same time.

Karen swallowed, feeling tears press behind her cheekbones. "What should I tell Mr. Sidwell, then?"

"I've already told him. I'm not interested in his plea deals, so he can stop bringing it up. Just tell him to get me the hell out of here. That's what I'm paying him for."

Correction, she thought. *You're not paying him for any-*

thing; I am. But that didn't seem like an important distinction to make at the moment. It was bad enough that her employer had met with this insolent man and associated him with her. It was all the humiliation she needed.

"I think you're making a mistake," she said. "But it's your life."

"I think my time's up," he said, glancing over his shoulder at the guard who stood by the door.

"I love you, son," she said, pressing her free hand against the dirty glass, no matter what she imagined might be on it from past visitors.

He gazed at her hand, ducked his head, a sour look passing over his face, the first sign that he felt anything in this place at all. "I love you, too," he mumbled, but never moved to touch the glass between them. He hung up the phone, swung out of his chair, and disappeared through the door leading back to his cell before Karen could even replace the receiver.

She'd tried to call Kendall dozens of times since New Year's Eve, and always the call went directly to voice mail, without even ringing. As if she'd been blocked. Or as if someone was looking at her number and rejecting the call.

Regardless, she tried again after leaving the jail. She sat in her car, the heat blowing feeling back into her body, warming the sweater, thawing her frozen fingers.

To her surprise, someone picked up.

"Hello?" A male voice.

Karen pulled the phone away from her ear, double-checked the number she'd dialed. "Um, hello? Is Kendall available?"

"Who's this?" the man asked. Guarded. Chip on his shoulder.

"This is Karen. Travis's mom."

"Who the hell's Travis? Hey, Kendall! Who the hell's Travis?" he yelled. Karen heard the pouty whimper of a toddler in the background.

Karen closed her eyes and leaned her forehead on the steering wheel. *Who the hell is Travis? His son is crying wherever you are, and you don't even know who he is?* she wanted to rail. But she didn't have the chance. She heard the crying come closer to the phone, paired with Kendall's voice, which was spouting curse words at a fast speed.

"'Lo?" she finally heard.

"Kendall? It's Karen."

"I know."

"I've just been wondering about the baby."

"Shut him up—I can't hear anything," Kendall said, away from the phone, and then came back. "What?"

"I've been wondering about Marcus."

"What about him?"

The pressure behind Karen's eyes got even stronger. "How is he doing? Where are you?"

"I told you that you wouldn't see him again if you didn't help me out. You didn't help me out, so we blew."

Karen took a deep breath, tried to steady herself. "Kendall, please. I've helped you so many times. He's my grandson. I care about him."

"Yeah, but who cares about me, huh?" Kendall said. Her voice sounded funny—staccato, strung out. "Your loser son didn't care, you don't care, my own family doesn't care. The only one who cares about me is Marcus. And I'm not going to share him with you so you can turn him against me, too. You know?"

"I wouldn't ever," Karen said. "I have never done anything but support you."

There was a puff of air in the phone. Sardonic laughter. "Oh, you would."

"I just want to know if he's close," Karen said. "Can you at least tell me if he's close? If he's safe?"

"What the hell? Of course he's safe. He's with his mother. What do you think, I'd let something happen to him?"

Well, something happened to Travis when he was with his mother, Karen thought wildly. *Something big and wrong.* "No, I wasn't saying that," she said. "I'm just wondering where you guys are."

"It's our business where we are. And with no money, who knows how long we'll stay here? Who knows how long I'll even have this phone?"

Gamey. God, how Karen hated gamey. She couldn't understand what had ever attracted Travis to this girl. She could only imagine what it must be like to be trapped in a relationship with her. Life would be one constant passive-aggressive threat. One betrayal or drunken fight after another. She supposed that was what Travis liked in a girl; they'd all been just like this.

Or maybe that kind of girl was the only kind of girl Travis could get—a thought that terrified and saddened Karen.

What kind of woman would Marcus grow up thinking was the best kind of woman? Would he perpetuate the cycle of jail and baby mamas and dying strangers in the hospital? Would there be no one in his life to help him break it?

"I'll give you money," she blurted in a panic. "I want to see Marcus. How much do you need?"

There was a long pause on the other end of the phone, and when Kendall spoke again, Karen was sure she could hear a smile in the girl's voice. "That's so nice of you, Mom."

"You should come over," Antoinette told her thirty minutes later. "Sal's out of town on business. I have wine and a spare bed."

"I don't know," Karen said, balling another tissue in her hand. She'd just spent the past half hour sobbing as she wired a couple grand to Kendall, on a prayer that the girl would actually do something right and show up with the baby after she got the money. She was finally able to find out that Kendall was in Iowa. Who, or what, brought her there, only the good Lord knew, but at least Iowa wasn't far. At least if Kendall decided to do the right thing, she would have only a few hours' drive to do it. "I don't want to be a burden."

"Oh, stop it, you are not a burden. You're my friend. Besides, I still haven't gotten the skinny on how the sexy accountant is in the sack."

"And you won't tonight, either," Karen said, wiping her nose. Truth was, she and Marty still hadn't gotten to that point. They'd shared the New Year's kiss, but then the nonsense with Kendall had come up and Karen had been too preoccupied to pay much attention to her relationship with Marty Squire. She wasn't even sure, in fact, if there still was a relationship. She wouldn't have blamed him if he didn't want one with her. He'd come over a few times, but all she'd been up for was watching TV and waiting for the phone to ring. They'd kissed, because once you start, you can't very well go back, but even those kisses were lukewarm.

He still called her daily. He was such a nice guy.

"Well, I'm not going to just listen to you cry about breaking into your savings for some criminal whore. I'm giving you the good wine. I'm willing to wash sheets for you, woman."

Karen laughed. "I'll come by. For one glass of wine. I won't stay. Leave the sheets dirty."

"Good enough."

Antoinette's house was technically one town over—a fifteen-minute drive through stoplights and traffic.

It was at one of those stoplights—the one at the corner where the Tea Rose Diner sat—that Karen saw a familiar figure walking along the side of the road. She nearly rear-ended the car in front of her, which had stopped for the red light.

Instead of going straight toward Antoinette's house, she made a quick veer into the turning lane next to her and steered into the Tea Rose parking lot. She jumped out, keys jingling in her hand, and jogged across the lawn toward the figure.

"Maddie!" she called. "Maddie Routh!"

The figure had reached the corner and turned and walked back the way it had come, now moving toward Karen. It was twilight, and her face had sunk into shadows, but Karen recognized the bony arms, the blond hair, the pregnant belly, which hung low and obvious on the thin frame. Karen kept moving toward her, every so often looking over her shoulder to make sure no car was about to swerve into the gravel and flatten her.

"Stop," she said breathlessly when she finally reached Maddie. She put her hands on Maddie's shoulders. The girl stopped. "Are you okay?" And when the girl didn't answer, she gave her a little shake. "Maddie? Can you hear me?" She gulped in air, her heart racing more than it should have been from such a short jog. "Oh, God, you're not trying to kill yourself again."

Maddie still didn't speak, didn't even lift her head. "I'm taking a walk," she said in a flat voice. She took a few more steps, pausing to scrape her feet along the area where the bus had gone off the road, and then moved on. "It's a free country," she said over her shoulder. "Anyone who wants to walk here can."

At first Karen thought she was being chastised for questioning Maddie's state of mind. But then she realized this was an invitation of sorts. It was a free country; if she wanted to join Maddie in her walk, she was welcome to.

She fell in alongside Maddie, on the grass side, so close their shoulders occasionally bumped. A couple of times she opened her mouth to ask Maddie what exactly she was doing, but she already knew. The girl was tracing the area where her husband had last been alive. She'd been hoping to catch a glimpse of the past there. Walking along the street was comforting to her somehow.

Karen reached into her pocket and pulled out her phone. She sent a text to Antoinette:

No wine tonight. Something's come up. Will explain when I see you Monday.

She and Maddie paced the stretch of highway in front of the Tea Rose Diner together, in total silence, until frost made the grass crunchy under Karen's feet and the headlights blinded them.

TWENTY

Melinda was in no mood for her partner Jason's bullshit. It was March, which meant spring break, which meant the numskulls who lived catty-corner from her house had gone to Key West, leaving their numskull teenagers at home alone. During spring break. Numskulls. Melinda had gotten barely any sleep, between the thumping music, the squeals and screams of what sounded like ninety billion teen girls, and the endlessly screeching tires. Paul had slept like a rock next to her—or at least she guessed he had. He'd gotten up soundlessly and left for work before her alarm had even gone off.

That was how their lives were now. Sure, he was back, and they were speaking again, but it was cordial speaking. Sex was cordial sex, like two business partners living up to their end of an agreement. Communication was cordial. *Did you see the news about the blizzard in Colorado? Oh, yes, I saw that. How horrible to get so much snow this late in the season. Speaking of weather, do you know what the temperature's supposed to be today? I can look on my phone. No, no, I can do that—don't trouble yourself.*

It was as if they were two strangers who didn't particularly want to get to know each other.

It broke Melinda's heart.

A thousand times she planned to sit him down and talk to him. Really talk to him. About what had happened. About her fears. About babies and children and the future, which they desperately needed to talk about if they were ever going to get past this.

About her plans to quit her job.

That was what it had come down to, she decided. Either she was going to lose the love of her life or she was going to lose the career she'd worked so hard for. It was no contest. She could work anywhere, but she could never find another Paul. Even as angry as she was at his reaction to what she'd done, she still knew he was her soul mate.

She hadn't definitely made up her mind yet about the job, of course. There was the small matter of paychecks and needing to find another job before she left this one. Joanna had promised to ask her boss about waitressing at the restaurant where she worked, and Karen said she'd look into openings at the law firm. But Melinda had applied for a few others as well. A hair salon needed someone to run the front desk and answer the phones. A psychology office needed a receptionist. A bank needed customer service agents.

None of these jobs felt right. The only job that would ever feel right to Melinda would be the one where she rolled up into the middle of a dire scene with rubber gloves in place and training in mind. But as long as she did any job that potentially involved watching people die, she would never work past this . . . this whatever-it-was that was keeping Paul and her apart.

Yet no matter how many times she intended to sit Paul down for a chat, she could never quite make herself do it. It was scary, what was happening to them. She felt intimidated and embarrassed and angry. She felt closed down.

So the cordiality continued.

And to make things worse, she'd had a more difficult time keeping tabs on Maddie Routh lately. Where she'd occasionally been able to follow her to the grocery store or shopping before, lately Maddie seemed to never leave the house. The white car remained in the driveway twenty-four hours a day now, and the only person Melinda ever saw step outside the front door was Maddie's mother, who seemed to look older and less put together every day. Occasionally, an aging man would pull up in an ancient blue and white pickup truck and go inside. Melinda guessed that man was Maddie's father, but he never stayed for long.

Seven months. It had been seven months since the accident, and from the looks of things, Maddie Routh had only gotten worse. She would be having a baby soon, and how would she care for it? She couldn't even care for herself without her mother there to help her.

Karen had said she'd caught her walking in front of the diner a month ago. Joanna had found her inside the diner writing names in a notebook before that. She was a ghost, floating around the most important place in her life, unable to rest in peace.

It was weird to think of a living person as a ghost, but some people were so on the fringes of their own lives, there was no other way of describing them.

So Melinda had been veering toward the edge for some time now, but after the all-night spring break rager and Paul's silent disappearing act, she was definitely not in the mood for Jason's bullshit.

"Whoa, someone hide your makeup today?" he asked the minute he saw her.

"Shut up, Jason," she said, without even looking up from the packet of sugar she was emptying into her coffee.

"Ouch, so it's PMS, huh?" He snickered, pouring coffee into his mug.

She tossed the empty packet into the trash and picked up her mug. "If I were you, I'd stop talking." She took a sip, grimaced. "Unless you want to wear that coffee."

"What the hell's your problem?"

She wheeled on him. "You know what? You are. Your attitude is terrible, and working with you is hell. You're nasty and rude and your wife is whiny, and I won't miss you when I'm gone."

He blinked at her. "Gone? You quitting?"

She flushed. She hadn't even made the decision yet. She shouldn't be spouting off things like that. She could end up being invited to leave before she was ready.

"Whatever," she said quietly, then blew across the top of her coffee and took another sip. "I don't have time to deal with your crap. And I'm not eating with you at any point today. I don't care how hungry you get. I can't do it anymore."

She watched as Jason's face filled up and twisted with red anger, his forefinger so tightly wrapped through the handle of his coffee mug it was white at the knuckle. She took some amount of satisfaction in seeing him that way, in being the one to elicit disgust for a change. "I don't know who flipped your bitch switch—," he started, but was interrupted by a call coming in over the radio.

An attempted suicide.

At 503 East Ninety-second Terrace.

An address Melinda recognized.

She heard nothing else Jason might have said. Only ditched her coffee mug on the counter, a splash of coffee sloshing over its side, and rushed to the ambulance.

The man whom Melinda had guessed to be Maddie Routh's dad was standing at the door when they arrived, frantically waving for them to come in. He was holding a bloody dish towel in one hand, and his face was etched deep with worry.

"She's in the bathtub," he said. "We've drained the water, but she refused to come out. Her mother's in there with her, trying to keep the bleeding to a minimum."

Melinda pushed past him, leading Jason through the house toward Maddie's mom's voice, which was equal parts frantic and anguished. She'd forgotten all about Jason, about the man at the door, about the time Maddie had kicked her out of this very house. She feared she'd even forgotten her job.

This was it, she realized. This was what it felt like when the emergency was yours. This was what she'd been avoiding all this time. This was what she'd trashed her marriage to escape.

How could she feel so deeply for Maddie Routh? Even she didn't understand the connection that had been constructed between the two of them. All she knew was that she couldn't screw this up. She couldn't let Maddie die, not the way she'd let Michael do it.

They rounded the corner into the hall bathroom, and at first all Melinda could see was the backside of Helen, who was kneeling next to the tub, her top half pressed inside of it as she talked, yelled, cried at Maddie. Another step inside and Melinda could see Maddie Routh, her eyes closed, tears streaming toward her ears. She wasn't responding to Helen's pleas, but Melinda wasn't sure if that was because she couldn't, or just because she wasn't.

Helen felt them come in and stood up. Her arms were covered with blood, and her mint green tunic was soaked with pink water. "Thank God," she said. "We thought she was just taking a long bath. There was so much blood in the water. It's her wrists. She's not dead, okay? Tell me she's not dead."

For a moment, Melinda was unsure she'd be able to tell Helen anything. She was completely focused on Maddie Routh's body, which had been covered with a towel, soaked through with blood and bathwater. There were red streaks up one side of her face, taking Melinda back to the day of the crash.

Help him! Save him—he's dying! Michael, don't die! Michael, do you hear me?

The kids. The kids had been crying. Some of them inconsolably. Hitching, shrieking cries. Some of them with broken bones, bloody noses. Their white T-shirts and pink backpacks sprinkled with blood. Their lunch bags burst open. Their bus driver dead and staring lifelessly through eyes glittered with shattered glass.

They were left. Even if only for a few seconds, until other adults could park their cars and run across the lawn of the Tea Rose Diner, they were alone in their horror. Their parents would be summoned to get them—at the bus barn, at the hospital—and they would be limp little sandbags in their parents' arms, their nightmare over, but their innocence blotted by its memory.

He had been dying. She'd had to leave the children. She'd had to help Maddie Routh. Pregnant and alone Maddie Routh, inconsolable as her own nightmare unfolded before her.

"You should wait outside, ma'am," Jason said, ripping Melinda out of her memory. She was jostled as Helen stepped around her toward the bathroom door. "We'll take care of her," Jason said, employing a sensitivity that Melinda would never have guessed he had.

It was enough to jar her into movement. She couldn't lose it now. She couldn't fall apart. She couldn't let both Maddie and Michael down.

She dropped to her knees next to the tub, placing two fingers against Maddie Routh's neck. There was a pulse, though the girl's face was extremely pale. Helen had wrapped two towels tight around Maddie's wrists. Red blooms patched through here and there, but not much, which led Melinda to believe that the bleeding had at least slowed down.

"Okay, honey, we're going to need to get you to a hospital," she said, smoothing Maddie's hair behind one ear. "But you're going to be fine."

At the sound of Melinda's voice, Maddie's eyes fluttered open. They landed on Melinda's face, at first looking startled, but quickly melting into a flood of emotions that Melinda couldn't quite pinpoint.

"Help me," Maddie said, and the look in her eyes told Melinda that she didn't just mean at that moment. It was what Melinda had been hoping to hear from Maddie Routh for months now. *Help me get through this. Help me live.* "Please help me."

"Okay," Melinda said, nodding. She felt a tear drip past one cheek—something that had never happened before on the job. "Okay, we're going to help you."

Maddie lifted her arms, stared at her wrists as if she had no idea what had happened to them. "Oh, God," she croaked, and then fell into sobs so deep they took her breath away. When she finally breathed again, it came as a rusty gasp. She turned to Melinda again, sitting up, spilling the towel into her lap, exposing her swollen belly. "I need you."

Melinda had to force herself to tear her eyes away from Maddie's belly—it was fine. Maddie was not fine, but the baby was fine. But when she did finally tear herself away, she clicked into professional mode. Not all the babies on their calls made it.

But, by God, this one would.

TWENTY-ONE

Joanna supposed she couldn't blame Stephen for thinking she'd pulled another one of her disappearing acts. She couldn't even blame him for being angry about it, even though he was wrong. She hadn't disappeared. Not on purpose, at least. She'd been gone only a few hours.

It just happened that she'd gotten Melinda's call about Maddie Routh moments after she'd climbed in the car to go meet Stephen to check out some reception halls.

There'd been no time to call. And she'd been too busy hurrying to the hospital to answer his call. And then she'd been too worried to be bothered with her phone after she arrived, and had turned it off for some peace and time to think.

Or . . . maybe this was just another way of saying she was disappearing again.

Maddie had been admitted. They would keep her for at least the requisite seventy-two hours, but that didn't stop Melinda, Karen, and Joanna from sitting in the waiting room for hours after they'd declared Maddie stable. Hours after Helen and the aged man who'd introduced himself as Cleve had gone, they were still there. It was as if none of them wanted to get too far away from her, just in case something else should happen.

"She cut fairly deep," Melinda said. "She caught a couple veins pretty good. I don't know if she would have died, but she might have, if her mom hadn't been there. She needs more than seventy-two hours in psych care. She needs real help."

"How's the baby?" Karen asked.

"So far, so good," Melinda said. "But she's like thirty-two weeks along. I can't help wondering what that baby's about to be born into, you know?"

"We'll help," Joanna said. "We can all help her. We've been doing it this long. Why would we stop?"

"I don't know about you guys, but I can't stop," Melinda said. "I need to make sure this baby is born safe and alive. I can't explain it—it's such a long story—but it's like every-thing in my life rides on this. If this baby comes out fine, I'm fine. If it doesn't . . . I think I'll lose so much."

Joanna shook her head as if trying to clear it. "I don't follow."

"Paul wants kids. I . . . can't get there. All I can think about are the dying kids and the scared kids and the hurt kids."

"And the troubled kids," Karen added. "Don't forget those. They'll kill you slowly."

"Yeah, those, too," Melinda said. "I'm sorry, Karen," she mumbled, and Karen waved her off. "Anyway, I don't see how anyone can do it. I would be such a nervous wreck all the time, I don't understand how it is even a little bit worth the time and energy."

"But it is," Karen said. She sat up straighter. "I mean, there's a lot of anxiety and stress, sure. And from what I can see, it never stops. But it's worth it. Travis is a shithead. He really is. And he's in so much trouble now, there's probably no fixing him. But there were so many good days with him. So many hugs and ice cream kisses that got my face all sticky and times when we talked—just sat and talked about our lives—and he loves me. It sounds selfish to say it's worth it to have kids because they love you, and I don't really mean it that way. I just mean it like when one of your kids tells you he loves you . . . it makes up for all of the hard parts of parenting." She gave an embarrassed laugh. "That probably sounds really hollow and stupid coming from me, huh?"

"Of course not," Joanna said. She reached over and put her hand on Karen's arm.

Karen lunged forward and gasped, grabbing Joanna's hand. "Is that an engagement ring? Stephen proposed?"

Joanna pulled her hand away, suddenly shy. "Yeah," she said, turning her hand over so that the diamond faced down into her lap.

"You're engaged?" Melinda asked. "Congratulations. I'm so sorry—you don't want to be listening to my depressing marriage problems right now when you're planning a wedding."

"When did this happen?" Karen asked.

"A while ago," Joanna admitted.

"You haven't said anything," Karen said. "Have I just been missing the ring?"

Joanna could feel herself blush. "No, I haven't been wearing it. It, um . . . makes my finger swell," she lied.

"Oh, an allergic reaction?" Melinda asked. "I've heard of that. Some people are sensitive to metals." She grabbed Joanna's hand, turned it over, and inspected the area around the ring, frowning. "Huh, it looks fine."

Joanna pulled her hand away again. "It comes and goes," she said.

"So when's the date?" Karen asked.

"We haven't set one yet. We were supposed to go look at a couple of halls tonight, but . . ." She gestured around the hospital corridor and shrugged.

"Oh, you should go," Melinda said. "We can handle this."

"No, that's okay. I want to be here," Joanna said.

"It's your wedding," Karen said. "We've got this. You go, be with Stephen."

"It's fine. He'll understand."

"Joanna, don't be silly. You can come back tomorrow," Melinda said.

"She'll be here until Wednesday, at the very least," Karen added. "We can't do anything until then anyway."

Joanna felt sweat pop out on her forehead. She wanted them to just stop talking. Why did she wear her ring today? Oh, that was right—because Stephen would definitely have noticed if she hadn't been wearing it. "No, really, I'm going to stay."

"Go, go," Karen said, and at the same time, Melinda said, "We'll have coffee in the morning and catch you up on any news." Each of them pushed and prodded at Joanna.

She began to feel her pulse in her temples, which were now so coated with sweat that her hair stuck to the sides of her face. She wasn't ready to let people know about the wedding. She wasn't ready for choosing a reception hall and she wasn't ready for setting dates and she would never be ready. She couldn't do this. All she wanted was to drive to the theater and watch Éponine sigh her last breath in Marius's arms. All she wanted to do was feel the brush of Sutton's fingers on her bare arm. All she wanted was to go back in time to that moment with Alyria in the makeup room, to go back and lean into Alyria and smell her perfume and kiss her and hold her hand at an ice cream shop and take her home for Thanksgiving.

She wanted to take back the disappearing acts.

She wanted to be done hiding.

"I'll call you later," Karen said. "When we're done here."

Melinda gave her another little push. "We'll see you tomorrow morning. So, go. Go, go, go."

"I'm gay," Joanna blurted, her eyes squeezed closed. She gulped, and then opened her eyes and repeated, staring at Karen, "I'm gay."

"Oh," Karen said. "I had just assumed Stephen was the one who gave you the ring."

Joanna nodded. She twisted the ring off her finger and

stared at it in the palm of her hand. "He was. Is. Whatever." And then suddenly she burst into laughter. "I've never said it out loud before." She covered her mouth with her palm.

"I'm confused," Melinda said.

Which only made Joanna laugh harder. "So was I. Oh, my God, forever I was confused. But it's so stupid, all this worrying and hiding. I'm gay. I'm in love with a woman named Sutton. But she's not the first. I've been in love with women for years and I've been running from it and oh, my God, I'm engaged to Stephen and I'm gay."

"Oh," Karen repeated. She paused. "What are you going to do?"

"She's going to break it off. Right?" Melinda said. "You can't stay with him if you're in love with someone else."

Joanna waited for the punch in the gut, the guilty heart slam, the emotion that would send her back into hiding. It had been so natural to her for so long to deny, deny, deny what she was feeling—to call it confusion or call it wrong or call it whatever, but it was what it was. She loved Stephen deeply, but she was in love with Sutton. And even if Sutton didn't return her feelings, she wouldn't suddenly feel the same way about Stephen as she had about Sutton. She wouldn't feel that way about any man. She'd known it since she was twelve years old. She just never felt safe admitting it—not even to herself.

She gazed at Karen and Melinda, who were both looking at her expectantly. Why was it she finally felt safe, and it was with these two ladies? They weren't the same ages; they had little to nothing in common, other than a shared morning on a beautiful, horrible September day.

But what they did have in common was huge. They'd watched a man die. They'd kept his wife alive. They'd come together in the single most defining moment of someone else's life . . . and had ended up defining themselves. Or at least Joanna had. She knew it now. There was no going back.

"Yeah," she said. "I'm going to have to break it off. Of course."

And it wasn't until she said it out loud that she realized what that really meant. Poor Stephen. She would break his heart. She would destroy him. She would destroy her mother, who wanted so badly for this moment to finally come. But she couldn't spend her whole life being silently shattered to spare a few people a few bad days.

"He's going to be so shocked," she said. "How do I do it?"

Melinda shrugged. "Just say to him what you said to us."

Joanna tried to imagine herself looking into Stephen's hopeful eyes and saying those words: *I'm gay, Stephen. I know we've made love countless times. And I liked it. I can't explain it, but I liked it while even wishing I was with a girl I know.*

It definitely wasn't going to be as easy as *Just say to him what you said to us.* But for the first time ever, it seemed doable.

Joanna did eventually leave the hospital. So did Karen and Melinda, when they finally decided that maybe leaving Maddie Routh alone in the hospital would be okay.

"You think she'll try again?" Joanna asked on the way to the parking lot.

"It's definitely possible," Melinda said.

"Especially after the baby is born and the postpartum hormones set in," Karen answered. "I had a heck of a time, and I was nowhere near suicidal before Travis was born. I saved that for after he turned sixteen." She chuckled. "Kidding. Bad joke. Sorry."

"It's okay," Melinda said. "We can't be holding our breath all the time. Do you think she'll keep the baby, or do you think she's going to give it up?"

"No way," Joanna said. "She wouldn't be able to give up Michael's baby."

"But she's tried to kill it several times now," Karen said. "And she went through that whole thing about the names, remember? I think she doesn't know what she's going to do once the baby is born. I think it scares her."

"It would scare me," Melinda said.

Joanna and Karen chuckled. "We know," they said in unison.

"I'm so glad you find the dismantling of my life so funny," Melinda said, but she was smiling when she said it.

"Of course it's not funny," Karen said. "But it definitely went without saying."

Melinda let out a breath of laughter. "I suppose you're right," she said. She stopped walking, and they each stopped with her. "Do you guys think I would be a good mother?"

"Of course," Joanna said.

"Yes," Karen said, as if it was obvious. "But you'll have to let go of some of your fears. Bad things happen to good kids. You can't help it."

"I guess not," Melinda said, and started walking again.

When they got to the parking garage and had to part ways, Melinda jangled her keys and asked if they all wanted to stop by the Tea Rose for some pie.

"I've got to get home," Karen said. "Marty is bringing over some dinner."

Joanna shook her head. "Not this time. I've got someone I need to see."

The show was sold out. It had grown increasingly popular and had been enjoying sold-out shows on a regular basis now. Not bad for a low-rent production filled with amateurs who would never get past community theater.

But it meant that Joanna had to pull around to the back entrance and wait. She parked next to Sutton's car.

She made the mistake of turning on her phone. Stephen had called multiple times. She deleted all the voice mails without even listening to them. She could guess what they had to say, and she couldn't blame him for being pissed or worried or both. She texted him:

Sorry something came up with Maddie Routh. I had to turn off my phone in hospital and now I'm

She paused, thought about how she might finish the sentence without outright lying. But the last thing she wanted was for him to show up here and make things even more difficult. She would talk to him, but she needed to sleep on it, to decide what to say.

—having an important meeting, she continued. Will explain tomorrow.

He texted back, right away, several texts firing into her phone at once, demanding to know where she was. Wondering if Maddie was okay, if she was okay. Telling her he'd been thinking the worst, and the least she could have done was text him earlier. Telling her that they'd missed the guy at their first choice for reception hall and probably wouldn't be able to get another appointment before the wedding. Which was interesting, she thought, since they still didn't have a date in mind.

She ignored those texts, placed her phone facedown on the passenger seat, slid back in her chair, and turned up the radio.

She didn't realize she'd dozed until knocking woke her up. She jerked awake, swimming to consciousness only to find Sutton grinning outside her window, a black coat with fur collar buttoned all the way up to her chin. She waved when Joanna looked at her.

Joanna rolled down her window. "Hey," she said sleepily. "You startled me."

"You always sleep in back alleyways behind theaters, or were you waiting for someone in particular?" Sutton teased. She winked. She still had on her stage makeup, and Joanna wanted to feel the thick lashes up against her cheek.

"I was hoping to scalp some tickets to the hottest show in town," she joked back.

Sutton poked one hip out to the side and tapped her chin. "I think I might know someone who can help you out," she said. They both giggled. "Seriously, though, aren't you sick of watching it? You've been here so many times."

"Not a chance." A slow grin spread across her face. "You've noticed me at the shows?"

"Of course." A gust of wind blew, and Sutton tensed against it.

"Oh, here, you should come inside," Joanna said, unlocking the doors. Sutton trotted around the front of the car and hopped in.

"Thanks. I am so ready for spring to actually get here for real." She rubbed her hands together as Joanna turned up the heat. "So why are you here, really?"

Joanna's mouth felt very dry, and her palms were clammy, but otherwise she was far less nervous than she expected to be. The engagement ring was in her pocket. She planned to tell Sutton all about it, but not there.

"I was hoping we could go get that drink tonight?" she asked.

Sutton grinned. "I thought you'd never ask. Should I get Theo? I'm not sure if he's still in there, but I can look."

"Nah, just the two of us," Joanna said. "If that's okay. I want to toast a brilliant Éponine."

Sutton brushed her fingers against Joanna's, biting her lip. "It's definitely okay," she said.

Joanna put the car in reverse and pressed on the gas. She knew she had a lot of battles ahead of her. A lot of unpleasant conversations. Tears. Pain. But for the first time in her life, she felt truly happy and free.

TWENTY-TWO

The biggest April Fools' joke that had ever been pulled on Karen was the one where Kendall took her money and never showed up with the baby.

Emphasis on *Fool*, Karen thought. She just happened to be the biggest fool she knew, handing more cash over to that dishonest little liar. She could just hear her mother, who would undoubtedly be going on and on about a fool and her money soon parted. She could hear her lecturing—*This is why Travis is the way he is, Karen, because you want to be a friend and not a parent.*

Wrong. She didn't want to be Kendall's friend. She didn't want to be Kendall's parent. She didn't want to be Kendall's anything. She wanted to have her grandson in her life. She wanted to see him grow up.

Of course, Kendall had disappeared again. Only this time, her phone was also disconnected. She didn't know why this made the baby feel even further out of her reach, but somehow it did. Even when Kendall wasn't answering, at least there was a sense that she was out there somewhere, that she was real and pinpointable, if someone was wanting to pinpoint her.

Karen called and listened to the recorded operator voice at least twenty times, each and every time hoping it would say something different—maybe give her a new number to call, maybe add the word "temporarily" to "out of service." Anything. But, no, it was always the same— *number disconnected, please hang up, blah blah blah.*

Finally, she gave up, and just set about wondering where Marcus might be on any given day. Every newscast she saw, every viral video she clicked on, every crowd behind the *Good Morning America* set, she scanned the faces, hoping to see a familiar button nose or flyaway blond hair on a little boy. But that never happened. It was as if Marcus had simply ceased to exist.

Next thing she knew, it was mid-April, and it had been weeks since she'd sent the money to Kendall. It had been weeks since the number went dead. It had been weeks of waiting for Kendall to make the short trip from Iowa to Missouri. It didn't take weeks to get from Iowa to Missouri. It didn't take weeks to get from anywhere to Missouri.

She'd stopped spending her mornings at the Tea Rose Diner. They all had. Instead, they'd spent rotating shifts at

Maddie Routh's house, relieving Helen when they could, working alongside her when she refused to leave.

"She's my daughter," she would say, stoically clutching a glass of red wine at the end of the day. "This is where I have to be."

Cleve would come around periodically as well, floating through the house with a hammer or a tape measure or a can of WD-40, a maintenance ghost. He never seemed to have much to say—definitely the quiet one in the relationship—and seemed to toil through his fate with grim acceptance. Karen liked him. He reminded her somewhat of her grandpa, back when she was growing up. Tough, quiet, smart, bowled over by the women in his life. She missed her grandpa, God rest his soul.

When Maddie had come home from the hospital, she'd spent most of her time in bed, sleeping round the clock, as if she hadn't closed her eyes since the accident. And maybe, Karen thought, she really hadn't.

With a lack of anything else to do, Melinda, Joanna, and Karen decided to do something practical. Helen had shown them a back bedroom, which housed a plain white crib and a small dresser, a few Target bags filled with clothes tossed on top.

"She's been trying, but this is all she has so far," Helen had said. "Cleve and I have been here with her, so it's been hard to get out and buy things. Plus, well, it's just been hard . . ."

She'd trailed off, but Karen could guess what she'd been getting at. It had been hard to be excited about the baby, given everything that Maddie had been going through.

Karen could imagine Maddie, blindly pulling things off racks at Target, the stitches still in her head from the accident. Buying onesies in a Windbreaker soaked with tears. Picking out a crib online and leaving the box on the front porch until frost collected on the top of it and Cleve finally dragged it in and put it together.

"Let's finish it," Melinda had said, standing in the doorway.

"What if she doesn't want it?" Joanna asked.

"The baby? Why would you think that?" Helen asked, startled. "Of course she wants it. We all want it."

"No," Karen had said. "I think Joanna meant, what if she doesn't want the room finished?"

Joanna had nodded, though Karen wasn't sure this was exactly what Joanna had meant. They'd all wondered, of course, about what the fate of the baby would be after it was born. But the room, even partially finished, spoke of Maddie's hope to make a life together.

"She wants it," Melinda said. "I don't know what makes me say that, but I just know she does. The baby needs a room. She just needs some assistance. We won't do anything major. Just maybe paint the walls and buy a few more things."

"Diapers," Karen said. "I don't see any diapers."

"And a mobile," Helen added.

"Maybe some Winnie the Pooh decorations or something," Joanna said, hopefully. "I've always loved Winnie the Pooh. The baby should have something cute."

And so they'd spent the next few days painting and buying and arranging, taking shifts opposite their work shifts, trying to overlap where possible so they could catch up quickly before the others had to leave.

The room began to take shape—soft yellow walls with dim lamp lighting, bumblebees hanging from a mobile cresting on the wave of warm air when the furnace kicked on. Melinda had repurposed a rocking chair. Cleve had built a toy box. Joanna and her friend Sutton had filled the dresser drawers with a rainbow of T-shirts and pajamas.

Which left Karen the task of buying diapers, a shopping trip she enlisted Antoinette for. She seemed all too thrilled to go. Between Travis's drama and Kendall's nonsense, Maddie's difficulties, and having Marty Squire in her life, Karen hadn't had as much time for her friend as she used to.

"I'm so glad you called," Antoinette said as they pushed a cart down the grocery store aisle. "I've been thinking it's been way too long since I bought a couple cases of diapers. Let's see, when was the last time? Oh, I remember. Never. I have never bought diapers in my life."

Karen smacked at Antoinette's shoulder. "Yes, well, it's a thrill, I can assure you. Prepare to have your world rocked."

"Really," Antoinette said. "I feel like it's been forever since we talked. Your work hours have been weird. You've been ditching me at lunch for *that man*." She gave an elaborate roll of the eyes.

"Stop right there," Karen said, holding up a finger as she tried to dodge a child pushing a cart twice the size of himself. "Need I remind you that you were the one who practically begged me to start dating *that man*?"

"No, of course not," Antoinette said. "And I'm glad you

two have your thing going. I'm just saying, it would be nice to have another payroll meeting like we used to. The Cheetos don't taste the same without you. And the gossip is a lot less tasty. I've been reduced to watching one of those all-female daytime talk shows. Do you know how many fashion segments I've had to sit through?"

"Point taken," Karen said. "Next week. I promise." She veered down the middle aisle, which was choked with parents picking up last-minute Easter items.

"Speaking of Marty Squire," Antoinette said. "Have you two gotten . . . you know . . . close yet? Surely you have by now. You're holding out on me. I'm watching the latest on stiletto trends when I should be getting the down and dirty on your down and dirty."

Karen pursed her lips at her friend. "Shhh, there are little kids around here. And no." She slipped between two carts, leaving Antoinette to shove her way through the mob.

"Why not?" Antoinette stage-whispered when she caught up. "He's so cute. Aren't you curious? My Lord, when was the last time you did that? I would think you'd be dying."

Karen spotted the overhead sign for infant wear and headed for it, sighing. "It's been a long time, but, no, I'm not dying for it."

"How long exactly?"

Karen stopped; Antoinette nearly bumped into her with the cart. "Truth?"

Antoinette nodded.

"Since Travis was born. When Doug took off, I guess I just sort of gave that up."

"What?" Antoinette howled. Karen quickly started walking again. "Are you sure it still works down there? It's probably all full of cobwebs and dust."

Karen couldn't help laughing. "Everything is just fine down there. And besides, it's not like I'm turning down scores of men. It just hasn't come up."

"Clearly. Well, surely it's come up with Marty."

"Actually, it hasn't. Here they are." Karen had, thankfully, found the diapers. It hadn't come up, mainly because Karen had let Marty know in no uncertain terms that she wasn't available for that. Not now, probably not ever. He seemed fine with it.

Although lately he'd taken to feathering her collarbone with his fingertips when he kissed her, and she'd started to think that never was a very long time.

She grabbed two boxes of diapers and heaved them into the cart, then went back for two more. "If I recall, she's going to need a lot of newborn diapers. Seems like Travis went through a diaper about every half hour."

Antoinette grabbed a box and held it for Karen, who took it and tossed it on top of the others. "And how is she doing?" she asked. "Maddie."

"Better," Karen said. "Last night she ate dinner at the table. And Joanna said earlier in the day she sat in the rocking chair in the nursery. She's not sleeping as much. And she's not crying as much. So progress, I guess."

"Is it an act to get you guys to go away so she can off herself?" Antoinette asked.

Karen had to admit, it was a question that had probably

crossed all their minds at some point. She'd learned through her years with Travis's nonsense that manipulation could be very, very hard to spot, and sometimes you realized that you fell for something obvious only a long time after the fact. Was Maddie simply "acting better" so they would stop watching her every move?

But Maddie wanted help. She and Melinda had talked about it a lot. Melinda thought they'd turned a corner, so it was possible that they really had.

"I—," Karen started, but was interrupted by her phone ringing. Her heart leapt—maybe it was Kendall—and she set down the box of diapers she'd just started to pick up so she could dig her phone out of her purse. It was an unknown number.

She answered, and a machine told her it was a collect call from the correctional facility.

Oh, God, what now?

She okayed the call, and after a pause, Travis's voice filled her ear. "Hello? Hello?"

"I'm here," she said. "What's wrong?"

"Is it true, Mom?"

"Is what true?"

"What Kendall said about the guy."

Her hand tightened around her phone. "You've heard from Kendall? Where is she?"

"I don't know, shacking up somewhere in South KC. That's not why I'm calling."

"South KC?" Karen interrupted. "She's back in Missouri? When did she get here? Does she have Marcus with her?" Travis hadn't called about Kendall, but Karen didn't care. Kendall's whereabouts were the only thing she cared about right now. Kendall's, and Marcus's.

"I don't know." She could hear the annoyance in Travis's voice, but she ignored it. After all that she had been through for him, it was the least he could do to humor her for a change.

"But you've heard from her?" she asked.

"Yeah." More annoyance. "She called this morning to say that guy woke up. Said no residual problems. Is it true?"

"What?" Karen asked, but realized she had heard him and was asking only for herself. "Curt MacDonald woke up?"

"What?" Antoinette barked, and leaned into Karen's shoulder to get a better listen. Karen tilted the phone away from her ear so they could both hear.

"If you can believe Kendall," he said. "Which I don't. I thought maybe you'd know."

"I don't," Karen said. "Oh, my God, Travis, it would be a miracle."

"I know, right? I could get the fuck out of this place. You could get that Sidwell guy to go ahead and arrange a plea. I want out."

"No, I mean, it would be a miracle for the guy to live. And with no residual problems. Imagine how relieved his family must be."

He could get married to that adorable girl, she thought. He could give her faith a real kick in the keister. They could live happily ever after and he could smile at his kids and think back on the day when he was brutally attacked in a bar for no reason whatsoever. He could marvel that he lived through it, so life must be a blessed thing indeed, and he would never take a moment of it for granted.

"Yeah, whatever. I don't care about him. I just want to go home," Travis said. "Can you find out for me? Call Kendall or something?"

"Of course," Karen said, realizing that she wanted to know. She had to know. Had Curt MacDonald lived? Had all her hoping and wishing and praying actually worked? "But I can't call Kendall. Unless you have her new phone number?"

He made a blowing noise into the phone. "Like that bitch would give me anything."

Karen threw her phone back in her purse and hurried the diapers up to the cashier.

"So we're definitely not going to the house to deliver these," Antoinette said, as Karen tossed the diapers into her trunk.

"Are you kidding? No way," Karen said. She slammed the trunk shut and climbed into the car, having trouble containing herself long enough for Antoinette to return the cart and join her inside the car.

"You know I owe you, right?" Antoinette said as they pulled out of the parking lot.

"What do you mean?"

"I promised you that if the guy ever woke up, I'd tell you what Marty Squire said about you that time I ran into him."

It took a moment for said promise to click, but when it finally did, Karen found herself somewhat curious. She was high on good news. "Okay," she said. "Lay it on me. What did he say?"

"He said, 'I'm going to marry that woman someday.'"

"He said that?" Karen asked. Antoinette nodded. "Well, that's just ridiculous. I already got my one miracle." Karen cracked the window open and laughed as the wind blew through her hair.

Antoinette waited in the car while Karen practically sprinted into the hospital, moving past the information desk so quickly the elderly woman manning it barely had time to look up from her novel, much less offer to help. But Karen didn't need any help anyway. She knew exactly which elevator would take her to 502.

She had to force herself to slow down, catch her breath, calm herself before the elevator doors opened. When they finally parted, she saw the same sleepy floor as before, only this time no nurses were in their station. Karen could hear someone talking inside a room to her left, but she veered right and marched straight to Curt MacDonald's room.

The door was wide open, and she could tell from the light spilling into the hallway that the curtain was drawn as well. She took a breath, braced herself, and stepped inside.

A girl in scrubs was taking the bedding off the bed Curt MacDonald had been lying in before. She was the only one in the room.

"Oh, hi," she said when she saw Karen. "Can I help you?"

Karen pointed blankly at the bed. "The man who was here. Curt?"

The girl turned her mouth down in a fake pout. "You just missed him."

"He left?"

The girl nodded. "Like, literally minutes ago. You might still be able to catch them downstairs if you're fast. I wish I'd seen him go. They forgot a bag." She pointed to a black-and-white striped tote, which was leaning up against the leg of one of the chairs.

"So he just . . . woke up, and walked out of here?"

"Well, he left in a wheelchair. Hospital policy." The girl's eyes averted above Karen's shoulder, and Karen turned just in time to see Curt MacDonald's fiancée— Katy—hurry in.

"I forgot my bag," she said, a little out of breath herself. She walked over and picked it up, and only then seemed to notice Karen. She stopped abruptly. "Oh."

Karen's eyes glistened with tears. "He came out of it," she said.

Katy nodded warily. "I don't think you're supposed to be here," she said. The girl in scrubs wilted and went back to her bedding.

"There's nothing wrong with him?" Karen asked, ignoring her. "Nothing long-term?"

Katy's dimples popped up. She just couldn't help herself. "Walks, talks, feeds himself, everything. Doctors said they've never seen anything like it. But I don't care. All I care about is having my Curt back. What's the difference how it happened, right?"

"Exactly," Karen said. "Congratulations."

Katy glanced at the girl in scrubs and took a timid step toward Karen. "Listen," she said. "I don't want to be rude or anything, but I think you should stay away now. Even though he woke up, I don't think his mom would want you around. You seem like a nice person, but I don't think she'll understand."

"Of course," Karen said. "I won't be. I'll leave you alone now."

She turned and walked toward the door, feeling like she was floating above the tile. For the first time in months, she had hope. She stopped at the door and turned around. "Oh, and Katy? Have a wonderful wedding day."

The dimples popped out again. The girl's eyes absolutely sparkled. "Thank you. We will."

The next morning, Karen was the first one in the office. The hallways were silent, the cubicles abandoned. Mr. Sidwell's office door was closed and locked. She headed for the basement, which was chilly and dark, and turned on the lights, switched on the copier and the printer, and started a pot of coffee in the break room. She went back into her office and fired up her computer, listening to it gurgle and click as it blinked to life. She'd never noticed how quiet it was when you were down there alone. Her antics with Antoinette were a lot noisier than she'd realized.

She sat in her chair, leaned back as far as it would go, and closed her eyes. Once again, as she had several times the night before, she felt relief wash over her. Curt Mac-Donald's limbo state had been weighing on her heavier than she'd ever guessed.

But the relief she felt was not relief for Travis, who would now be much easier to get off the hook. Rather, the relief was for Curt MacDonald, who could now have the life that had nearly been taken from him. Relief for his mother, who'd stayed faithfully by his bedside, who would be fighting for him even now that he was out of the woods.

Relief for herself, for what she was about to do.

As soon as she began to hear the clack of shoes on the break room floor, she got up from her chair and headed upstairs. Antoinette hadn't arrived yet, but that was no big surprise. Antoinette was frequently late, and usually with a good story to tell by way of explanation. Karen decided to take Ant to lunch, so she could hear it all.

Mr. Sidwell was in his office, but still wore his jacket. She knocked lightly on the doorjamb. He turned, a flicker of irritation passing over his face.

"Can I come in?" she asked. "I won't take much time."

"Sure," he said. "Let me take my jacket off." He shrugged out of it and hung it on a hook in the corner, where an assortment of walking sticks and caps and golf clubs transformed the corner into a man jungle. He began sorting through papers on his desk. "What's up?" he asked, not even bothering to look up from his work.

"Curt MacDonald is up. Up and walking right back into his normal life," Karen answered.

"I see," Mr. Sidwell said, as if she'd simply told him she'd brushed her teeth that morning. "And I suppose your son has had a change of mind in light of this new development."

"Actually," Karen said, "you're fired."

Mr. Sidwell looked up sharply. "Excuse me?"

She held her palms out. "Just from working with Travis. He has had a change of mind, but I'm no longer helping him. So you're fired."

"Have you told him about this?" Mr. Sidwell asked, still looking none too pleased.

"Not yet. But I will. It's time for him to learn to deal with his own problems. If I keep swooping in and helping him out, we will never get past this cycle he's stuck in. He needs to learn a lesson. And if that means he learns it in jail, that's the choice he's made."

Mr. Sidwell sank into his chair, the mail temporarily forgotten. "This is a pretty big lesson."

Karen leaned forward. "With all due respect, Mr. Sidwell, he almost beat an innocent man to death. He needs a big lesson."

Mr. Sidwell tented his hands, and pressed his fingers to his chin. He nodded, and finally a smile crept onto his face. "I think you're doing the right thing, Karen," he said. "And I suppose in light of what you're telling me, I don't mind being fired."

"About that," she said. "I might need some legal counsel on another subject."

"Oh, really? And what is that?"

Karen scooted back in her chair, crossed her legs confidently, and said, "What can you do about grandparents' rights?"

TWENTY-THREE

"I have to go home early today," Melinda said, fussing with the new curtains, trying to get all the pastel balloons to line up. "Is it right?"

Maddie Routh looked up from the rocking chair where she was sitting, smoothing the pages of a baby journal in her lap. She'd been writing, Melinda could see, but she didn't know what. She knew only that it was good to see Maddie doing something. Something productive. Something other than simply trying to survive a day.

"You've got a weird wrinkle on the left side," Maddie said. "But it looks fine."

Melinda peered at the curtain and began rearranging. "Anyway, I have to leave in a bit. I've got something I need to do. But Karen is coming for dinner, and Joanna should be here in the morning."

"You know you don't have to keep doing that," Maddie said. And Melinda did know that. Maddie had come a long way. She smiled sometimes now. Laughed at Melinda's jokes. They'd gone shopping together, twice, and had put together Maddie's overnight bag for the hospital. They'd even gone to the park and eaten ice-cream cones, and Maddie had talked about being at that same park as a child, about being at that same park with Michael. She was able to talk about him wistfully now. She was able to talk about the baby. She was calm and hopeful.

"It's fixed?" Melinda asked, leaning back to assess the curtain.

"No. I mean, yeah, it looks fine now. But what I meant was you don't have to keep babysitting me. I feel so bad about how much I've disrupted all of your lives."

Melinda stepped off the stool she'd been standing on and wiped her palms on her jeans. "We're not babysitting. We're supporting. You haven't disrupted anything. And I thought you were okay with it."

"I am. I was," Maddie said. She ran her hand over the open page of her book again, nervously touching the writing. "I mean, I think I'm getting better now. You can't do this forever."

"That's great," Melinda said. "But we still want to be here for you. It's not forever. Just for a few more weeks, balloon girl." She reached out and patted Maddie's belly, which felt tight and hard under her palm. "We're not doing this because we have to. We're doing this because we're your friends. I'm your friend." She patted the belly again. "You're about to pop. Any day now. We're about to find out soon if it's a boy or a girl."

"It's a boy, I just know it," Maddie said. She rubbed her belly, something Melinda had seen her do more and more often lately. She'd also heard her humming softly while rocking in the chair. Maybe she really was feeling better, like she said.

"Is this for the baby?" Melinda asked, lifting the corner of the book in Maddie's lap and letting it drop again.

Maddie let out a big sigh. "Yeah. I've been filling out the family history part. It's really helped, telling the baby about Michael. They didn't give me enough room, though." She flipped to the back of the cover and pulled out several folded sheets of paper, each filled with her tiny handwriting. She ran her finger along the fold of the pages. "He was so amazing. You can't sum up a guy like Michael in one page."

"This baby will be amazing, too," Melinda said. She knelt in front of Maddie, resting her hands on the arm of the rocker. "You know that, right? It may not seem like it now, but as soon as you hold him, you will feel how amazing he is."

Maddie nodded. "I know. This baby has stuck with me through all of this, so I already know he's a fighter. Michael made him that way. And I kind of do feel it now, how amazing he is."

"It makes me so happy to hear you say that," Melinda

said. "But you've been fighting right along with him, so I think maybe you made him that way, too. Or her."

Maddie managed a smile. "Now, go. Do what you need to do. We're fine here."

Melinda fussed with the curtain for a few more moments, not sure if she was trying to get it perfect, or if she was just being reluctant to let go of Maddie.

"Hey, Melinda?"

She turned. "I know. It looks good. I should go."

"No." Maddie picked at the edge of the page open before her, looking uncomfortable. "I just . . . I'm your friend, too. I wanted to make sure I said that. Because I've said a lot of hateful things to you, but you never gave up on me. I know it's all three of you who've helped me, but you're the one who kept pushing. Thank you."

Melinda smiled. She supposed she was the one who kept pushing. The one who first had the idea to find Maddie at all. The one who pulled her out of the bathtub and insisted she keep living. Maddie wasn't the only fighter. She was a fighter, too.

And she had her own life to fight for.

She looked over her shoulder one last time as she headed out the door. Maddie was bent over the journal again, writing intently with one hand and rubbing her belly with the other.

Melinda was home before Paul, which gave her plenty of time to set the stage the way she wanted it. She started with dinner, which she hadn't made in so long she'd almost forgotten how. It seemed pointless to cook for two people who would only eat in awkward silence. But today would be the start of something different. Melinda was determined.

So much had happened. There was so much hurt. Yet she saw how Maddie Routh had fought. How she'd fought for Michael. How she'd fought for the baby that she'd so desperately wanted and then so desperately resented. How she'd fought for the love she'd once forged for herself. What would be Melinda's excuse for letting her love just fade away?

While the chicken roasted and the potatoes boiled, she changed out of her uniform and hung it over the treadmill just like she'd done a hundred times. Habit. She picked up the leg of her pants and rubbed the fabric between her fingers. She'd worked so hard to earn this uniform. It was one of her pride points, being an EMT. It was the only thing she'd wanted to be for so long. But the uniform also held a lot of memories, and a great many of them not good. Some of them the stuff nightmares were made of. She used to think this made her special, her ability to keep her cool when confronted with a grisly scene or a stunning trauma or a tragic moment. But now she knew the truth—that only a part of her kept its composure. The rest of her hung on to those moments and let them take her down, slowly and completely, on the inside.

She whisked the pants off the treadmill and took them to the mudroom, where she stuffed them into a garbage bag. Her two weeks were up. Come Monday, she would be wearing scrubs to work. A formality, really, for the person answering phones at a dental office, but she supposed she would welcome the comfort.

She went back into her bedroom and gathered up her other uniforms and took them out to the garbage as well, shoving them deep within.

She walked into the kitchen just as the oven timer sounded that the chicken was done. She put it on a platter and mashed the potatoes. She dumped the roasted Brussels sprouts in a bowl. She found a book of matches and lit the candles on the fireplace mantel. She combed her hair. She brushed her teeth and put on soft music. And then stood next to the kitchen island wondering if this was trying too hard. Was it too romantic? Would Paul be put off? Were they past this stage? And, if so, would they ever be able to get back?

But before she could make a move to change anything she'd done, the mudroom door opened and Paul stepped in, blinking in confusion.

"Hey," she said.

"I didn't expect . . ." He trailed off. "Is something going on tonight?"

"Yeah, kind of," Melinda said, busying herself by searching for a spoon to put in the potatoes. "Maddie is doing much better, so I decided to spend some time with you."

"Why?" he asked. He let his messenger bag slither down his arm and land on the floor.

Melinda slid the spoon into the potatoes and turned to

him. "Because I love you," she said. She started to say more, but decided instead to let it sit.

He broke his gaze first, clearly uncomfortable. "I mean, sure," he said. "It's just you haven't done that in a while."

"There are lots of things we haven't done in a while, Paul," Melinda said. "I miss you."

His jaw worked a few times while he contemplated what she was saying. "I miss you, too," he said. She could see the familiar wall push its way up between them again. He was trying so hard to shut her out, but she could see something else as well. Something in that working jaw. He still loved her. There was a hope they could get back.

"I don't know what you did all that time you were gone," she said. "And I don't need to know. I really don't. I trust you. You've never betrayed that trust."

"No, I haven't," he said, accusation dripping off his words.

"I know," she said. "You haven't. So I don't need to know what you were doing all that time. But what I'm hoping you didn't do is talk yourself into giving up on us forever. Because you came back, which makes me think you want to make this work. But you haven't really talked to me since, which makes me wonder if it ever will."

"You haven't exactly been talking, either," he said, and again Melinda could hear the blame in his words. He was so defensive he almost couldn't speak to her without it. "That's what started this whole mess, if I remember correctly."

"I know," she repeated. "But I'm ready to change that. I want to talk to you. I want to cook for you and do things with you again. I guess I'm just saying that I want to try to get us back. I'm willing to do anything."

"I see." Still wary.

"So I quit," she said.

"Quit what?"

She picked up the potatoes and took them to the kitchen table. "My job," she said. "I quit. I turned in my notice two weeks ago. Today was my last day. Jason didn't even bother to say good-bye, by the way. Not that I really expected him to."

Paul slumped against the counter. "You quit your job and you didn't even mention it to me? This is what you think is going to bring us back together? Jesus, Melinda, is this what our lives are going to be like now? You doing whatever the hell you want and hiding it from me?"

"I start at Danforth Dental on Monday," she said. "Making more money than I was making before. Plus free dental care."

He nodded. "I still would have liked to have a heads-up."

"The hours are way better," she said.

"I'm sure they are," he said. He started to argue more, but she cut him off.

"That way I can be home more for the kids." She swallowed. "When we have them."

Paul stared at her harder. She could see the wall begin to chip and crumble. Could feel him leaning toward her, like a flower to sunlight. She could feel it and see it even behind the anger in his posture. "If," he said. "I think you mean *if* we have kids."

She came to him, took his hands in hers. "I was so worried about the pain of someday losing a child that I forgot about the pain of losing you," she said. "It's the worst, Paul. I kick myself every day for what I did, but I never did it because I don't love you. I did it because my love for you is terrifying, and if loving you scares me, what will loving your child do to me?"

"You made a fool out of me for months," he said. But his hands twitched around hers. He wasn't pushing her away; he wasn't letting go.

"And I'm so sorry about that. I want to make it up to you. If you want to have kids, we can have them."

"You can't just change your mind like that," he said. "It's not the way it works."

"Yes, I can just change my mind like that. I'm willing to try, anyway. No, I *want* to try. It's not a sudden change. It's been months in the making. Months without you, even when you're here. It's been months with Maddie Routh and Karen and Joanna, and listening to Jason bitch, and I can't explain it all, but I've learned some things about myself. I quit my job, Paul. I'm serious about this."

She looked up into his face. His eyes were closed, and wetness had gathered beneath them. "This hasn't gone too far?" he asked, his voice raspy.

Melinda leaned her forehead against his chest, feeling his warmth soak into her. "Please, try," she whispered.

Paul let go of her hands, causing her to blanch with fear. But then she felt his hands, pressing flat against the small of her back, moving to the center as his arms wrapped around her, and then slowly floating up the length of her spine until they were cupping the back of her head. He held her tightly against him. She felt such relief circle through her that she almost felt dizzy. Her arms found their way around his waist, as she turned her head and laid her cheek against his chest.

She could hear his heart beating.

It was a sound she never wanted to forget.

TWENTY-FOUR

I t was Sunday, and Joanna was slow to get up. Saturday nights at Café Fellowship could get pretty late, especially if her boss got a bee up his ass about prepping for Sunday brunch. She thought she'd never get out of there, and when she finally did get away, her fingers were red and pruney from all the vegetable prep.

She hadn't even gone straight home. Instead, she and Sutton and Theo and his boyfriend had gone out—beers and script run-throughs for *Vanya and Sonia and Masha and Spike* auditions. Sutton had somehow managed to talk Stan into allowing Joanna back into his good graces. Joanna felt like she was returning to family, or maybe truly joining a family for the first time, and although she and Sutton had still not taken anything beyond a hug, the moments between them were electric as hell.

It was right. Nothing confusing about it. *Confusion* had become Joanna's least favorite word. It was a lie. It was a crutch. It was an oppressor.

Fortunately, Helen always brought Maddie breakfast on Sundays, and stuck around to work on laundry, so technically Joanna didn't have to be over at Maddie's for a couple of hours anyway. Not that she thought it was really all that necessary anymore. Maddie had improved so much—she and Melinda had been doing things together for a while now, and she'd even gone grocery shopping with Joanna last week. Joanna had accidentally driven past the Tea Rose Diner, and while Maddie had given the lawn in front of it a long look, she hadn't shed a tear. Progress.

Joanna was still in bed, blinking at the ceiling, remembering that she had the day off, and planning out way more things than could possibly get done in one day, when the phone rang. She reached over and picked it up, thumbed it on without even looking, assuming it would be Sutton.

"Hello?"

"It's me," her mother answered. "You sound sleepy. What are you doing?"

Joanna yawned loudly. "Well, sleeping. It's not even noon yet."

"Nearly," her mother said. "Guess who I ran into this morning?"

"Who?"

"I'll give you a hint. Your father and I decided to have breakfast out for a little treat, so we went to LaEats, and guess who was working the Sunday brunch?"

Joanna grimaced and sat up. She had not told her parents about the breakup yet. It hadn't seemed necessary—she'd never announced their engagement to them, even though she'd told Stephen that she had. She thought she might save the news until her birthday in May, when she would be expected to bring him around for a family gathering. Not that she wanted to keep her parents in the dark—she hated that, actually—but she was still uneasy about the conversation that would likely follow. She was out, and loving it, but that didn't mean she wanted to discuss things with her mother, who loved Stephen, or her father, who probably didn't even know for sure what the word *lesbian* meant.

"Did he wait your table?"

"Yes," her mother said. A pause. "So I take it what he told us is true?"

"I don't know, Mother. What did he tell you?" She really didn't need to know. The answer was as plain as the ice in her mother's voice.

"He said you broke up with him. But the real shocker was that he said you'd been engaged. He seemed to think we already knew that part. Is it true? You never said a word. Surely you weren't engaged without even telling your own mother."

Joanna closed her eyes, a wave of guilt washing over her. Her mother was not the type to show pain, but Joanna knew it was there all the same. "I'm sorry, Mom. I didn't tell you because it just never felt right. I think I knew deep down that we weren't going to get married and I didn't want to disappoint you."

"Not knowing that your only daughter is engaged is pretty disappointing," her mom said.

"I'm sorry." Joanna climbed out of bed and headed to the kitchen for a bottle of water. Her mouth was so dry she felt like clouds of dust were puffing out with every word. Hearing her mother's upset voice only made it worse.

"I would ask you what it possibly could have been about him that you didn't like, but he told us something else, too, so I think I already know."

Joanna stopped drinking. Stephen had outed her to her parents? How could he do that to her? He knew how hard this was for her. He knew the struggle. He saw the way her hands shook when she told him the truth. He heard the tears of regret as she handed him back his ring. He witnessed it. How could he tell?

She set the water bottle on the counter and massaged the back of her neck with her free hand.

He was that hurt by her; that was how. He felt that betrayed. And could she blame him? No, probably not. If Sutton suddenly told her that she was straight, Joanna would probably feel pretty bitter about it, too.

"Joanna?"

"I'm here."

"So it's true, then."

"Yes. I'm sorry."

"You're sorry."

"Yes." Joanna could envision her mother, sitting in "her spot" at the kitchen table, running an emery board over her nails, the phone tucked between her shoulder and ear, legs wound into a pretzel beneath her, as usual. "I'm so sorry."

"Well, I don't know what you have to be sorry about. If you're gay, you're gay. So what? I mean, I wish you had told me yourself. And I wish you would have come to us. I wouldn't have pressured you so much about Stephen. Is that why you haven't come to Sunday dinner?"

"Kind of," Joanna said, reeling in disbelief. *If you're gay, you're gay. So what?* Of all of the possible scenarios she had run through her head over the years of how her mother might react to her news, *If you're gay, you're gay. So what?* had never been one of them.

"That's just silly. We always want to see you, Joanna. If there's any place you can just be you, it's here. We love you."

Joanna slid down the side of the refrigerator until she was sitting on the floor. "Thank you, Mom," she said, her heart so full it hurt.

"So tonight you'll be here?"

"Sure."

"Good. I'm still mad at you, but it'll be good to see you. Now, tell me, is there a girl?"

Joanna reached up and found the water bottle, drank from it. "Kind of. I like her, and we've been getting together, but it's nothing official yet. I really loved Stephen. I still do, actually. It was just a different kind of love. I think I just need some time. This is new to me. Not the part about liking girls, just the part about liking them in public."

"I see. It's smart of you to give it some time," her mom said, and started to say something else, but Joanna's phone beeped in her ear.

"Hang on, Mom, I've got another call."

She switched over. "Hello?"

"Joanna?" Desperate. Breathy.

"Maddie?"

"I'm in labor. I can't get ahold of Melinda." She let out a wail that made Joanna hold the phone away from her ear. "Can you get me?"

It took Joanna a moment to process what she was hearing. She had known this day would be coming soon, but not this soon. And she always assumed she would be getting the call from Melinda, with Maddie safely tucked away and labor-breathing in a hospital bed nearby. She never expected to be the one to get the call.

"Where's your mom?" she asked. "Are you alone?"

"She's home, sick. It's just me. I've been having contractions all morning, and just all of a sudden it's really bad. Please come? I'm scared."

"I'll be right there," Joanna said.

She didn't even bother to change out of her pajamas.

TWENTY-FIVE

The baby was coming early. Karen hoped that was not a sign of something bad. A problem. She had wondered through most of the pregnancy if it was possible for the baby not to be affected by the tsunami of Maddie's grief.

The same elderly lady sat at the information desk—a different paperback this time—but Karen veered into the chapel before approaching her. Maybe it was because of Curt MacDonald's miraculous recovery, but she felt that taking a moment to pray, or whatever you could call what she did inside this bare chapel, would be a good thing.

To her surprise, Joanna was in the front row, sitting quietly.

"Hey," Karen whispered, sitting next to her. "Everything okay?"

Joanna nodded. "As far as I know. Melinda got here, and things had slowed down, so I took a break. Thought I'd come here and . . ." She shrugged. "Can't hurt, I guess. Right?"

"This chapel worked a miracle for me once before," Karen said, "so I'm not going to doubt you. How's she doing?"

"Pretty good, actually. She's scared. She wants Michael, and that's been pretty intense. Her mom can't go in there because she's got some sort of viral thing going on. So it's a good thing we're here. Otherwise, she'd really be alone. Can you imagine?"

Karen stared at the candles. Only three or four were lit today. She made a mental note to find a dollar and light one for Maddie's baby on her way out. A part of her wanted to stuff a whole wad of bills into the box and light every one. Get miracles for everyone. "I wonder if that's why," she said.

"Why what?" Joanna asked.

"If that's why we were all there that day," Karen said. "At the diner. I mean, don't the odds seem strange to you? We were all there—we were the only ones there—all wrapped up in our own problems, and this thing happened. And we all went out there and we all did what we could to help without any one person taking charge. We all watched this man die."

"And we all kept coming back," Joanna said.

"Yeah," Karen said. "Do you think it was meant to happen that way? That maybe we were purposely put there so we could help Maddie get through today?"

"I never thought of it that way, but you're right, it's possible," Joanna said. "We definitely are a weird little family."

"And growing," Karen said.

Joanna smiled. "And growing," she repeated. "Right at this very moment."

It was decided that Melinda would go into the delivery room with Maddie. She'd tried to spin it like she was the only one with medical knowledge, and who had delivered half a dozen babies on the job, and was used to blood and nakedness and all of that, but Karen suspected there was more to it. Somewhere along the line, Melinda had become the one closest to Maddie Routh. And it was only right—Melinda was the person who'd first suggested they find her, after all. It was a full-circle thing.

But Melinda had also been the one to save Maddie when she'd tried to kill herself, and she'd been the one Maddie continually reached for throughout her recovery. She'd gone from the person afraid to park the car and approach Maddie's house to the person coaching her through childbirth. Funny how life worked sometimes.

Karen and Joanna sat in the waiting room, along with another family, who seemed to be very excited about their newest member being born. They whooped and hollered and giggled and paced around, balloons and gift bags adorning their chairs. Every few moments, it seemed another family member joined them. The waiting room was filling up.

"So how's your son doing?" Joanna asked.

"Trial has been set. He's got a new lawyer who seems to think they won't give him too much time, and that he'll get time served."

"You don't sound too happy about that," Joanna said.

Karen absently opened a magazine, even though she had no intention of reading it. Maybe a part of her wasn't happy, which made her sound like a terrible mother. But the truth was, Travis hadn't learned a thing from this go-round, either. And she feared what that would mean for him. How much worse would it have to get—how much higher the stakes—before he would finally turn things around?

"I'm happy that he's taking care of it himself. But there will be some changes when he gets out. For one, he's going to help me find my grandson. For another, he's going to have to find his own place to stay, no more money from me. And he's going to have to accept Marty."

Joanna grinned. "You guys are really becoming a thing, huh?"

Karen couldn't help but smile. The night before, things had gone to a whole new level. It had taken every ounce of courage that Karen had—and a stout shot of tequila—but she had made a promise to Antoinette.

They'd been on her couch, watching TV as usual, when

Marty leaned over and kissed her on the top of her head—
something he did often.

"Whatcha thinking?" he'd asked.

Karen had swallowed past the lump in her throat. "I'm
thinking you should kiss me," she said, hating how she
sounded. Rehearsed. Ridiculous.

But he did kiss her again, and this time she'd run her
hand through the back of his hair, and he'd pulled back
questioningly, but she'd kissed him again. He'd leaned into
her, knocking the TV remote to the floor, and she lay back,
thrilled with the feeling of want, of being wanted. She'd
forgotten so long ago how good it felt to have the weight of
a man on top of her; it was almost like having it happen for
the first time all over again. She'd kissed him with everything she had, not worrying about inexperience or mother-
ing or heartbreak. She just focused on Marty Squire, not
stopping him when his hands roamed.

"You're sure?" he'd asked before unbuttoning her shirt.

She'd nodded. "More sure than I've been about anything in a long time."

She'd awakened in his arms this morning, filled with
nothing but happiness. She'd hated having to leave him to
come to the hospital. But she loved that when Joanna
brought him up, she could remember the night before without feeling shame or guilt or as if she'd wrongly chosen
herself over someone else. She just felt . . . good.

"Yeah, I think it has potential," she told Joanna. "What
about you and Sutton?"

Joanna scratched the back of her neck. "We're working on it."

Just then the double doors opened and out came Melinda, looking flushed and dazed, a yellow paper gown and hat thrown over her clothes.

Joanna and Karen both stood.

"It's a girl," Melinda said. "A healthy, pink little girl."

She came to them, and they fell into a circle of hugs, all laughter and tears and clutching arms.

TWENTY-SIX

Melinda couldn't get enough of the baby. She could think of nothing she wanted to do more than hold her. Count her fingers and toes over and over again. Run her hands across the soft spot on her head. Touch her cheek to see the reflexive yawn of her mouth. Smell her.

She was beautiful and fragile and perfect. Anything could happen to her. Anything. She could be president or the person to cure cancer or she could end up like Karen's son, Travis, or she could blink out of existence when she was six. But Melinda instantly knew, by the weight of her sweet little body, that whatever journey this baby went on, it would be worth it to take it with her. No matter when or how or if it ended.

Maddie had mostly slept after the baby was born—conking out the way she had when she'd come home from the hospital after her last suicide attempt. But Melinda didn't mind. She would sit with the baby as long as was needed. She didn't want to ever put her down. Paul understood. He was waiting for her at home, but he knew this was something she had to do. He knew it was something she wanted to do.

Karen and Joanna had gone home. Joanna had a dinner to get to at her parents' house, and Karen wanted to turn in early before work the next day. Helen and Cleve had come and gone, surgical masks over their faces. Helen refused to hold the baby, in fear of getting her sick, but Cleve had held her, big tears soaking into the top of his mask. They both kissed the sleeping Maddie on the temple before leaving, their arms around each other's waists.

Finally, when dinner arrived, Maddie woke up.

"Mommy's awake," Melinda said to the baby. She walked to Maddie's bedside. "You want to hold her, sleepyhead?"

Maddie yawned, nodded. She held out her arms and Melinda placed the baby in them. Maddie stared into her face for a long time as the infant squirmed and wriggled. She would be waking up soon, wanting to eat. "She looks like him," Maddie said. She brushed the baby's nose lightly with her fingertip. "Right here. He would have been so upset that she got his nose. He always thought it was big."

"I think it's perfect," Melinda said.

"It is, isn't it? I think I was most worried that I wouldn't be able to see him in her at all. Like, if I couldn't find him in her, it would be proof that he was completely forever gone. But there he is, right in the middle of her face."

"You'll see him every time you look at her," Melinda said. "You'll be surprised how many things she'll do that will remind you of him."

"I hope so." She went silent, running her fingers along the contours of the baby's face, arms, hands, seemingly mesmerized by the shape of her child.

"Have you thought of a name for her yet?" Melinda asked.

Maddie nodded. "Rose. Tea Rose Routh. But I'll call her Rose for short."

Tea Rose. A unique name for a unique baby born in the most unique circumstances. Ordinarily, Melinda might have snubbed her nose at such uniqueness. Might have thought it too theatrical, kitschy. But somehow it really fit this baby. Somehow it was not theatrical or kitschy at all, but more of a badge. *Look what I survived*, the badge seemed to say. *Look who I am.*

"Rose," Melinda repeated. She smiled and wiggled the baby's fist with her finger. "Hello, Rose."

"You think Michael would like it?" Maddie asked.

Melinda reached over and clutched Maddie's hand with hers. "I think he would love it."

EPILOGUE

Baby's First Birthday
When . . . April 30th
Where . . . At our house, a backyard party
Who Was There . . .

They say you have friends for a reason, friends for a season, and friends for a lifetime. From the moment I met your father, Michael Routh, at a fraternity fund-raiser my sophomore year in college, I knew he would be my friend for a lifetime. I just didn't understand that the lifetime would be so short.

I know I've written so much about him in this journal already, Rose, and maybe you're even sick of hearing about him. Maybe you wish I'd write more about you, so that you can look back and know who you were. Were you born with the stubborn cowlick that will cause you all kinds of problems when you're a teenager and you want your hair to just obey? (Yes, you were.) Did you always sleep on your back with your fists flung up alongside your ears? (Yes, you did.) Was your voice always so deep and melodic and full? (Yes, it was.) But, for me, it's not that easy. Because when I see that cowlick, I think of your father's cowlick, in a different spot, but just as unruly. When I watch you sleep or listen to your voice, he is there. He is always there. And so it's not easy for me to separate you from your father. And I feel as if I need to say it when I think of him, because I'm the only one who can. If you're reading this, hoping to get a glimpse into who you were, know that you were him.

He would have been so excited for today, Rose. He would have hired ponies or bounce houses or ponies and bounce houses and magicians and jugglers and a whole damn carnival if he thought it would make you happy. I don't know how I know that, except to say that I know he would have done those things for me, and he wanted you just as much as he ever wanted me. He loved you just as much, too. Maybe even more.

So even though technically he wasn't here for your first birthday party, I'm writing about him anyway. He was the first to arrive. I saw him, as soon as I opened my eyes this morning. He was standing at the foot of my bed, grinning that goofy grin of his, the one that meant he was either excited about something or up to no good. It hit me like a punch to the chest, Rose, because I realized he had been grinning that same way right before he died. The last thing he knew, in full consciousness, was that he was excited for something. That something was you. Realizing this makes me love you even more.

So he was here, and he brought the best gift either of us could have ever asked for: comfort.

But, aside from your father, your first birthday party was filled with lots of family and friends. Gammy and Pappy, the silly names my parents had given themselves, were there. They brought so many gifts, we had to save some to open later, after the party. Stuffed toys and dolls and blocks and—your favorite—a little red wagon. Oh, how your eyes lit up when you saw that wagon. You immediately climbed in, the ruffles on the seat of your panties showing out from under your dress as you struggled to get footing. You wanted a ride, and Gammy took you around the yard so many times I thought you might get dizzy.

Gammy is your best friend, Rose. "Gammy" was actually your first word. Not "mama," and certainly not "dada." "Gammy." I didn't mind. I understood.

I spent the first four months of your life wanting to kill myself. What little progress I'd made during the last months of pregnancy just seemed to fly out the window as hormones and reality slammed into me. I had no money. I had no husband. I had no future, yet I was supposed to give you, this beautiful precious girl with eyes full of hope and expectation, a future.

I barely got out of bed. I wasn't sleeping. I was lying there thinking of all the ways I could die. I was lying there wishing for it. But, dammit, I couldn't do it. Because you were counting on me, and I knew what it was like to have the one person you counted on ripped away from you. It was a pain I would be surprised to survive. It was a pain I would never want to repeat.

I tried imagining what your life would be like if I died. Gammy and Pappy would take care of you. Of course they would. They wouldn't hesitate for a second. But no matter how hard they loved you, no matter how much they treated you like one of their own, you never would be their own. You would have nobody to remember your first flutter of movement. And you would always wonder. You would wonder about me the way I wonder about your father—*Is he okay? Did he know I loved him? What would he have been like in twenty, thirty, forty years?* But you would also be wondering about yourself. *Why would my mother choose death over being with me?* you would be forced to think. *Am I so bad?*

What a horrible thing to have to speculate on about yourself.

So I got up. I started helping out where I could. My meds started kicking in. And when I'd catch you in profile, I would see him, and the grief would hit with such intensity, I would have to disappear into my room and try to remember the way he sounded when he said my name.

Eventually, I stopped being able to hear it. That was when I knew it was time to move on.

Thank God, Gammy was as willing to let you go as I was to let her have you.

Our neighbors, Yvonne and Richard, came to your party, too. They brought their little boy, Austin, who is older than you by a few months. You were cute together, even though you fought bitterly over your new toys. Still, I hadn't ever really talked to Yvonne and Richard much. They were always two pairs of curious eyeballs trying not to be noticeable across the yards when I was sulking on the back porch in my nightgown or when I was screaming and throwing breakable things at nobody or even that time the ambulance had to come and take us away—you in my belly, and me covered in drying stained bathwater. The fact that they were willing to embrace me when I was ready to be embraced said a lot about them. They brought you a piggy bank. It's one of those kinds that you have to break to open. I've been tucking notes in there. Just little things, like something cute that you said that your father would have laughed at, or a little encouraging quote just in case you should need one. I want you to open that bank someday and find that the riches inside aren't the bills with the presidents' faces on them.

Your father's entire family came to the party, too—aunts, uncles, cousins, the whole shebang. It was overwhelming—there were at least twenty of them—but I was happy to see you interact with them. Michael loved his family, and I saw ghosts of him wisping around their conversations. His mother would periodically look off into the distance, hands propped on her hips, teeth working her lower lip.

"I'm so glad you came," I said, sidling up to her next to the fence. She had been watching you climb in and out of that wagon.

"I'm so glad you let me," she answered.

"You're always welcome. Michael would have never wanted you to be apart from Rose."

Second Chance Friends

She turned to me and I could see white lines on her cheeks where tears had eaten away her makeup and the wind had blown them dry. "I hate that we have to say things like that. *Michael would have wanted this* or *Michael would have been happy about that.* He should be here."

"I know," I said. I leaned into her, rested my temple on her shoulder.

She tilted her head on top of mine and let out a long sigh. "I miss him so much," she said.

I didn't say "I know" that time. Because I didn't know. I knew what it was like to miss Michael, yes, but I had no idea what it was like to miss your child. I couldn't take that extra grief away from her. It was hers alone, and one I never want to experience. I'd been completely self-absorbed for most of the early months of your life, and still I couldn't imagine being without you.

You are sunshine. You are birdsong. You are the tinkling of golden coins. You are everything.

Your "aunties" Melinda, Karen, and Joanna came to the party, too, of course.

Melinda looked nearly ready to pop, as she once told me I had looked. She said her back was hurting and her ankles were swollen and she couldn't wait to get this baby out of her. She already knew she was having a boy. She'd already named him. Paul Junior. Not very creative, but given the hell the two of them had gone through to get to this point, it seemed pretty perfect.

She told me, over huge breakfasts in the back booth that faced the bus crash divots, that she was still terrified. She said she had nightmares where she was still at her old job, and they got a call, and when they arrived, it was her baby who needed the ambulance. She said she'd had that nightmare a dozen times and never once was she able to save Paul Junior. When she told me this story, her fingers shook around her fork and she stopped eating.

"Do you ever wish he hadn't been in your life in the first place?" she asked.

It took me a minute to even figure out what, or who, she was talking about. And then it dawned on me that she was talking about Michael. "What? Of course not," I said, and I'd said it so quickly and with such certainty that it really hit me for the first time. Even if I'd known, way back during that frat party, that I was going to lose your father so soon, I still would have loved him. I still would have married him. I still would have tried to get pregnant with you. My memories with Michael are some of my most precious. Why would anyone want to give those up for safety?

Melinda nodded and went back to eating, smiling as if I'd done her a big favor just then. She was the one who'd given me the gift.

Auntie Joanna came carrying a huge teddy bear. So big I couldn't even see her head over the top of it. She laughed when she sat it on the ground, and you immediately toddled over and tackled it, toppling over it clumsily. Joanna had broken up with her girlfriend, Sutton, a few months before, her only reason that she wasn't quite ready to be tied down. She wanted to catch up on the dating the rest of us had done in high school and college, when she'd been too busy hiding. She wanted to try out love and lust and hand-holding and innocent kisses in public. She was currently dating a girl named Heather, but it wasn't serious. Joanna didn't have time for much dating, anyway. She'd gotten a huge lead role in a production at the community college. She was going back to school. She smiled a lot and told me funny stories and sang for me and once, last September, we ate slices of Boston cream pie right there on the lawn of the Tea Rose Diner. You slept in your infant carrier next to us, the sunlight making your eyelids nearly translucent.

Karen and Marty came to your party together. Karen had cut her hair, colored and straightened it, and bought some new clothes. She looked decades younger. She brought her grandson, Marcus, with her. Marcus is probably your best playmate right now, Rose, and he is so protective of you. Like a little mother hen, following you around, telling you "no" when you reach for something dangerous.

Her son, Travis, who you've never met and probably never will, was back in jail, this time for robbing a convenience store. Sometime during the weeks that followed, Travis's girlfriend, Kendall, disappeared. Took a bunch of jewelry from Karen's jewelry box and split. Karen was now a parent to a nearly two-year-old boy. But she seemed very happy about it and kept going on about do-overs and how you can't predict life, no matter how hard you try. I've already learned that with you, Rose—that as a parent, you always wonder if you could have done it better.

Things were so busy at the party, with the cake and the presents and the chasing around toddlers and cousins and refilling drinks, I barely had the chance to talk to Melinda, Joanna, and Karen at all. Not that not talking to them would be a huge deal. We talk every single day. We meet for coffee at the Tea Rose Diner most mornings, even if for just a few moments. It's our spot. The spot where we all got our second chances.

But as people began to clear out, and you curled up on the giant teddy bear and dozed off, I made my way over to them.

"Crazy," I said, raising my eyebrows. "Are birthday parties always this exhausting?"

Karen laughed, bouncing Marcus on one knee. "Only if you have them."

"Well, I will be having them, so go ahead and mark your calendars now," Melinda said.

"Your baby isn't even born. How do we mark our calendars for a birthday that hasn't happened yet?" Joanna asked.

Melinda rubbed her belly, thinking. "Just go ahead and block out the entire month of May for the rest of your lives."

Marcus wiggled out of Karen's lap and ran toward the tricycle that you had gotten and temporarily forgotten about. "Don't get hurt," Karen called, her hands trailing after him, as if she didn't want to let go. That was when I noticed her finger.

"You're engaged," I said.

The other two gasped as she held her hand up for inspection. "Last night," she said. "Isn't it beautiful? I know I'm old to be starting over, but . . . life is funny sometimes, isn't it?"

Second Chance Friends

Life is funny sometimes. You can go from holding poster board next to this adorable frat guy to saying, "I do," to watching that frat boy die, to watching his baby eat fistfuls of cake on her first birthday without even taking a breath between any of those things.

You can go from happiest girl in the world to sitting in a bathtub full of your own blood before your eyelashes bat once.

You can go from husbandless and friendless and hopeless to admiring the engagement ring of one of your best friends in the instant it takes to put your foot on the wrong pedal of a speeding bus.

Remember that, Rose. Remember that life is funny sometimes. Remember that things can change so quickly and so completely that you could never have predicted them, even if you'd been told to let loose your wildest thoughts. Maybe that was why your father was sent into our lives, Rose. Maybe he was here to teach us that you can't predict life . . . but that unpredictable doesn't equal bad.

"I should put Rose down for a nap," I said, hurrying over to you. I plucked you out of the bear's lap and felt the sweaty contours of you against my arms. You had a smear of icing across one cheek. Your dress was grass-stained. You smirked in your sleep, just the way Michael always had. I kissed your cheek, a perfect moment in the midst of a billion imperfect ones.

I carried you past Karen, Melinda, and Joanna as they chatted excitedly about wedding plans and baby kicks and theater. I listened to them all the way inside, until the walls muted their voices to whispers and then to silence. I smiled at my fortune. Can you believe that, Rose? I smiled at how lucky I was. How lucky I still am. Those three ladies kept me alive. Karen, Melinda, and Joanna were the reason I could smile.

On September 2, my husband, Michael Christopher Routh, was killed instantly when a school bus lost control on Highway 32 and crashed into our car.

On that day, I met Karen Freeman, Melinda Crocker, and Joanna Chambers.

They say you have friends for a reason, friends for a season, and friends for a lifetime.

Somehow I got lucky and got all three at once.

Second Chance Friends

Jennifer Scott

This Conversation Guide is intended to enrich the
individual reading experience, as well as encourage us
to explore these topics together—because books,
and life, are meant for sharing.

A CONVERSATION WITH JENNIFER SCOTT

Q. Second Chance Friends *begins when a perfectly ordinary day in the lives of three different women, all of whom are having breakfast in a local diner, is disrupted by a car accident in the intersection outside. Why did you want to use that particular event to kick off the novel?*

A. I love stories that explore connections. I think one of the most important tasks of our lives is making connections, even just in ordinary moments. But I've long wondered about connections made in extraordinary times as well. A few years ago, there was a horrific accident involving a school bus at a very busy intersection in my town. Certainly, there were many witnesses, and my heart went out to them. I began to wonder what would happen if a few of them continued to meet—even if accidentally at first. How would the uniqueness of what they experienced together affect their relationships with one another? Would they feel more connected? Would they forge friendships? Would they help one another get through the healing? This book had been writing itself in my head ever since.

CONVERSATION GUIDE

Q. As the novel moves forward, the chapters are told from the perspectives of three different women: Karen, Melinda, and Joanna. They're unique women with very different personalities. Yet you develop each one with rich details and careful attention. When you write different characters, do you love them all? Do they come to you fully formed or do you discover them along the way?

A. I do love them all, but there is usually one who will endear herself to me a little more than the others. She will speak the loudest and seem the most human to me. That doesn't mean the others don't also speak and seem human—it only means they're a little quieter than she is. In this case, I felt a particular connection with Joanna. She had all this love and passion that she wanted to share, yet fear kept her in hiding. I think we can all relate to that on some level—fear of being who we really are—and know how painful and damaging that anxiety can be. I was really rooting for Joanna.

I like to get to know my characters as real people before I begin writing, so I spend a lot of time writing character sketches before I start each novel. I get to know their appearance and mannerisms, their worries and desires, their family dynamics and their motivations. Yet even after all of that work, they always still manage to surprise me at some point in the novel. So, yes, I begin with fully formed characters in mind . . . and, yes, I discover them along the way, too.

Q. There is, of course, a fourth woman in the novel, Maddie, who is pivotal to the story. We see her in many of the chapters, but we are shown her perspective only in the epilogue. Why did you make that choice?

A. Mostly because Maddie's perspective would have been so bleak throughout most of the novel that I think it would have been too heavy and hopeless. With Karen, Melinda, and Joanna, they had their problems, and even had moments of real pain, but they were hopeful. They were reaching out and connecting with one another. Maddie had no faith, and she was pulling away, shutting herself off at every opportunity. It wasn't until she'd begun to see that she had a future that I felt it was safe for her voice to shine through.

Q. Despite the seriousness of the subject matter, you've also used quite a bit of humor in the book, especially between Karen and her friend Antoinette. Was it hard to balance the light and dark moments as you wrote?

A. Even though my novels often revolve around more somber subject matters, I have written a lot of humor, too. In fact, I wrote a weekly humor column for the *Kansas City Star* for more than four years. So humor comes very naturally for me, and sometimes I think we need those moments of levity, even in the gloomiest hours, just to take a breath and keep our sanity. It's human nature to seek relief. So I wasn't so much bogged down by

trying to keep a balance as I was popping up with a reminder that there is a "better" out there waiting for the
four friends (and for us) to arrive.

*Q. At the end of the book, Maddie reflects, "They say you have
friends for a reason, friends for a season, and friends for a
lifetime." This quote has the ring of knowledge handed down
through the ages. Is it something you've heard before? Or
something that came to you in the writing of this book?*

A. I've heard this saying many times, and have always
loved the truth of it. Sometimes I've even heard it taken a
step further, that when you figure out which one of those
things someone in your life is, you will know what to do
with that person. I've tried to find the origin of the saying,
but it doesn't have a clear attribution that I can find.

Q. In your first work of women's fiction, The Sister Season,
*you wrote about three estranged sisters returning home to the
family farm. They are coming to celebrate the holidays, but
they are also coming to bury their father. What one might
have expected to be a joyful event becomes quite complicated.
Here, you've begun with a tragic accident, and yet the four
women the story focuses on actually grow through that event
and rediscover joy at the end. Is it your hope to explore the
unexpected emotional journeys we take in your stories?*

A. Yes, I think life is one big unexpected emotional journey, and it's what we do and learn along the way that makes us remarkable. I think that it's in the moments of great joy and great sorrow that we find parts of ourselves we never knew existed, and sometimes what we find can be so profound as to change us forever. It's rather amazing, when you think about it, how much there is to discover in even the darkest, dustiest, most frightening corners of our souls.

Q. Second Chance Friends is a rich, complicated book that will impress readers in different ways. Is there something you especially want readers to come away with after they've turned the final page?

A. That there is always opportunity for reaching out and connecting. I would hope for my readers to come away looking for places where they can connect with someone else, likely or unlikely, and be the blessing in that person's life, even if only for a season.

Q. What's next for you in your writing life?

A. One of the things I love most about writing is that I'm never quite sure what's up next! I love to experiment and follow new stories and ideas and genres. But one thing I can be certain of is that I will continue to weave the threads of hope in tragedy, and the blessing of human connection—in ordinary times and extraordinary ones—into all of my stories.

QUESTIONS FOR DISCUSSION

1. Small-town diners are often pictured as meeting places—places where we can see familiar faces, catch up on the neighborhood gossip, and enjoy a sense of inclusion. This story begins in such a place. But with the rise of social media and electronic devices, we're also finding virtual communities. Do you still find a sense of community in places such as diners and bookstores in your neighborhood? Do you participate in virtual communities? Do you find these two things at odds with each other? Do they enhance each other?

2. The story is told mostly from the point of view of three different women: Karen, Melinda, and Joanna. Did one of them resonate with you more than the others? If so, why? Do you find yourself often drawn to the same types of characters in the books you read?

3. After the accident, Karen, Melinda, and Joanna decide to search out Maddie, the young woman in the accident. They come, unbidden, into her life. Do you believe them

when they say they're acting purely out of concern for her? Are they being nosy? Are they being supportive? Are these two sides of the same coin?

4. Discuss the different issues of motherhood the characters struggle with as the story builds. Think of Karen and her wayward son, or Melinda, who quietly deceives her husband to avoid having a child, and Maddie, who initially doesn't want the child she'll have. How do the women help one another through these issues? Does one of these issues resonate with you more than the others?

5. Romantic love and sexual identity are also issues confronting the characters. Think about their different conflicts in this area. Joanna, of course, comes readily to mind. But think also of Karen, who is in a very different phase of her life, and of Melinda, who is married. What challenges are they facing in their romantic lives? Do you think they work through them successfully? Do you feel they have work left to do when the story ends?

6. There are many secrets in this book—secrets the characters hide from themselves and from others. List the secrets you observe. Do they remain at the conclusion of the story? Do you have secrets you keep—from your friends, your family, or yourself? Do you think revealing them would help enrich your life? Are there times secrets are best kept concealed?

7. For women who become mothers, balancing the physical and emotional demands of a job with the role of motherhood can be difficult. In this story, Karen seems to be able to use her job to strengthen her position as a parent and grandparent. But Melinda decides she needs to leave her job as an EMT in order to be a mother. Do you understand their decisions? Do you believe them? Do you feel you've had to make similar choices in your own life?

8. For Joanna. the arts, and in particular theater, play a crucial role in her personal development. Has artistic expression helped you understand something about yourself?

9. The epilogue is a critical part of this story. What role does it play? Why do you imagine the author chose to write it in this format? And are the characters where you thought they might be in their lives?

10. This book begins with a tragedy—with an accident that claims lives. Yet it ends with great joy—a child is born and friendships have blossomed. So would you call it a sad book? A happy book? An honest book? Why? Have you had experiences that you feel are similar to what the women here have shared? Do you believe we can heal from the tragedies we've endured? Do they weaken us? Strengthen us? Or perhaps simply change us?

t was what should have been dinnertime in the Epperson house when the phone rang. Of course, it wasn't actually dinnertime. Not officially. It hadn't officially been dinnertime in the Epperson house since Kevin, leaving a trail of balled socks and loose change and mementos of a lost age—football cards stuck upright in the cracks of the baseboards, a Sanibel sand dollar plucked from the ocean an impossibly short decade ago, figurines from the imaginative days of childhood—left the house with a passport and only half a harebrained plan. And quite a bit of cannabis, from the smell of him. Oh, he could deny it, but a mother knew when the eyes of her child weren't right.

Her youngest. Her baby. A once-treasured bedroom now home to only forgotten Super Balls and soccer pads and slippers, rock band posters and a rat's nest of old phone chargers, and the college textbooks he'd foolishly purchased before he'd decided to admit that he wasn't planning to go, all abandoned.

He'd left with a jacket, a pocketful of snacks, and a sleeping bag harnessed along the underside of a backpack, for Christ's sake. *Isn't he taking this backpacking-across-the-world business a little far? How can he possibly have packed enough to live off of in that thing?* Brenda had asked Gary, who'd sat on his parked motorcycle looking one-tenth worried for Kevin and nine-tenths envious out of his gourd. *Oh, he'll be fine, Brenda. Let him explore. This is important. You don't want him to turn around in thirty years and regret that he never went.* Bren had rolled her eyes. Of course Gary would make this about himself. Ever since the man turned the corner into the back side of his forties, he'd managed to make everything about himself. God love the old oafish bastard.

And so Kevin had hugged her and made promises about phone calls and postcards and a future that she knew would never come true and had hopped into his friend Tony's idling 2000 Toyota, checked his pocket for his passport one last time, and set off for the airport—a flick of his wrist through the passenger-side window for a wave, a fog of alternative music the last souvenir of her son to leave the block he'd grown up on.

Epperson family dinners whisked away, just like that.

At last check-in—it must have been at least three weeks ago—Kevin was just pulling into Český Krumlov, which Bren had made him spell so she could look it up on the Internet. Somewhere in the Czech Republic, he'd said. He'd dropped his iPod in the Vltava River, but he didn't care, he'd said. He'd met a girl, he'd said. Her name was Pavlina; she was an artist—*like, a real artist, not one of those weird girls who use creative stirrings as their excuse not to shave their pits, Mom.* Pavlina didn't believe in shoes, and she was the most beautiful thing he'd seen yet, and that included all the Roman sculptures and paintings combined. He was smitten, but was telling Bren this as if dictating a travelogue, as he always did. Sounding removed, dutiful. Bren forever fretted that there would be a test at the end of his phone calls. She never talked to him without a pencil and a pad of paper—what she thought of as her telephone pad—so she could write down all the confusing foreign-sounding things he said. When they hung up, she felt like a completed chore. A *confused* completed chore.

This time, the ringing phone had a +66 country code at the front of it. Bren, eating cheese on toast—her fourth piece—and idly filling out a magazine quiz while the news droned on the tiny kitchen TV, a persistent buzzing of negativity and fear-mongering that both frightened her and made her feel superior, jumped at the receiver.

"Hollo?" and then, covering the mouthpiece with her palm, "Gary! It's Kelsey! Kelsey is calling!" Then, back into the phone, "Hello?"

A strange click, some faraway hissing. "Mommy?"

Bren's breath caught. She loved that her daughter had never gotten too old to call her Mommy, but had to admit that hearing the word *Mommy* coming out of her daughter's mouth, even at twenty-four years old, even married and a whole continent away, brought to mind skinned knees and Barbie dolls, an eight-year-old Kelsey who would never grow any older.

"Kelsey!" she exclaimed. "How's Thailand?"

"Oh, Mommy, it's beautiful. The rain has stopped and it's so warm. Perfect, really. We're getting ready for Loi Krathong here. Do you know what that is? Have you ever seen it?"

Bren scrambled for her telephone pad and pencil, flipped to the *Kelsey* page, and scribbled down *Loy Rithong.* "I've never even heard of . . . Did you say *Rithong* with an *R*?"

Kelsey giggled. "A *K*, Mommy. A *K*. Krathong. We make these little boats and fill them with flowers and candles and coins. We're making ours out of bread to feed the fish—our boat. That was Dean's idea. Isn't that a great idea, Mommy, to make it out of bread?" Bren nodded, but there wasn't time to speak between Kelsey's breathless sentences. Kelsey always got that way, especially when she talked about her new husband. "He's so smart about things, even though we're still learning. It's like he's lived here his whole life. Anyway, so, you float these little boats down the river during the full moon. It's like an offering, Mommy, but it's also symbolic. It symbolizes letting go of your hatred and anger and bitterness, and there are lanterns, so many lanterns, and, gosh, it just sounds so beautiful. Doesn't it sound beautiful?"

"Yes, beautiful," Bren said, but she'd gotten behind on her notes. "Wait—you have hatred and anger?"

"It's symbolic, Mommy."

"Symbolic hatred," Bren said, writing down the words as she spoke them.

"So, what are you and Daddy doing this evening? It must be about dinnertime there. I just woke up. I'm waiting for Dean to get out of the shower. We're playing hooky and going to the beach today. I'm telling you, Mommy, someday you and Daddy simply must come visit us. We have space. Dean said he would make space—isn't that the sweetest? He's so thoughtful that way, you know. Always worrying about everyone else. He would probably give you our bed and would sleep outside on the ground if that was what you wanted. You must come and let him be thoughtful to you, Mommy. It would mean the world to him. And you would be amazed by these beaches. The water—it's so clear. You've never seen water like that in Missouri—I can tell you that much."

Ah. There it was. The requisite Missouri-bashing that both her kids had to do on a regular basis now that they had moved on to such exotic locales. As if nothing good ever could have come from a place as bland as the Midwest. As if they both had not come from the Midwest themselves.

Bren wrote the word *beache*—misspelled, after over-thinking that it might have some foreign iteration like all the other things she'd been writing down—then scratched it out and wrote *hooky* instead, then scratched that out, too, and put down her pencil.

"So?" Kelsey asked.

"*So* what?"

Impatient grunt, followed by a giggle. Kelsey's signature. The girl moved like a hummingbird, always zooming on to the next thing, the next conversation, the next song, the next location. "So, what are you and Daddy doing tonight?" she repeated.

"Oh, that," Bren said. Her head felt swimmy, stuffed too full of information. She placed her hand over the phone receiver again. "Gary!" Nothing. She went to the garage door and pounded on it with the flat of her hand three times, marital code for *Get your ass in here.* "Gary!"

"Daddy in the garage again?" Kelsey asked. "Still working on that motorcycle?"

"Yes and no," Bren said. "He's onto dune buggies now. It's a long story. I suppose we're not doing anything tonight. Although I'd hoped to catch up on some of my recorded shows."

"Well, that's boring. Honestly, Mommy, you should get out sometimes."

Bren's hand went to the back of her head. "I get out. I went to the hairdresser today."

"The hairdresser? What, are you ninety? I mean *get out* get out. Do something fun. Go dancing. You're empty nesters now. You have freedom!"

Don't remind me, Bren thought, thinking for the thousandth time what an awful term *empty nester* was. So lonely, evoking images of things dried and barren. It was bad enough to feel that way without putting a name to it, too.

Bren found herself stuttering, nothing intelligible coming out, as her daughter continued to talk over her with suggestions of things to do—fancy dinners, romantic river cruises, day trips, double dates, clubs—followed by condemnation for sitting around and rotting at home, then doomsday predictions of what happened to old couples who didn't thrive, old people who didn't leave the house.

"They die younger, Mommy. Did you know that? Retired people who get out and do things live longer."

Excerpt from The Hundred Gifts

"We're not retired," Bren found herself saying bewilderedly. "I'm only forty-five. Your father's not yet fifty."

"It's here before you know it," Kelsey said in a very sage voice, as if a twenty-four-year-old knew the first thing about the advancement of time.

There was a thundering of footsteps, and Gary came into the room, reeking of gas, wiping his hands on a filthy towel. Grateful for the excuse to interrupt this discussion, Bren set the phone on the table and hit the speaker button.

"Hey there, princess!" Gary said without waiting for an opening. *Exactly where Kelsey got the chatty gene— right there.*

"Daddy!" Kelsey squealed. If they'd been visiting in person, she would have wrapped her entire body around him the way she always had. Such a daddy's girl. He took her marriage and moving much easier than Bren thought he would. Although Bren still wasn't allowing herself to fully think about it yet, either, so she had no real idea how hard she was going to take it when she finally let down her barrier and allowed it to sink in full force.

She'd always had a vague fear that one of her children would move away. *Away* away, not college away or different town away or even different state away. But she'd never have guessed that one of them would actually go and do it. Not to mention both of them. Where had she gone wrong that both of them suddenly wanted to be *away* away?

Kelsey had been married for exactly forty-six minutes before she'd made her way to the middle of the reception dance floor, grabbed the mic, and announced that Dean was accepting a new job (pause for polite applause) and that it was a really great opportunity (pause for excited grin) and that they would be moving (pause for hopping on toes) to exotic and beautiful Thailand (pause for confetti and balloons and a goddamned unicorn shitting heart-shaped puppies all over the place). Bren had smiled and clapped with the others, all the while trying to remember whether Thailand was a place with big, scary insects or a place with big, scary diseases or a place with big, scary kidnappers. Or maybe all of the above. She was quite possibly the first mother of the bride in all of history to wonder aloud, at the reception, whether her daughter was up-to-date on all her immunizations.

Oh, Gary had taken it hard at first. But he'd gotten over it so quickly. How did he do that? Kelsey had now been gone for six months and it already felt like six years, but to listen to Gary, to watch him as he putzed around on his dune buggy without a care in the world and as he casually chatted with his daughter on the phone—no pad and pencil required—you would never have known the girl had been gone at all.

"How are things Down Under?" he asked.

This got the usual giggle from Kelsey. "We're not that close to Australia, Daddy."

"Oh, does that mean you haven't a pet kangaroo yet? Well, then, I'm never coming to visit."

More laughter. They were so cute together, those two. It made the bridge of Bren's nose ache. She pinched it, wondering whether she should write down *kangaroo*. Out of nowhere, her shoulder itched. She shrugged a few times, the friction from her bra strap scratching it.

"How's Dean-o?" Gary asked, his voice booming, making Bren flinch.

"Oh, he's just great. His project is going well and it looks like he may get a contract extension, which we're so excited about. We haven't seen nearly enough of Thailand yet. We'd like to stay a few more years."

"Years?" Bren barked, and then slapped her mouth shut. She'd vowed to never make either of the children feel guilty about their decisions to live lives separate from hers—even if they were so carelessly breaking her heart—but she couldn't help it. Years was a long time. Years was long enough for her to miss the birth of a grandchild. Years was long enough to put down roots, real roots, the kind of roots that you don't want to dig up.

"Well, you tell him we said hello and to keep up the good work," Gary boomed as if Bren had never said anything at all. Thank God.

"So, I can't talk for much longer," Kelsey said, her voice going down at the edges. "Trying to save money where I can."

"That's my girl," Gary said. "Levelheaded."

Bren shot him a look. As if saving pennies by shortchanging her own parents on phone calls while lollygagging on a beach all day instead of working was a fiscally responsible decision.

"I just wanted to say hi. And to tell you I miss you both bunches."

"Bunches?" Bren repeated. Her pencil scrawled it out of its own accord, but she was drowned out once again by Gary.

"We miss you, too, pumpkin. You take care of yourself down there. Don't forget to put another shrimp on the barbie."

Kelsey's laughter tinkled through the phone speaker again. Bren had more than once wished she could bottle that laughter, keep it safe, keep it handy. It was a sound of such pure joy. But now it only sounded far away, dulled by distance. A joy that she could only admire but never fully experience again.

"Oh, just a reminder, by the by, that Dean and I won't be coming home for the holidays."

"Yes, yes, you've told us," Bren said tiredly. Did her daughter have to keep reminding her of that? Did she really think that having her first ever Christmas apart from her children would be something Bren would absentmindedly forget?

"Got big Christmas plans?" Gary asked.

"Not really. It's mostly Buddhist here, so not a lot of Christmas celebrating goes on, I don't think. Plus, the place will just be flooded with tourists, from what I hear. We'll probably have a quiet dinner. Maybe some noodles, some fish. Just the two of us."

"Same here," Bren said. "Just the two of us. Only without the noodles."

"Well, enjoy that!" Kelsey cried out, right back to her sunny self. "A romantic Christmas dinner for two, for the first time in, what . . . ?"

"Twenty-four years," Bren supplied.

"Wow, twenty-four," Kelsey said. "You are long overdue."

"I suppose we must be," Bren said. She didn't have the

heart to tell Kelsey about their cafeteria dinner plans, or about the dune buggy or the cheese on toast or the pad and pencil with all the foreign words, or even about her incessant nightly scouring of the Internet for cheap flights halfway around the world.

"That we are," Gary said, snaking an arm around Bren's shoulders. She resisted the urge to pull away, though she knew she was going to smell like that damned buggy now even if she did.

Their good-byes were, as always, over so quickly that Bren's head was left spinning. She clutched the pad and pencil, gazing at the words as if trying to memorize the conversation, file it away so she would have it to pull out on her next lonely evening of filling out magazine quizzes and listening to the nightly death report.

Gary drifted away, taking the rag and a glass of iced tea with him. Terse, typical conversation would now return, as the amiable guy with the big smile and the cute turns of phrases was snuffed out like a candle on a birthday cake.

"You eat?"

"Just some cheese toast."

"Huh."

"You want me to make you something?"

"Naw, I'll grab a bite later. Working on the buggy."

A shuffling of footsteps toward the garage again. "You gonna be long?"

Garage door opening, an echoey answer that drifted into inaudible murmurings and then a shut door: "Got to get to bed. Meetings tomorrow . . ."

Bren stared at the pad of paper. *Bunches* was the last word she'd written.

But off to the margin was the sad face that she'd drawn when Kelsey had told them she hadn't planned to come home for the holidays.

Suddenly the cheese toast looked congealed and disgusting, postsurgery fleshy. She could feel the bread perching at the base of her esophagus, coiled, ready to launch as soon as she lay down for bed. She could practically see little orange pustules of grease popping into the pores around her mouth, on her cheeks, her forehead, suffocating them, making her skin dull and cheeselike itself. The very thought made her tongue curl back in a gag.

She got up and carried the plate to the sink, snatching up the remote control and turning off the TV as she went. The room hummed with silence. The sun had fallen.

She padded to the bedroom, where her black long-haired cat, George, lay waiting for her, curled at the bottom of the bed. He made a *brrr* noise as she slid headfirst into the bed, then moved so the cat's hind end pressed warmly into her side.

It was barely seven o'clock, but Bren Epperson went to bed anyway, thanking God, as she drifted off, for the short days of autumn.

Jennifer Scott is an award-winning author who made her debut in women's fiction with *The Sister Season*. She also writes critically acclaimed young adult fiction under the name Jennifer Brown. Her debut YA novel, *Hate List*, was selected as an ALA Best Book for Young Adults, a *VOYA* Perfect Ten, and a *School Library Journal* Book of the Year. Jennifer lives in Liberty, Missouri, with her husband and three children.

CONNECT ONLINE

jenniferscottauthor.com

facebook.com/jenniferscottauthor